Camp 22

Escape from Tyranny

By

Warren Miner-Williams

First published as Kindle edition in 2021 by Warren Miner-Williams

Revised August 2023

POD 11/2021

ISBN 978-1-99-115613-6

A CIP catalogue record of this book is available from the National Library of New Zealand

If I have seen more clearly than others it is because I have stood on the shoulders of giants.

Sir Isaac Newton, English mathematician & physicist, 1642 – 1727, (adapted from a quotation in a letter to Robert Hooke, February 5, 1675)

To my family: Lynda, Cheryl, Corinne and Ruth

Prologue

In the remote north-eastern corner of the Democratic People's Republic of Korea (DPRK), close to the border with Russia and China, is the country's largest concentration camp. Hidden in the mountains, just 20 kilometres outside the city of Hoeryŏng, lies Camp 22, a bestial, godless place. Larger than Auschwitz or Dachau, it holds over 50 000 political prisoners and their families, and for good reason, it is called the "Killing Compound".

Concentration camps in North Korea came into being at the close of World War II after the country was liberated from the Japanese. Those considered "adversary classes" were rounded up and imprisoned in large labour camps, similar to the Russian gulags. Although these sprawling death camps increased in the late 1950s and 60s, their number has decreased in recent years to just six. However, estimates of between 400 000 and 1 million political prisoners have perished in these camps since 1972. Termed *kwan-li-so*, political penal-labour colonies, camps such as Camp 22 hold more than 200 000 men, women and children. So-called political offenders face life sentences without trial for offences as trivial as failing to bow to portraits of Kim-Il-Sung, "Great Leader."

One frightening aspect of North Korea's system of social control is that of collective responsibility or the *yeon-jwa-je*, the three-generation family incarceration system. Just as those who allegedly commit political crimes are condemned, so too are their parents, siblings, wives and children, three generations or more, regardless of guilt or innocence. Such political prisoners are deemed to be "factionalists". As in Nazi Germany, fear, intimidation and political subjugation dominate every aspect of DPRK society. The people of North Korea are terrified of betrayal by a friend, a neighbour or a relative, quislings of the most repressive nation on earth. Factionalists are a threat to the revolution; they are class enemies who have to be destroyed like weeds.

The government of North Korea outlaws Christianity. If caught, Christians aren't simply killed; they are starved, tortured and shipped off to the concentration camps. Christians have to worship secretly, rarely outside the family group, terrified they will be betrayed to the authorities.

For more information and satellite imagery of the concentration camps in North Korea, see:

1. North Korea's Largest Concentration Camps on Google Earth: http://freekorea.us/camps/
2. The hidden Gulag; exposing North Korea's prison camps: https://www.goodreads.com/book/show/13618690-the-hidden-gulag

3.   Amnesty International: North Korea: Political Prison Camps: https://www.amnesty.org/en/documents/asa24/010/2013/en/

4.   Concentration camps in North Korea: http://en.wikipedia.org/wiki/Category:Concentration_camps_in_North_Korea

5.   Hell on earth': Detailed satellite photos show death camps North Korea still deny even exist: http://www.dailymail.co.uk/news/article-2039542/North-Korea-Satellite-photos-death-camps-deny-exist.html

Part I

North Korea

1. Camp 22.

It was a grey, ugly day, with dark, ominous rain clouds scudding across the sky. A bedraggled group of prisoners huddled together in the middle of a square of black asphalt situated in front of the Kim Il-Sung theatre. A freezing wind, rolling down from Manchuria in the north, cut through their thin tunics, the prison clothes issued on their arrival. The frightened children were crying, it was so cold, and they hugged their parent's legs in a vain attempt to keep warm. From the northern corner of the square, sixty metres away, a small group of officials emerged from the camp director's office. The six soldiers guarding the prisoners quickly stamped out their cigarettes and brought their rifles to bear.

"Come on, you worthless bastards, get into line." Shouted a sergeant, prodding David with his bayonet.

David and his family were Christians and had all adopted names from the Bible. Ko Jong-Su was known as David, a name he never used outside the family. At 1.79 metres, David was taller than most of the other prisoners and could see across to the beginning of the column of prisoners. At thirty, his black hair was already turning grey at the temples. Apart from a chickenpox scar on his forehead, his skin was unblemished. With little facial hair, his complexion, in the fiercely cold wind, was sallow and dry around his eyes. David had an athletic build which he had developed while at university. In his youth, he had trained as a 400 and 800-metre runner, but as he had only ever achieved average times, he was told to think of another career. After studying biochemical engineering at Hamhŭng University, he was employed at the massive 'February 8' Vinalon Complex in Hamhŭng. But that was a lifetime ago. Although a past Arirang Festival taekwondo champion, it would not help him in the camp colliery. Soft-spoken and slow to anger, he would have to toughen up if he wanted to survive.

As the adult prisoners tensed and shuffled into line, the children started to cry even more.

"Get those snivelling curs in line, or one of them will end up skewered on my bayonet."

Screamed the sergeant of the guard closest to him. The sergeant was a short, stocky man with the neck and shoulders of a bull. His nose, broken many times, pointed across his pockmarked face towards his right ear. He spoke in hisses and snarls, with spittle accumulating at the corners of his mouth. His eyes were cruel and bloodshot from years of bestial bullying and hard drinking. If Camp 22 was a Godless place, he was the devil incarnate.

The parents of the children shepherded them into line, consoling them with kisses and hugs. As the camp director and his entourage approached, an anxious quiet settled over the group, prisoners and guards alike.

The director looked at the prisoners with disinterested eyes; these souls were just the same as the tens of thousands that had passed through the camp during the fourteen years he had been in charge. Most would not leave and end their lives in slavery and torture. He cared nothing for the individual, only the camp's productivity; in this respect, the children were worthless.

"Is this the latest group to arrive, sergeant?" enquired the director Rong Song Il. The director was a man of small stature, a sixty-year-old with cruel piercing eyes. Sporting a basin-cut hairstyle, he was as ugly now as he had been as a child orphan.

"Yes, director, one hundred and twenty-four, including children. This group here are all the same family, Christians." He spat out the word Christians as if they were lepers that might contaminate them all. "I have the details here, sir." Said the sergeant proffering his clipboard.

"Separate the women and children from the men and be quick about it." Commanded the director, ignoring the clipboard.

As the guards brutally tore the families apart, it brought more sobbing from the children. When the sergeant moved to hit one small girl, her mother quickly moved between the two. The blow to the side of her head was swift and cruel. As the woman slumped to the floor unconscious, the sergeant instinctively kicked the woman in the ribs.

"Stop that, you imbecile." Shouted An Sang-Ho, one of the military medical staff. "She is of no use to us injured. You'll lose a day's pay for that, you idiot."

The sergeant stepped back and came to attention. "Yes sir, sorry sir." The timbre of his voice betrayed his fear of the camp doctor.

An Sang-Ho, a reincarnate Josef Mengele, walked around the group of women, as might a farmer selecting stock at the market. Now and then, he would prod one of them, testing how much fat they had beneath their ill-fitting clothing. As he went around the group, he scribbled notes about each of them, referring to the numbers stencilled on the tunics. As he approached prisoner F18472, David's wife Rachel, he smiled menacingly;

"This one is excellent." He said as he pushed the sharp end of his pencil under her chin, forcing the woman's head up.

"Yes, my dear, you'll do nicely." He hissed ominously. Her husband, David, prisoner M16284, moved out of line towards the doctor to defend his wife, but before he could say anything, one of the

4

guards struck him across the bridge of his nose with his rifle butt. Although David staggered backwards, he did not fall. With blood pouring from his nose, he was pushed brutally back into line at the point of a bayonet. Staring across at his tearful wife, Rachel, he glowered at the doctor. His reward for that was another blow to the side of his head. David sank to his knees, the agony pulsing in his head like a slowly fading echo.

"Step out of line again, you son of a whore, and I'll slice your daughter into little pieces before your very eyes." Screamed the sergeant.

As David slowly looked up, he saw his wife shaking her head, her eyes pleading to stop him from doing anything else. They had been married sixteen years, she was his soul mate, and he would forfeit his life instantly if he thought he could save her and the children. He squeezed his nose to stem the flow of blood and nodded slowly. Rachel's eyes smiled at him, almost as if she could read his mind, compelling him to obey the guards. David closed his eyes and remembered the many times she had quelled his frustration with that same look, much like when he was about to shout at their two-year-old daughter for scribbling on his graduation certificate. As he opened his eyes again, he found the doctor staring at him.

"Well, my dear, that was gallant of him, wasn't it? If he moves again, I'll kill him myself." The doctor hissed in her ear.

The doctor turned slowly away from his prey, his eyes cold and heartless.

The camp director spoke next. "Sergeant, take these women to the family quarters. The children can go with them; they're all related so I'm sure they won't mind. The able-bodied men should be transported to the Chungbong Mine. The old ones I'll leave to your discretion, sergeant." With that, the group of officials turned in unison and marched away to the warmth of the administration building.

***

As David shuffled to the rear of a truck parked on the edge of the square, he watched the three most precious people in his life – his wife, Rachel, his daughter Ruth, and his son, Joseph – being herded away at the point of a bayonet. He thought he would never see them again. As more prisoners were forced into the truck, David was crushed by the others. As the rear doors closed, they were engulfed in darkness. The fetid atmosphere was heavy, with the smell of fear and urine. So many bodies were crammed into the back of the truck that David struggled to raise a hand to cover his nose. When the diesel engine coughed and struggled into life, the exhaust fumes added to their torment, reducing the quality of what little breathable air was available.

David had recently celebrated his thirtieth birthday. It had been a wonderful family affair. David's father, mother, brother and sister, with their children, his wife's parents and siblings, had all gathered at their small home in Hamhŭng. With years of significant shortage, the party had been modest but happy. Although there were no expensive presents or fancy delicacies to eat, all the family shared joy, happiness, and love. Rachel had made a phenomenal cake despite the shortages. David had blown out a dozen candles on his first attempt. As he gathered Rachel, Ruth and Joseph around him that day, he wished the whole family could escape North Korea and live with his elder brother Peter in South Korea.

Peter had miraculously escaped to the South 15 years ago. His Aunt had a small food company in Wŏnju, Gangwon province, which manufactured bean curd, tofu. Having graduated from Yonsei University, majoring in food technology, Peter had brought the company into the 21st century as a multi-national with an annual turnover of 300 million U. S. dollars.

But now his birthday celebrations seemed a lifetime ago. Crushed together with men from other families in the back of the truck, David closed his eyes and tried to recollect the horror of the last ten days. David had been arrested at work on the first of October by the military police. His administrative staff had stood in silence as he was dragged from his office by two Ministry of Public Security officers. He had not been given any explanation for what he had done wrong and knew nothing until he was pushed into a cell at the central police station. To his horror, he saw his wife and children handcuffed to a steel ring at the base of the rear wall. David barely had time to hug them before he was handcuffed to a second ring in the far corner of the cell. Rachel then told him that their neighbour, an officer in the State Security Department, had reported him for criticising the government and Great Leader, Kim Jong-un. Before the day was out, they were joined by David's mother and father, his younger brother, together with his wife and children. During the night, Rachel's mother and father, her handicapped sister, and her two brothers with their families had also been arrested.

In the morning, he had asked one of the guards why they had been incarcerated. The guard spat in his face, saying they didn't need a reason to lock up scum like him.

The next day, still with no official explanation as to what they had done wrong, they had all been loaded into the back of a large cattle truck. Most of the shutters were closed, and very little light penetrated the confines of the truck's interior. Its recent use made it smell of manure, and the terror of the animals it had held was palpable. The current human inhabitants felt the same. All the children were sobbing, their mothers unable to console them. All of the men were silent and shivered with fear. There was no food, no water, and just a bucket as their only toilet. It was bitterly cold, and with only light clothing, huddling together was their only means of combating hypothermia.

The interminable journey northeast to Ch'ŏngjin, North Korea's third-largest city, took a week. Broken only by infrequent stops for small amounts of food and water, they arrived at Ch'ŏngjin, exhausted and psychologically broken. They were transferred to a boxcar in the main train station's goods yard. Although it was dusty and the toilet facilities were the same, this was a palace compared to the cattle truck. When the goods train moved off, they had no idea in which direction they were travelling. The next stop was Hoeryŏng, a city in North Hamgyŏng. The boxcar remained in a siding for the best part of the day, during which they had no food or water. Finally, the boxcar was coupled to another train that took them the final 20 kilometres to Hoeryong concentration camp, Camp 22.

***

The Chungbong mine lies some forty kilometres from Camp 22. If Camp 22 is hell, the mine is the devil's anvil. Few witnesses to the barbaric conditions in this labour camp exist, as few, if any, escape its cruelty. From the moment David arrived at the concrete assembly area, another massive square, he knew that life here was cheap and his survival would be difficult. Simon, David's younger brother, saw something shiny on the ground and bent to pick it up. Standing next to him, the guard immediately hit him across the head with his billy club. Simon fell to the floor like a sack of potatoes, his scalp split open and pouring with blood. As David went to help him, he received a similar blow. David staggered at the ferocity of the impact and the blinding agony that followed. His father, Paul, caught him as he slumped to the floor.

"You worthless piece of shit. I didn't say you could bend down, did I?" The guard screamed at Simon, kicking him viciously in the ribs. A loud popping sound signalled several breaking bones. Simon moaned as the blows rained down on him, still aware of the pain even though he remained unconscious.

"Stop, please stop." Shouted his father, Paul.

The guard swung round to face the old man; his face flushed with anger. "Did I ask you to speak?" he shouted, punching him in the face. David pulled his father away from the certainty of another blow. "Now, you stupid bastards, I give the orders round here, and you won't piss, shit or eat unless I tell you. Now you meddling shitheads, pick this fucker up and get in line."

Simon regained consciousness briefly as his brother and father picked him up. However, he soon relapsed once the pair had shuffled him into line. He was a dead weight, and it was almost impossible to keep him upright. Both men realised that Simon would not survive another beating if he fell.

"Now, you bastards, this is your new home." Shouted the chief guard, another sergeant. "Here, you will earn your rights to call yourselves children of our Great Leader, Kim Il-Sung. Your blood and sweat will earn you privileges, principally, eating and sleeping." His contempt for the men was reflected in his eyes, which were cold and cruel. "At the moment, you don't have any rights. You haven't worked or earned your keep, so you will remain here till your shift in the mine starts. Now over in that pile of boots, you will find a pair that fits you like a glove." His sneer betrayed the lack of concern he had for their feet.

"You have five minutes to find that pair. So, what are you waiting for?"

Timidly the men shuffled forward to the small pile of work boots, half expecting to be beaten for stepping out of line. There was no mad rush. Miraculously, David's first pair was a perfect fit, though a little stained. As he bent down to tie the laces, he realised that the stain was dried blood, and caught in the eyelets were small pieces of hardened flesh. His silent question was answered as he looked up at the nearest guard.

"Still warm, are they? Where do you think we get these boots from, you piece of shit, Nike? "Get a pair for that sleeping turd, and look sharp about it." The guard demanded.

"It's OK, David." His semi-conscious brother Simon whispered, "I can manage."

Of course, he couldn't, and David and his father struggled to find a pair to fit Simon. Just as the guard returned, his billy club raised, they thankfully found a pair.

"Get back in line, you shitheads and listen. Your shift starts at 4 am and finishes at 6 pm. You eat and sleep when you return to the barracks, and only if you have met your quotas. You lucky bastards have come to the best holiday camp in Hamgyŏng Province." Laughed the sergeant. "Now stand up straight and wait till I return in the morning."

David watched as the sergeant and five of the guards marched away, leaving the remaining four to watch over them till morning. After four hours, Simon collapsed. As the remaining guards didn't seem to care, David did not attempt to pick him up. After another two hours, they were allowed to sit. Simon was unconscious again. That night was the longest and coldest David had ever endured. Soon after dark, the air temperature plummeted and must have been below zero. Thankfully there was no wind, as combined with such a low temperature, any wind chill would have killed them all. As it was, they only survived by huddling together. The guards were no better off.

Although they wore woollen greatcoats, they, too, were freezing. Life was cheap here whether you were friend or foe.

It was still dark at 3 am when the sergeant and his cronies returned. After sending the night guard away, he again stood before the prisoners. Lit only by the distant floodlights behind, they could not see his face, but they heard the savagery in his voice well enough.

"Well, you lazy bastards, I hope you had a nice rest because you'll have to earn your survival from now on. Stand up, NOW." He screamed.

As David attempted to wake Simon, he realised his body was stiff and lifeless. Sometime during the night, he must have mercifully slipped into a coma from which he did not return. As David hugged his brother, tears streaming down his cheeks, his father, Paul, pulled him to his feet.

"He slipped away in the night." His father whispered. "He is the lucky one; he has escaped this hell for heaven. Leave him, David; we must look after the living; the dead are beyond our help."

"What the fuck is going on here?" The sergeant screamed, hitting David and his father with a bamboo cane. "Get this man up; get him up immediately." Swiping them once more with the cane.

"He's dead." Hissed Paul.

The sergeant's response to Paul's insubordination was swift and brutal. With lightning speed, he hit Paul across the side of his head with the bamboo cane, splitting his ear almost in two. Paul staggered back with the force of the blow as blood gushed from the torn flesh.

"Don't answer me back, you sorry piece of shit. Get him up now."

When David and his father picked up Simon's body, he was stiff from rigour mortis.

"That's better." Continued the sergeant. "Now throw him in that waste skip over there and be quick about it." As David and his father laboured with the twisted corpse, the sergeant screamed at them to move faster.

"Run, you lazy bastards, run."

Moving at any pace was difficult, for they were both stiff with cold, and Simon's body was stuck in an awkward death pose. All they could manage was a shuffle. All across the square, they were pursued by a guard, who swiped them with a cane every few steps. Having lifted Simon's lifeless body into the skip, they were forced to run back to the main group of prisoners as quickly as they could, receiving further swipes with the cane as they ran. There was no time to mourn Simon's passing. Their own lives were threatened at every step.

"Now, because we have lost time dealing with that lily-livered bastard, we'll have to run to the pit head. So, follow my jeep, and no slacking, or you'll answer with your hides," the sergeant said menacingly.

While the sergeant and one other guard crossed the square to a rusty American jeep, seemingly leftover from the Korean War, the other four guards herded them west at a jogging pace, past the Equipment and Repair Shops, then around the Security Bureau to the pit-head.

***

When they arrived at the ramshackle building labelled Safety Store, all the prisoners and guards were out of breath. One of the guards, who must have weighed 120 kilos, was hanging onto the corner of the building gasping for air.

"What the fuck are you doing?" Demanded the sergeant, swiping the fat guard across the back of his head with the bamboo cane.

"Set an example, you fat bastard; stand up straight and pull yourself together. If you can't run that short distance, perhaps I should send you down the mine with this heap of shit," he shouted, waving the cane towards the prisoners. "Perhaps I would get a fair day's work out of you then."

"Yes sir," spluttered the fat guard, "I… just arrived yesterday… I will get fitter."

"Dam right, you will or die trying. Now get out of my site, you fat tub of lard."

The sergeant turned to face the prisoners and addressed them once more.

"Right, listen up, the shift supervisor here," he said, waving his cane at a short, stocky man dressed in dirty navy-blue overalls who had suddenly appeared in the doorway of the Safety Store, "he will give you a helmet and light, then tell you what you will be doing and where you will be working. This is a dangerous place, and we don't want you hurting yourself; that's my fucking job." He chuckled menacingly at his own joke. "Mr Shim over to you."

"OK, sergeant. You bastards will call me sir from now on, and be warned; your life depends upon it. My men will soon give you a helmet, a lamp and a belt. You will do exactly what I'm about to show you. Thread the battery box onto the belt and buckle it around your waist, the box at the back. Then bring the lamp over your left shoulder and clip it to your helmet. Adjust the strap and put it on your head. Got that?"

"Yes, sir." Some of the prisoners mumbled.

"I didn't hear that. What did you say?"

"Yes, sir." They all shouted in unison.

"Now, another thing." Shim continued. "On each battery box is a metal disc with a number on it. This number identifies you." He said, pointing at the body of the prisoners. "At the start of every shift, you will write your name on the blackboard in the lamp room and put the disc number by your name. Before you descend the shaft, you will give that disc to the lift operator. He later checks the board with the discs he's been given. This is so we know who is down the mine and that no one is missing, injured or dead. If you fuck up the board, you will find yourself travelling down the shaft by gravity, because I will personally kick your arse over the edge. It's about 450 metres straight down, so you'll have plenty of time to contemplate your mistake before you end your miserable life as a red stain at the bottom of the shaft. Am I making myself clear?" He shouted.

"Yes, sir." Came the unified reply.

"Good, now file into the lamp room and do as I told you.

In ten minutes, they were equipped and once more standing in front of Mr Shim outside the lamp room.

"OK, this is your squad leader Sohn Kwang-Ho. He is a prisoner like you. But he has earned the privilege to lead a team like you lot in glorious toil for our Great Leader, Kim Il-Sung. His privileges depend on your productivity. Fuck up, and he will kick your arse down the shaft. Got that?"

"Yes, sir."

"Now I understand that you were a little tardy coming over here. So as a reward, you will use the ladder roads. Climbing down 400 metres or so of the ladder roads will pep you up for the day ahead. If you are lazy at the coal face, you will climb back up again at the finish of your shift. You will have missed your food ration by the time you get up here. So put your backs into it today and prove the sergeant wrong. He thinks you are worthless pieces of shit, unworthy of working in the mine. He just wants to beat you to death for fun. So, work hard if you don't want to end up in the same skip your relative did earlier. And if you want less strenuous work, work harder still. OK, Sohn, they're all yours."

"Come with me then." Said Sohn Kwang-Ho. "I'll take your discs and set you off down the ladder roads. You'll have 35 minutes to get down to the bottom. Don't make me wait for you."

***

Colonel Doctor, An Sang-Ho watched the death throes of EHF18472 (Experimental Human Female #18472). Clawing ineffectively at the glass walls of the experiment chamber until she slid down to her knees, her face twisted in agony. Her face was grossly distorted, her tongue swollen, and her bloodshot eyes bulged from their sockets. Large blue-red blemishes had developed on her pale skin, and blood flowed freely from her nose. Just six minutes after the nerve agent had been injected into the chamber, she began the violent convulsions that signalled the extinction of life.

"That concludes the testing on Batch B. On average, it kills two minutes faster than Batch A, Doctor." Said Song Min-Su, An's enthusiastic lab technician.

"Yes, yes, we have saved our nation a few more minutes," Sang-Ho replied wearily. Though Min-Su was behind him, Sang-Ho saw the technician's shoulders drop, reflected in the glass panel gas chamber. Sang-Ho turned to him. "You have done well, my friend. Once the Professor sees these results, we will start mass production of N.A. – nerve agent – 6B. I will ensure the Professor knows how hard you have worked on this project." Sang-Ho smiled at his friend and patted his shoulder heartily. "It is regrettable that we won't be working together on the new project."

"But Doctor, why? Haven't I worked hard enough to move to the new laboratory with you?"

"Yes, of course, you have, but I thought you'd want to finish the work on 6B."

"No, no, sir. I want to continue working for you if you will permit me?"

"Are you sure Min-Su? You will miss out on the praise and glory that goes with the end of a project."

"I am happy with that choice, sir. It is a privilege to work with such a genius as you."

"Stop with the worship stuff. You know I hate such servile fawning."

Min-Su was crushed and turned away to the control panel. As he switched on the powerful extractor fans, he wondered if he did want to work with An Sang-Ho anymore.

"I'm sorry Min-Su. That was cruel of me. I will speak to the Professor today. I'm sure he will allow you to transfer to the new lab. Call the guard and get some of those bastard prisoners to shift this carcass out of here."

Although Min-Su smiled at An Sang-Ho, he was still smarting from his insult. As Min-Su picked up the telephone, he bit his lip, fighting off the urge to change his mind and stick with the 6B project.

A heavy, triple-sealed door at the rear of the experimental chamber swung open, and two prisoners dressed in rags shuffled in to clear away the dead woman. With one at the shoulders and the other at the feet, they dragged the body across the concrete floor and dumped it unceremoniously into a two-wheeled barrow before re-sealing the rear door.

2. Chungbong.

A continuous draft of hot, dusty air swept up the shaft, sometimes gusting so strong that David thought he would lose his grip on the ladder and become the red stain Shim had spoken of. The ladder roads were a nightmare – step after step, monotonous, mind-numbing, and seemingly endless. Throughout David's descent into the bowels of the earth, the muscles in his thighs and forearms burned and quivered as they screamed out for oxygen.

The ladder roads comprised of thirty fifteen-metre ladders and just as many narrow, rickety platforms. Each ladder was 40 centimetres wide, with a similar separation between each rung. From above, the ladders seemed to spiral down the shaft. Occasional rests on the narrow platforms gave David only brief respite from the agony in his chest and limbs. With each step, his breathing became more desperate and tortured by the physical effort needed to keep climbing down one ladder after another. Each passing minute of this torment dragged on and on until time blurred into a unified misery.

When David's foot touched solid ground near the bottom of the shaft, he could not believe he had made it. His whole body ached from the exertion, and although each new breath helped him to recover, it was a painfully slow process. Behind him, his father-in-law Isaac was doubled up gasping for air; his asthmatic wheezing was audible over the background noise from working machinery at the pit bottom. David stood beside him, encouraging the old man to breathe deeply and more slowly.

Sohn Kwang-Ho waited in the shadows for all the men to arrive at the pit bottom. When he had counted them all down, he stepped forward to address them.

"That took forty-three minutes; that's eight minutes too long."

The gasping and wheezing group of prisoners collectively sighed in horror as they imagined climbing back up the ladders at the end of the shift. Some of them knew they wouldn't make it. A look of despair spread across their faces like a Mexican wave at a soccer match.

"However," Sohn continued, "I know my watch is unreliable, so this morning, I'll let you off."

He winked at them and smiled, ensuring they realised how lucky they were. David breathed a sigh of relief. He was convinced that if the mine supervisor, Shim, had been waiting for them, they would not have easily escaped the climb-out. He would soon discover that Shim and the mining engineers only made inspections twice a week, and they never supervised the prisoners. There were no military police either. The supervisors were all trustees, and the productivity targets they had to meet ensured that they pushed the prisoners just as hard as any guard would have done.

***

Sohn Kwang-Ho led the men from the pit bottom, along a service tunnel, to a crosscut in the main entry tunnel, where they were told to get into the empty ore cars that would take them to the coal face. It was forbidden in most modern mines because of the risk of injury. Later Sohn Kwang-Ho told them that if any activity increased the productivity of the squad, then it was allowed.

The one-kilometre journey along the main entry – haulage tunnel – took them to another crosscut tunnel where they exited the ore cars. Sohn Kwang-Ho issued them with picks and shovels before they walked the final 200 metres to the coal face. Although they used a longwall mining technique, they had no machines to help them. The panel being excavated was over twenty metres wide, with a coal seam just one metre high. The roof of the excavated seam was held up by pine pit props 150 mm in diameter, secured with timber wedges. David's first task was to knock away the props holding up the roof of the goaf – the area left to collapse after coal extraction, then erect them in the part of the panel that the other men were currently excavating. Kneeling within the excavated panel, the men used short-handled pickaxes to cleave the coal from the one-metre seam. Behind them were others who shovelled the coal to the rear. It was hot, remorseless, back-breaking work. A gang of four men loaded the coal into the ore cars before David's father and father-in-law pushed the fully laden ore cars down the gate roadway – access tunnel – to the main entry. They would couple the cars together for the journey to the pit bottom, then push empty cars back to the excavation panel.

David's father-in-law Isaac was barely coping with this task. He was older than Paul and suffered from arthritis in his back. Although Isaac put on a brave face, Sohn Kwang-Ho soon realised that the squad's productivity targets might not be met. Three hours into the shift, Sohn Kwang-Ho blew a whistle that signified a water break. Minutes earlier, two boys in their early teens had carried buckets of water, from somewhere down the main entry, to the squad's excavation area. No sooner had they deposited their burden; they disappeared back down the gate roadway and into the gloom beyond. The work, within the airless confines of their panel, was hot and very dusty. If the work didn't kill them, black lung – coal workers' pneumoconiosis – certainly would. Black lung is a chronic disease caused by breathing in excessive amounts of coal dust. The dust becomes embedded in the lungs, causing fibrosis, which makes breathing very difficult. Unlike a modern coal mine, there were no water sprinklers to minimise the dust in Chungbong.

They were allowed just one cup of water but no time to savour it. It was brown with tannins, warm, stale and far from refreshing. As David looked at the other men, their sweaty bodies grimed with black dust, he wondered how long he could suffer in this hellhole.

"You swap jobs with this old man and keep those cars moving. We're judged by how many of our cars reach the surface, and we need to catch up. Take the chalk from Isaac and mark the cars 32A. Your father will show you." Instructed Sohn Kwang-Ho. "Now get going."

"Yes, sir."

It had been a break of just six minutes, hardly enough time to recover properly. As David took the chalk from his father-in-law, he wanted to reassure the old man that he would look out for him. Anticipating what he was about to say, Isaac smiled at his son-in-law and patted him on the shoulder.

"Don't worry about me, David; I can do this; I'll be OK."

And when David moved to speak, Isaac put his forefinger to his lips to silence his concern.

"I'll be OK. Now go push some coal."

It was evident to David that Isaac couldn't cope with the physical hardship for long, and another eleven hours of their shift were left.

When the whistle blew again, there was water and rice gruel, a cup of each. The gruel may have tasted better if it was hot, but cold and full of coal dust, it was terrible. David would have retched if this hadn't been the first food he'd had for 48 hours. However, that hardship was still not enough to make the gruel palatable.

Lunch, if you could call it that, was twenty minutes. None of the men was used to such physical labour, and being so tired, no one spoke throughout the whole break. David sat with his back against one of the roof props in the gate roadway. There were two bulbs in their headlamps, a main with a spot beam and a reserve, much weaker and more diffuse. They had all been advised to switch to the reserve at the start of their break. Even though they were not working, there was no respite from the heat. There were no drafts of fresh air; it was just stale and rank. As well as coal dust, the air was full of sounds; the clangs and bangs of others working further down the main entry and, curiously, the constant dripping of water. Plink, plink, plink, regular and monotonous. With such discomfort, the heat, the darkness and the strange noises, David's mind started to play tricks. Shapes in the half-shadow moved before his eyes; the face of the sergeant at Camp 22 loomed towards him, his face twisted by hate and cruelty. It wasn't easy to know where the fantasy ended and reality began. David shook his head to rid himself of the demons. With such a low level of light in their section, the darkness pressed in on him. He was not claustrophobic, but the darkness was oppressive; it felt like it was smothering him. As the demons returned, he had to switch his main light on to reassure himself that others beneath the dull, glow-worm points of light shared the same small space he occupied.

Before the whistle went again, Sohn Kwang-Ho swapped everyone's tasks except for Isaac. This time David and his father were shovelling the excavated coal into the ore cars. Some lumps were so heavy they required both to lift them into the ore car. It was a good job. There weren't many of them that size, as they could feel their remaining strength leak away twice as fast. The two men, who were charged with the task of rolling them down to the main entry, David had not seen before. One of them, Jang-Ho, couldn't stop talking. He was a short, wiry man with very little hair and a permanent smile. His missing front teeth gave him an endearing, comical look. He had survived in the pit for five months. The smile was fixed to escape beatings from the guards; it had worked well for him. David liked him from the moment he spoke; it was good to know someone else in this Godless place, David thought. He told them that their squad leader, Sohn Kwang-Ho was the best; the others, he said, were cruel and regularly beat their crews. The work was horrendous on its own, but with someone bullying you, it would be impossible. Jang-Ho also told him that their squad had the best safety record.

"A friend of mine is in another squad," he said smiling, "They've had two deaths in the last two weeks. One from a roof collapse in their panel, and the second man was pushed down the shaft. Their squad leader, Noh Sung-Uk, is worse than some of the guards, a real bastard. He has a piece of rubber hose that he hits you with. My friend could hardly raise his arms above his head last week; he had been beaten so severely. Stay away from him if you can; he'd kill you without a second thought.

"Who pushed the guy down the shaft?" Asked David

"The squad leader, Noh Sung-Uk, of course. When my friend was being beaten, this new guy, I don't know his name, stepped between Noh and my friend. He told Noh to stop. Instead, Noh hit him with the hose and broke his nose. At the end of the shift, Noh told the whole squad to climb the ladder roads. When the new guy reached the top, Noh was waiting for him. He just pushed him off the top landing."

"What happened to Noh? Surely, he was punished."

"Yes, he was. Sergeant Ji, who brought you over here, kicked him in the balls and told him he did all the killing around here."

David looked at Jang-Ho in horror. "Is that all?"

"Yep, They like Noh. He's one of their informants. He tells them anything he can find out from the other prisoners. Say he finds out that someone's planning an escape, he tells them to wait for them to make their move and then catch them in the act. That's when we have a public execution to attend. I tell you, keep your head tucked in, don't draw attention to yourself, otherwise…" Jang-Ho drew his finger across his throat and made a squelching sound.

"Sounds like good advice to me," said David, "we'll remember that, eh Father?"

"Seems life in Chungbong is like swimming with sharks, and you don't know which one will bite you first." Replied Paul.

"Oi, you lot," shouted Sohn Kwang-Ho, "get on with some bloody work. There's no time to chat. Or do you want to climb out of here?"

"Sorry." Shouted David.

"Don't be sorry; just put your back into it."

***

In the heart of the detention centre of Camp 22, Haengyong, Colonel Doctor, An Sang-Ho, surveyed his new laboratory with great pride. Now he could undertake the research project he had dreamed of all those years ago after he had graduated from Pyongyang Medical University (PMU) in 1951. Professor Jin, his supervisor, introduced him to the fascinating world of parasitology. For his PhD, he studied parasite-induced changes in host behaviour, specifically the fatal attraction of rats to their top predator, cats. Once infected with *Toxoplasma gondii*, the protozoan can alter the behaviour of its intermediate host, in this case, the rat, to infect its definitive host, the cat. The parasite forms cysts in the rat's brain, which release chemicals that suppress the rat's innate and pronounced defensive reaction to the odours of its predators. Effectively it causes the rat to move towards the cat, not away from it. Such suicidal behaviour advantages the parasite, allowing it to complete its lifecycle inside the cat. Now An Sang-Ho had convinced the medical experimentation committee that his theories regarding parasite-induced behaviour modification could greatly benefit the Democratic People's Republic of Korea. He, An Sang-Ho, would develop a simple and effective bio-weapon that could change the course of human history. An Sang-Ho couldn't wait to start.

The lab technician, Song Min-Su, saw An Sang-Ho staring out the window towards the distant Hamgyŏng Sanmaek Mountains. The lab tech always found him a complex man to read. There was no doubting his genius, but he was hardly personable. Five years ago, when Min-Su started to work for An Sang-Ho, the doctor was affable and gracious. In those early days, An Sang-Ho assisted Song Min-Su with his studies, even paying for some of his courses. However, since the doctor's wife had died of breast cancer 18 months ago, he had become dour and prone to periods of depression. In the last few weeks, his demeanour had changed yet again. His son had recently graduated top of his class at PMU, and he had come to work with his father here at the institute. Though his son was now finishing work on the 6B nerve agent project, he was expected to join his father within the month once the project had moved to its production phase. Although the doctor seemed free of his depressive states, he was still prone to outbursts of temper. Yet, the lab tech still respected him through all the tempestuous times. Much of the glory generated by An Sang-Ho's brilliance as a biochemist had rubbed off on him too. Song Min-Su was an accomplished technician respected by the many project leaders in the institute. He and the doctor made a good team. Although not recognised internationally – as their research contravened the international ethical guidelines for biomedical research involving human subjects – it was still broadening the knowledge base of human physiology. He justified the cruel experiments as such protocols were only guidelines, near-sited, sentimental rubbish, published by the Council for International Organizations of Medical Sciences (CIOMS). An Sang-Ho and Song Min-Su worked with condemned prisoners who should be exterminated anyway because they were factionalists, a threat to the revolution and all peoples of the DPRK. The lab tech was honoured to work for such a dedicated officer of the revolution.

"I never tire of such a view Min-Su." Said An Sang-Ho emerging from his reverie. "I am sure my wife is in a similarly beautiful place. She always loved the mountains, the crisp, clean air, untainted by the revolution." The colonel doctor turned to face his faithful technician and smiled. "When we walked the mountain paths and trails and made love beside the streams of Mount Paektu-san, we luxuriated in the sights, smells and sounds of a different world. Our ambition was always to move closer to the mountains, near Namhasŏ, on the pine-forested slopes of Kwanmobong. I can tell you we were a world away from this hellhole." An Sang-Ho turned once more to the window and the distant mountains. "This place has the smell of death around it. My darling wife hated it here and, in a small way, hated me too for being here."

"An Sang-Ho, you mustn't talk of these things. There are spies, jealous, small-minded people who would gladly see you hang for such talk."

"Yes, you're right. I mustn't forget that others are stoking the fires of hell as we speak. We are the champions of this institute, and thus we've become the targets of the little people. Tell me, what do we still need for our experiment?"

"We are still waiting for the vials of *Toxoplasma gondii* from the PMU School of Parasitology. I rang them again this morning. They said that we should get the consignment tomorrow. The cats and rats are already in the small animal containment lab. I have recruited some prisoners to care for them. They're women who did a similar job before their internment." Song Min-Su saw the concern on An Sang-Ho's face and anticipated his next question.

"Sir, I trust them; they have impeccable qualifications. Besides, they know their families will suffer if they fuck up."

"Yes, yes, that is all good, but this research is so critical. We can't allow anything or anyone to fuck it up, as you say. They must be supervised Min-Su."

"And they are, sir; I have another technician rostered on whenever they're in the lab. Believe me, An Sang-Ho, everything will be OK."

"Well, OK, if you say so. But you will be accountable if anything goes wrong."

Song Min-Su didn't answer the veiled threat; it was what he had to put up with working with An Sang-Ho.

"I've also commissioned the workshop to make the maze you designed. That will be ready by the end of the week. They are the only two things we're waiting for. When will your son be joining us, sir?"

"Well, he's still caught up with the nerve agent project. By the end of the month, I should think. But he'll need to catch up with the theory stuff before he gets here."

"I, too, am unsure of what we will be doing. What will be our goal, An Sang-Ho?"

"That is classified and known by just myself, Professor Jang and the senior members of the experimental research committee. Needless to say, Song Min-Su, when we develop the behavioural manipulation of the protozoan *Toxoplasma gondii* to its full potential, it will be very useful to our glorious nation.

***

Thankfully when the men of Sohn Kwang-Ho's squad finished their shift, they rose from the bowels of the mine in the cage elevator and not via the ladder roads. Having collected their tag from the lift operator, they handed over their lamps to the lamp-room supervisor. Unlike miners in other commercial DPRK mines, the prisoners had no showers. Kwang-Ho took them to a large concrete shed that contained a trough the size of a small swimming pool and told them to get out of their work clothes and wash off. The men of David's family were aghast at the thought of stripping off naked on such a cold winter's evening.

"We'll surely freeze." Said Isaac, voicing the concern of the others.

"Come on, you babies," shouted the ever-smiling Jang-Ho, "if you get washed quickly, you won't feel the cold. Besides, the cold is your ally. It numbs the pain of everything else.

Such strange logic was lost on David; he couldn't see filthy, freezing cold water being anyone's friend. But as Jang-Ho stripped off and jumped into the trough, David felt the ice-cold wind tear at his flesh through his working tunic. They were all complaining about the heat down the mine, and now they were complaining about the cold. David did not want to stay filthy, so he reluctantly stripped off and joined his new friend in the water.

When the bitterly cold water ran down his back, it was so cold it took his breath away. Jang-Ho laughed and rubbed his skin with a bar of hard soap he had fished from the trough: more water, more torture. David washed Jang-Ho's back and then turned to watch his father and brother going through the same agony that he was. Realising that Isaac had not even taken off his clothes, David grabbed him, stripped him and then pulled him into the water. He was shivering so hard that his tremulous voice and chattering teeth reminded David of washing his son in the sink of a rest area toilet block near Wŏnsan. Joseph had been playing near an old iron ochre mine and was covered in red iridescent clay. Despite Joseph's protestations and his father's mechanical scrubbing, his son's skin remained red for the rest of their holiday. As David climbed out of the trough, another prisoner grabbed him by the shoulder and pulled him backwards. He fell back into the water and completely submerged for a second as he lifted himself out of the water, coughing and spluttering. The other man grabbed him by the throat.

"I'll have the soap now, fresh meat."

David thought he had lost it in the water, but he recovered it quickly and handed it to the stranger.

Before David could speak, Sohn Kwang-Ho intervened. "I see you've met one of my new squad members, Noh Sung-Uk. Let the poor guy go; he doesn't know who the important people round here are yet."

Noh looked up at the other squad leader standing just a metre away and stared at him. Their hatred for each other was plain for all to see. They obviously had a history. David scampered out of the trough while Noh was distracted. Suddenly he realised he wasn't cold anymore.

Once they were dressed in cleaner rags taken from a heap near the trough, Sohn Kwang-Ho escorted them east across the camp to the prisoner's barracks. The barracks consisted of four large buildings just a few minutes from the assembly area where they had spent the previous night. Inside the barracks were the mess hall, some washrooms and the dormitories. The windows were black with coal dust, so the lights inside were permanently on. A few low-wattage bulbs glowed a dull orange, their intensity constantly oscillating as the electrical supply surged and ebbed away. The atmosphere inside the barracks was uninviting; it reeked of stale boiled cabbage and sweat. A constant echo of shouts and cries emanated from behind closed doors along the endless corridors.

"This is it." Declared Sohn Kwang-Ho, as he opened the dormitory door with his foot. "This is where our squad sleep and rest our weary bones. Choose a bunk without bedding, and then I'll issue you a blanket."

David and the other family members filed into the room and quickly migrated to the far side of the dormitory to choose a bed. The bunks were constructed entirely of wood and resembled six-foot by three-foot trays. There was no comfort in them at all. David chose the top one and Isaac, the bottom bed. David was worried about the old man and wanted to watch him closely. Soon after Isaac climbed onto his bed, he was fast asleep.

Minutes later, Sohn Kwang-Ho issued them a traditional sleeping mat, called a *yo* and a blanket.

David shook his head in disbelief when he saw what the squad leader was handing out, unlike the acrylic mink blankets that David and his family were used to. These were coarsely woven woollen squares that smelled of stale sweat, just like the rest of the building.

"Don't turn your nose up at these; they are valuable. They may smell a bit now, but they'll smell a lot worse once you buggers have had them a while." Laughed Sohn Kwang-Ho. "Now you know where we live; we'll go and get our food ration." Suddenly his demeanour changed. "A warning to you all, you're new here, you know it, and so do the other lifers. For your protection, we should move around the barracks as a squad, safety in numbers and all that. Just as you met Noh Sung-Uk earlier, so you will face confrontation with the others in the block. Keep your eyes to the floor, keep out of other people's business, even though you will witness jungle brutality. Don't look up if you witness a beating; that's the best way to end up dead. Now wake up your father-in-law, and let's get some food.

David and the others sat at a long wooden table and waited for their squad to be called to the servery. Sohn Kwang-Ho and Jang-Ho collected the food in two cut-down vegetable oil cans. Each team received a bowl of salted cabbage soup into which small amounts of corn and potatoes had been added. There were no other vegetables and certainly no meat.

"Is this it?" Protested Isaac. "Where is the meat?"

"This isn't some fancy hotel, you old fool." Laughed Jang-Ho.

"We do have meat sometimes," said Sohn Kwang-Ho, "but we have to catch it ourselves. So, I suggest you leave a small piece of that potato. You might catch a nice rat with it if you're lucky."

"Occasionally, we might catch a snake or a frog." Added Jang-Ho, the ever-present smile on his face.

"Oh," Isaac said lamely as he scooped his last spoonful of cabbage soup into his quivering mouth.

"You look like you've just swallowed a rat, Isaac." Added Jang-Ho. At that point, the whole squad erupted in laughter; that single comment was the catalyst that dissolved much of the fear the newcomers had for Camp 22. Jang-Ho slapped the old man on the back and showed him a piece of potato that he was saving. "Don't worry, old man; you can share my rat."

Another peal of laughter chorused around the squad. Laughter was the best medicine.

***

That night was very noisy as the older squad members snored through until the next, inevitable dawn. Many newcomers couldn't sleep as they relived the horrors of the last forty-eight hours. Paul thought of his son, Simon, who mercifully had left the hell the living were facing. He remembered the happier times they had shared in their Hamhŭng home. He thought of the firsts, his first steps, and his first day at school. Of his marriage and the couple's first child, his first grandchild. Then he thought of his grandson's firsts, his first ride in a cattle truck, his first railway boxcar, his first concentration camp, and the last time he saw his father. The old man held his hands to his face and wept.

David thought of his wife, Rachel. He thought, too, of the best times they had both shared during their courtship and marriage. Their first child had been Joseph, a handsome lad who most resembled his granddad, Paul. Not so their second child Ruth who was a mirror image of her mother and the apple of her father's eye. David also thought of firsts, the comical moments, the proud moments. The continual competition between Joseph and Ruth, who could run the fastest, or jump the furthest, who was best at school, or simply competing for their parents' love and affection. David remembered the last time he saw his wife when she had urged him to keep silent, to stay alive, to fight the battles he could win and to look away from the ones he couldn't. With that thought, David felt ashamed, cowardly even. If there was any chance of saving his wife and children, he could not risk his life or his fitness. He could survive any horror as long as there was just a single grain of hope that they could be saved. Hope that would keep David alive.

3. Sohn Kwang-Ho's Story.

Sohn Kwang-Ho singled out David after they had eaten what little food there was on a cold and rainy evening in late November.

"I need to talk with you alone." He said, ushering him around the corner of the building. "Let's get out of earshot of the others. Hopefully, we can stand under the eaves without getting wet."

Outside, his father, Paul, and brother, Luke, were already waiting. It was a cold, bleak evening, as dark storm clouds piled up before crossing the Chinese border in the north. The rain beat the ground like a drum, splashing mud over the men's feet. While gusts of wind frequently blew the raindrops sideways, that cumulatively soaked their tunics.

His heart fell when he saw his father and brother, for he knew that Kwang-Ho must be the bearer of bad news.

As his father hugged him, David anticipated what Sohn Kwang-Ho would say.

"I'm afraid I've bad news for you all," whispered the squad leader, "I have a friend in Camp 22; he works in the detention centre as a clerk. He often sends me news of what happens in the camp. David, your wife is dead. She died the same day you were brought to Chungbong."

The colour immediately drained from David's face. He felt his legs turn to jelly and would have collapsed had it not been for his father's support. His face turned ashen grey, and despite the cold, tiny beads of perspiration appeared above his mouth and across his forehead. He felt light-headed and nauseous. Sohn Kwang-Ho stepped forward to help Paul while Luke, equally shocked, turned his face to the wall.

"How can you be sure?" Mumbled David.

"He files away all the medical reports from the experimental research laboratory. I'm so sorry, David." He said, gently holding David by the arm.

"How, how did she die?"

"You don't need to know that. In any case, I don't have the details. She's gone now; she's beyond suffering, free from the misery which we, the living, share. She is with God now, with your brother Simon. Be strong, David; she needs you to be strong for the rest of the family."

Through the haze of his misery, the mention of God caught Paul's attention. "Are you a Christian Sohn Kwang-Ho? He said gently.

Kwang-Ho looked at the old man, searching his eyes for any hint of disapproval. Admitting you were a Christian anywhere in the DPRK, let alone in a prison camp, was as good as signing your death warrant. He had told no one of his beliefs. Except for a fellow Christian in Camp 22, no one else knew. Had he made a fatal mistake? He hesitated before answering Paul.

"Relax, Sohn Kwang-Ho; we're all of the same belief here. We share the same God. How else do you think we can survive in this place?" Said Luke as he turned to face the group.

"Yes, I'm a Christian." He said nervously. "You, too, must be careful who you share your belief with. If the guards knew, you, and all your family, would be sent to the gallows. I have heard you whisper to each other using Christian names; you must not do this when others are around, as that is a certain path to the hangman."

David looked up at Sohn Kwang-Ho, his eyes filled with tears. "Thank you for trusting us. We will keep your secret safe." He whispered; his heart so filled with emotion he could hardly speak. "And yes, we will be careful what we say to each other."

"Have you any news of the others?" Pleaded Luke.

"Yes, I'm afraid I have." All three men faced Sohn Kwang-Ho, terrified of what he had to say next. "Your brother Simon's wife, Na-Young, also died at the hands of the scientists. I didn't want to tell Isaac myself; he isn't as strong as the rest of us. I thought it best come from you."

"You did the best thing telling us first." Said Paul. "I don't know whether he'd cope with that right now. I think we shouldn't tell him. What good would it do?"

The other squad members looked at Paul, unsure that keeping silent was the best course of action.

"Wouldn't you want to know if your daughter had died?" Asked Luke.

"Yes, of course, I would, and sadly so would Isaac. But that's not important now. Isaac is frail physically and psychologically; news like this could break him. I truly believe he would lose the will."

"It's wrong to keep silent; he has a right to know what has happened." Stated Luke.

"It's not a matter of rights to break a man with news of something that can't be changed. We must protect the living. What of his wife, Min-Hee? Is she still alive?

"I have no other news. I am guessing the other women are alive, and I haven't heard about any children being killed." Sohn Kwang-Ho declared. "The camp authorities are cruel and heartless, but they usually hold the family responsible for the welfare of its children. So, I can't be certain, but I suspect that the rest of the women are alive and looking after the children. They will remain alive if they're still useful to the regime, either by working on the vegetable farm, in the food or furniture factories." Though he spoke the words, he did not fully believe them. He, too, had a responsibility to keep these men alive. To do that, he would give them hope, and hope would foster their will to live, regardless of the privations of Chungbong.

As the family patriarch, Luke and David looked to their father for guidance.

"No, we shouldn't tell him, not yet, a while anyway." Said Paul, shaking his head as if ridding himself of a decision he would regret later.

"Can your friend find out about the remaining women and children?" Implored David.

"He is risking his life, sending me information as it is. They would torture him to get at us if he was caught searching records or asking improper questions. I can't ask any more of him; I can't. He knows of your family, and I trust him to tell us if anything else happens."

As David opened his mouth to argue, his father held his fingers to his son's lips. Obediently David was silent.

"Can't we do anything for the women? If we escape, can we rescue them?" Asked Luke.

"No, we can't. They are forty kilometres away, which is why it has taken weeks for the news I have given you to get here. If you escape from here, you would have to break into the main camp, past armed guards and killer dogs, to get to them. Then you would have to break out again, with the women and children in tow. I'm sorry to break your hearts, but they are beyond rescue." Sohn Kwang-Ho saw David's shoulders drop as the reality of his words hit home.

"Look, there is hope," he continued. "you, David, are the one who has been deemed guilty of sedition. It is your life that is forfeit. You will never be set free, but the womenfolk; are only guilty by association. If they survive the deprivations of the camp and accept re-education, they could be released in just a few years."

"Really?" said Paul, latching onto the slender strand of hope that Sohn Kwang-Ho offered. "Can we improve their situation and help them survive the camp?"

"No, not really, it would be far too risky for us. Look, they have less strenuous jobs and access to more food than we do." Kwang-Ho lied. "They have a greater chance of surviving than we do. All we can do is pray and hope. My friend will send us news about your family if he can. Be patient, please."

The reality, Kwang-Ho knew, was quite different. If they worked on the farm, their work would be backbreaking, and if they were caught stealing any of the produce, they would face the garrotte or worse. It would be a miracle if more than the strongest survived. And the chances of the children surviving were even less.

A cloud of despair shrouded the small group of men. Although they couldn't abandon all hope, neither could they believe they would see their families again. Squatting now on their haunches, they stared at the rain bouncing off the muddy ground beside the barracks.

As David watched the ground swallow more and more of the raindrops, the clearer he envisaged Camp 22 consuming the endless stream of innocents. As the rain flowed away across the dark earth, all hope for the future flowed from his heart. Could his children survive? Because that was all, he had left.

***

Song Min-Su had fed twenty rats the *Toxoplasma gondii* oocysts that he had earlier extracted from the faeces of cats infected with the parasite. A further twenty rats, free of the parasite, were used as controls. At the end of the study, Min-Su killed all the rats to confirm whether they were, or were not, infected with the parasite by microscopically examining macerated brain tissue for the presence of cysts. Both sets were fourth-generation, wild-laboratory hybrids rather than rats taken from the wild. This ensured that the rats were initially parasite free whilst having behavioural patterns comparable to their wild counterparts.

The experimental maze was two metres square, with six different routes, each ending in a chamber similar to nest boxes where the rats were typically housed. Bedding material, in the end, chambers had been taken from other nest boxes that had previously housed rabbits, cats, or other rats. Similar bowls of food and water had been placed in each chamber.

Because the rats were essentially nocturnal, Min-Su started the experiments in the early morning. Each rat was released at the start of the maze, and its behaviour was observed, in low light conditions, for thirty minutes. Each change of direction and the number of visits to each scented chamber were recorded. At the end of each run, Min-Su had wiped down the maze channels with scent-free paper towels before another rat was released. He had repeated this experiment every night for the past week, starting with a clean maze with different bedding in each chamber. This would ensure that the rats entering the labyrinth would not be imprinted by routes they had previously taken.

After 100 hours of observed behaviour, a clear pattern emerged. Firstly, the infected rats were more active than their uninfected counterparts. In particular, wild animals are innately neophobic, suspicious of new environments and odours, yet the infected rats were measurably more inquisitive. Rats elicit a strong aversion to cat odours, yet in his experiments, Min-Su had shown that although uninfected rats avoided cat-scented areas, the infected ones did not. Infected rats visited the cat-scented nest boxes twenty-five per cent more often than the uninfected ones. Importantly Min-Su observed no other differences in social behaviour between the infected and uninfected populations.

He would repeat the same experiment tonight, except that instead of using scented bedding, he had tethered, in the various chambers, either a cat, a rat or a rabbit. He thought that if the parasite modified the behaviour of its secondary host and infected rats would be positively affected by cat odours. Such a fatal attraction should result in more infected rats being killed by the cats than uninfected ones. He had another forty rats to prove his case.

Long into the night, the piercing screams of cats, rats and rabbits echoed down the corridors of the experimental research wing of Camp 22's detention centre.

***

Kwang-Ho sat mumbling at the back of the dormitory, his head in his hands, his voice so low that his words were unintelligible. David had not seen him like this before and was concerned for his friend as he appeared to be crying as well. David sat beside the squad leader and waited for him to look up.

"Kwang-Ho, what's the matter?" said David when he was eventually silent.

"Today is the second anniversary of my arrival at Camp 22."

"I know coming here is hardly something to celebrate, but you're so upset. Can it help to talk about it?"

Kwang-Ho looked into David's eyes, searching for any sign of insincerity. His survival at Camp 22 and Chungbong was only possible because he kept his personal life hidden. He talked to few and trusted none.

"My family and I came here in similar circumstances to you." This was the second time he had shared some part of himself with this stranger.

"I'm sorry to hear that…" said David sympathetically, hesitating before he completed the sentence. "Are they still alive?"

Again, Kwang-Ho was reluctant to reveal any more of his story. As David smiled and patted his shoulder, he saw something in his eyes, confirming that he could trust this man. It was the birth of a friendship forged from extreme hardships, which would last a lifetime. Kwang-Ho smiled at David. He had bottled up his emotions for too long; purging himself of the emotional turmoil within his heart would be therapeutic, a release. A cathartic release of conflicting emotions that had begun to poison his very soul. Entangled in the love he had for his wife and three daughters was hate, frustration and anger. Hate for the butchers who watched his family die in agony, frustration and anger that he could neither save them nor meter out justice on the perpetrators of such a crime. Kwang-Ho was also ashamed of himself for allowing such a beautiful thing –the love for his family – to become contaminated by such an ugly emotion as hate. As Kwang-Ho turned away, massaging his temples, he began his story.

"My family and I lived in Kanggye; I was an architect, and my wife, Sung Su-Jung, was a nurse. My daughters were in high school. Eun-Su was fifteen; she wanted to be a doctor. Jin-Sook was thirteen and wanted to be a teacher, and her twin Sun-Hee wanted to be an architect like her dad. My father, Young-Ho, who lost his wife in a car accident ten years ago, was reported for praying in tongues at her graveside. He was so angry when he was arrested that he called Kim Il-Sung a murderer." Always conscious that someone might hear what he was saying Kwang-Ho paused for a second, looking around to ensure they were not overheard. "I think his actual words were that he was a corrupt murdering bastard." Kwang-Ho smiled as he repeated his father's words in a whisper.

"My father had blamed the state for her death because she had died of an infection that might have been prevented if the hospital had had an adequate supply of antibiotics. What little they had was reserved for party members. The Korean Worker's Party that's a joke; my father was a worker. He had worked on the railways all his life, but thirty years of loyal employment counted for nothing. They had the drugs to save her, yet they chose not to give her any. My father had kept that burden to himself for ten years; when he was arrested, the floodgates opened, and he hurled abuse at the regime."

"Like you, we were transported here. Most of my wife's family live in the South. When we arrived, my father was tortured in the detention centre before being publicly flogged and hanged. His body was so broken I didn't recognise him when they dragged him up the scaffold steps. I was sent here to Chungbong, and ironically, my wife and the girls were sent to work in the pharmaceutical factory, if you can call it that, in the south section of the camp. They weren't making drugs, though; they were making sarin gas. Sarin is similar to some commonly used insecticides, such as malathion, which they use on the vegetable farm. Hence, they make both. As I understand it, she worked there for six months before being moved to the detention centre. I have no idea why. One day Yang Suk-Chul sent word that Sung Su-Jung had been killed in the gas chamber; they were testing some new form of the nerve agent. I can only imagine her dying in agony, as must your wife. I was devastated by the news and would easily have committed suicide had it not been for our girls." Kwang-Ho paused the pain of the memory etched on his face.

"What has happened to them? Are they still alive?" asked David sympathetically.

"I have no idea. I hope so. They haven't been in the detention centre because Suk-Chul would have sent word. They have just disappeared off the radar. I heard from another inmate that three girls matching their descriptions worked on the vegetable farm, but no one has confirmed that. I suppose that's because they are just three of the fifty thousand prisoners in the camp. They have become anonymous, just numbers on somebody's roster. Now, I live from day to day, hoping they are still alive; it's that hope that keeps me going, day, after day, after day."

"You still need to be mindful about praying though Kwang-Ho. If you're caught, you're dead."

"Yes, I know. I was just melancholy, I suppose, feeling sorry for myself, trying to take comfort in my belief that God will prevail and my daughters will survive."

"I'll remember them in my prayers too. God's bound to listen if we pester him enough." Said David lightheartedly. "Come on, or we'll miss our two-course dinner, bread and soup."

"Yes, you're right; I've moped around enough."

As the two men left the dormitory, Noh Sung-Uk, stepped back into the shadows. He hadn't heard the whole conversation but had heard enough to make him suspicious. There was something strange about those two, he couldn't pin it down yet, but he would. He hated Kwang-Ho.

***

"It's incredible, sir, over sixty-five per cent of the rats infected with the Toxoplasma parasite, died after they fearlessly approached the cats. Yet, less than ten per cent of the uninfected rats made the same fatal mistake. It seemingly switches off their neophobia and innate suspicion of cat odours; they don't recognise the cats as dangerous." Declared Song Min-Su, proudly.

"That's good, Min-Su; I think that confirms our hypothesis, don't you?" replied An Sang-Ho, smiling at his assistant. "OK, so we know that the parasite modifies the behaviour of its secondary host, the rat. Next, we need to find out how the parasite affects humans."

"I'll have to build a bigger maze then. Perhaps we could get a couple of tigers as well." Laughed Min-Su.

"I don't think that will be necessary." Replied, ignoring Min-Su's joke. "However, we will need several human subjects to ensure the results are statistically reliable. How many have we available at the present moment?"

"The camp director has acceded to our request for children; there are seventy-six of a suitable age, both girls and boys."

"Good, we must be certain they have as little parental imprinting as possible. Secondly, I want to test the different sexes independently. Male and female humans demonstrate different cognitive processes; they use different parts of the brain to learn. Higher levels of oestrogen in females affect their neural processing. Therefore, infected females may behave quite differently from their male counterparts. We must have two separate experimental populations; forty boys and forty girls. Then if we observe them before and after infection, the experiment won't be subject to a systemic error resulting from cognitive bias." When Sang-Ho saw his technician's eyes narrow, he added: "We take individual differences between the sexes of our experimental subjects out of the equation. Although this is perhaps an ipsative assessment – each individual may react slightly differently to the infection – we should be able to see an overall pattern emerge."

"Well, I have access to forty girls but only thirty-six boys." Said Min-Su looking at his clipboard. "If we test the girls first, there will be enough boys when we get to the second experiment. Also, we have enough parasite stocks to start right away."

"Excellent. Now, if we test a single individual first, we will better understand what we will need for the full experiment. I suggest we observe the subject for five sessions, each of eight hours before and after infection. OK with you?"

"I'll set it up today.

***

"What do you know of Doctor An Sang-Ho?" asked David after the squad had their usual dinnertime cabbage soup later that week.

"Doctor Death? Not much, only what Yang Suk-Chul told me before I came to the mine. I know he's married and has two children, a boy about the same age as Joseph and a daughter about the same...as ..." Kwang-Ho stopped knowing that completing the sentence would cut David as severely as any knife.

David looked at his friend and smiled. "It's OK, Kwang-Ho; his daughter is the same age as Ruth. Just a sick coincidence, I suppose. Please go on."

"Well, I understand that he graduated from Pyongyang Medical University in the early fifties with a PhD in parasitology. When the war came in 1953, he joined the army and did a stint in a field hospital. I suppose it was there he learned about how much trauma the human body could withstand before death. After that, he was transferred to a research facility not far from here, just north of Hoeryŏng. He was working on the effectiveness of shock therapy in treating Combat Stress Reactions, – CSR – or battle fatigue as some call it." Kwang-Ho swallowed hard, fighting back the bile in his throat. "From what I've heard, he was using electroconvulsive therapy on CSR victims, by passing an electrical current through the brain to induce a grand mal seizure. This stuff was used liberally in the early part of this century for many psychological conditions. However, An Sang-Ho was involved in behavioural modification, and his use of ECT on non-anaesthetised victims; he was a legend at the institute. No one cared about these soldiers because, in the eyes of the state, they were cowards and were normally shot, so he could be as brutal as he liked with impunity. It's unknown how many brains he fried in the name of medical research, but many hundreds anyway."

David saw how his friend was fighting to control his emotions. "Kwang-Ho, you needn't carry on if it's too painful." He said, trying to give him a way out.

"No, it's fine. I'm OK. When the war was over, the source of his CSR victims dried up. He hadn't achieved anything significant anyway, so he came here. In Camp 22, he has been involved in several chemical and biological warfare projects. The latest is improving the lethality of various nerve agents derived from Sarin. Yang Suk-Chul tells me that he has been trying to get out of this project for some time; he's become bored by gassing his victims and wants to find more interesting ways of killing people. With the recent success of the nerve gas project, he has been allowed to pursue his old favourite, behavioural modification. I'm told that he's moved on from using ECT; he's now trying to generate a biological agent, which could later be developed into a weapon."

"What a monster," said David, realising how his wife may have been killed. "What an evil, heartless bastard. If word of this leaks out, this country will come under the spotlight of the UN and human rights activists. The developed nations of the world will ostracise us."

"I don't think the world gives a toss about what happens inside North Korea. We have been an international pariah since the end of the war. In any case, China knows what is happening here. Suk-Chul tells me that several Chinese scientists have visited Camp 22's medical research unit in recent years. So, you can bet that human experimentation data has been exchanged. DPRK data from camps like this for similar data from Japan's wartime Unit 731."

"Unit 731, wasn't that the place in China, run by a Japanese general in the second world war?" Asked David.

"Yes, a guy called Shiro Ishii. The unit was just north of here, near the Chinese city of Harbin. It's even open to tourists now. However, God knows why anyone would want to spend their holiday looking at where the Japanese scientists made over 30 kilograms of bubonic plague and then photograph the experimental chambers where hundreds of their victims died, choking and coughing up blood. At the war's end, Douglas MacArthur secretly granted all the medical researchers there immunity in exchange for data from their biological warfare research. The US wanted to prevent other nations, particularly the Soviet Union, from benefiting from Japanese research. The Japanese were up to the same stuff that goes on here; vivisection, biological and chemical weapons testing, amongst other equally immoral experimentation. The West knows about this camp, but they don't want another Korean war, so they choose not to do anything about it. Our hell is a quiet backwater that nobody cares about."

"How come you know so much about Unit 731 and the wartime atrocities?" Enquired David.

"My father hated the Japanese and was an activist after the war. He thought Japan should be brought to justice for its wartime atrocities. During the Tokyo War Crimes Tribunal, there was only one reference to Japanese experiments on Chinese civilians, and that was dismissed for lack of evidence. Only the Soviet Union pursued the case. At the Khabarovsk War Crime Trials, they prosecuted twelve top military leaders and scientists from Unit 731, such as General Otozoo Yamada, who had perpetrated the atrocities they were sentenced to hard labour in a Russian gulag."

David stared at Kwang-Ho in disbelief, horrified that such cruel war crimes should go unpunished.

"In contrast," Kwang-Ho continued, "many former members of Unit 731 re-joined the Japanese medical establishment as if nothing had happened. One was the director of the Green Cross, one of Japan's largest pharmaceutical companies, and many others had senior executive positions in Japan's post-war medical schools or the Japanese health ministry. So where is the justice in that?"

"Well, that's cheered me up no end." Said David dryly. "I think I need a drink of cabbage water."

There was a brief pause, and then both laughed in unison. As if life in Camp 22 wasn't challenging enough without taking on the injustice of history as well.

4. The Bleak Times.

Without heating and the wind finding gaps through the window frames, the night temperature in the barracks was below zero. The men who slept there survived by huddling together, two or three to a bed. Two people and two thin blankets could barely survive; anyone sleeping alone would not. At 3 am, the prisoner's misery increased exponentially. With five centimetres of snow on the ground and a raw, piercing wind from the mountains in the north, life in Chungbong suddenly passed from grim to appalling. Outside, the wind-chill index brought the temperature down to minus 37 degrees Celsius, a temperature that would freeze exposed flesh in just a few minutes. Although burdened by hunger and the freezing temperatures, the men trotted the half kilometre to the pit that morning, wrapped in their sleeping blankets. Even though they faced a day's hard labour in the pit, it offered respite from the freezing temperatures above ground. After changing into their work clothes, the men jostled for position at the pit head, eager to warm their malnourished bodies in the air rushing up the shaft from the workings below.

As David and the others rode the cage down the shaft's gaping maw, they smiled at each other for the first time that morning. They had survived another night. Although the barbaric privations of the camp drained them of physical strength, it had melded them together as a group, making them psychologically stronger. Even Isaac had toughened up. Although his body was weak, his mind was tougher than steel. As David looked at the menfolk of his family, it was obvious what the ravages of hard labour and near starvation were doing to them. Their pale, almost translucent skin was drawn taught over their facial bones. Devoid of fat, their gaunt faces and hollow eyes resembled Egyptian mummies more than the family he knew from their past lives in Hamhŭng. The musculature of their arms, legs, and torso was wasting away from the lack of protein in their diet. Life was becoming desperate; they couldn't continue like this. Trapped in this deathly environment, life was slowly being sucked out of them, just as a spider sucked the life force from a fly. The question that haunted David now was how much longer could they survive. Would it be months, or could it be years, as Kwang-Ho had survived? The answer that crowded his thoughts and extinguished hope was only months.

In the beam of his headlamp, Kwang-Ho saw the despair that filled his friend's eyes. He could sense the questions he was asking himself, for they were the same questions he worried about when he first arrived at Chungbong. Kwang-Ho had resolved this torment by realising that there was no answer to it. All he had was faith in God, for only He could predict the future. David would have to trust that God would see them through.

At the pit bottom, in the dimly lit main entry, the men picked up their tools for the day ahead and climbed aboard the ore cars that would take them to the panel they were excavating. It was hot at the main entry level, a warmth that embraced them and chased away the cold from their tired bodies. Soon they would be sweating as they toiled at the coal face, labour, which, ironically, every prisoner was eager to start.

When the squad stopped midway through their shift for what might euphemistically be called lunch, David sat alone, his mind tortured by what fate had in store for them next—every new day in the mine seemed to stretch like a cord of elastic, each day longer than the last. What would happen when they no longer stretched? Would they die, or would each day become mundane and boring, their edges blurring into a seamless mega-day that would eventually consume them all?

"You look troubled, David. Can I help?" Asked Kwang-Ho as he sat beside his friend.

It took a second or two before Kwang-Ho's words filtered through David's consciousness and ended his reverie. He looked up at the squad leader with tears forming in his eyes,

"We're not going to last much longer in this hellhole, are we?"

"I have." Replied Kwang-Ho. "I've been here two years, and they haven't got rid of me yet."

"Look around you; we're skeletons compared to what we were when we arrived."

Kwang-Ho put his hand on his friend's shoulder. "Look, the thoughts that haunt you now are the same that haunted us all after we'd been here a few months. It's natural for your mind to rebel against the tortuous conditions of Chungbong. Despair is a cloud that hangs over us all. You must look on the bright side; you've shed those extra kilos you thought you never could. Now that you're slim and trim, you'll be eligible to enter the internationally acclaimed Chungbong marathon."

David looked at his friend and smiled. He was in no mood for jokes. "We're wasting away; there won't be much left of us soon."

"We have all been through this, David. You will reach your fighting weight, so to speak, and won't lose any more weight. By then, you will wonder what you were worrying about."

"Isaac won't survive much longer. He can hardly raise his hammer now, let alone knock the roof props away. What happens when he can't even do that?"

"We'll cross that bridge when we come to it. You can't foretell the future any more than I can. You must stop worrying about what you've no control over; else it will eat you up."

"I can't stop worrying when my belly is empty, and my body is wasting away."

"We survive because we are strong here," said Kwang-Ho pointing at his head, "not because we are strong here." He concluded by pointing at the biceps of his left arm. "Toughen up, soldier, if you ever want another tomorrow."

"What's the point? Why should I look forward to another night and day as the last one? There's nothing left to look forward to, nothing."

"I had a teacher at high school who told me one day when I suffered from exam nerves, *nil desperandum*, which means; nothing must be despaired at, you must never despair. I know you're grieving for your wife and that you fear for your children, but thinking of these things doesn't help. One day they'll set us free, and we'll build our lives again. You have extended family, still free, look towards a future with them. Keep looking ahead, not behind."

"The only way we'll be free is to escape from here."

"Shhh," said Kwang-Ho lifting his forefinger to his lips, "even if we're caught talking about escape, they'll kill us."

"How can they kill us when we're already dead? They've already taken those I've loved most; my life was forfeit then. Taking my last breath won't make any difference."

"Don't talk like that, David. You've got to think about the living, your father and brother and the others; they need you to be strong. United we stand, divided we fall, isn't that what Aesop, the Greek slave, told us? Together we are unconquerable, and because of that, we have a responsibility to the others. If you give in, the others will surely perish."

David thought for a moment, alone yet surrounded by others. As he keyed into the muted conversations of the other squad members, he realised Kwang-Ho was right. His men folk were alive, and as far as he knew, his children were also. He also realised that it was his fault they were all here; it was his stupidity that condemned them. As long as they had hope, he was responsible to each of them to help them survive. From now on, that was his mission in life. He turned to Kwang-Ho and hugged him. He was a good man who cared for the well-being of all of them.

"Who the hell's Aesop anyway?" David responded. As the two men laughed in chorus, the other squad members stopped their conversations and looked across at them, curious to know what they had to laugh about.

***

Song Min-Su and An Sang-Ho watched the small child as she interacted with her peers. She was the twenty-first child they had infected with the *Toxoplasma gondii* parasite. She was a pretty girl, quite tall for her age, with long tresses of jet-black hair that reached down her back to her waist. Ordinarily, her hair would be shining and free-flowing, but now, through the lack of protein in her diet, it was dull and lifeless. Of the previous twenty children, this little girl was the most captivating; when she smiled, all those around her smiled too. Watching her from behind the one-way mirror, Min-Su felt fleetingly guilty that such a beautiful child was part of their study.

Although humans are not a usual secondary host for the parasite, and because cats do not eat them, they represent a dead-end host. It is, therefore, logical to assume that the evolved behavioural manipulation effects of the parasite in the rat would not be matched by similar behavioural changes in humans. Indeed, the marked differences in personality and intelligence quotient observed in subjects infected with *Toxoplasma gondii* were far more subtle than those observed in the rat. Rat behaviour is thought to be the outcome of the conflict between two behavioural traits, the fear of novel situations and the need to forage for food. Termed the omnivores paradox, such conflicting motivations, so pronounced in the rat, have also been observed in humans. Toxoplasmosis, the disease caused by *Toxoplasma* infection, exists in four distinct forms. The first, congenital toxoplasmosis, occurs when mothers infected with the parasite transmit the disease to their unborn children. This leads to congenital abnormalities and possibly spontaneous abortion. The second is the mild and relatively harmless acute postnatal form of the disease that can develop into the third and more serious chronic form of toxoplasmosis. However, the most common form of the disease is latent toxoplasmosis. In this fourth type, the parasite survives in cysts that remain dormant for the host's life.

Although latent toxoplasmosis is generally considered asymptomatic, it can develop into a severe neurological disease in humans that are severely immunosuppressed, such as in AIDS or during chemotherapy. Whilst most research has been directed towards the more virulent acute or congenital forms; little is known about the behavioural alterations in individuals with the latent toxoplasmosis form. What is known is that women develop more measurable behavioural changes than men. Women become more warm-hearted and easy-going; they also become more conscientious, persistent, moralistic and staid. Both men and women display stronger feelings of guilt. Those with latent toxoplasmosis are generally more placid and malleable in temperament. Just what an autocratic regime needs its populace to be.

One question An Sang-Ho wanted his research to answer was; would the intensity of these subtle behavioural changes increase with the duration of the infection? To this end, most children subjected to this experimentation would be studied for many years. Just a few would be killed to confirm the presence of parasitic cysts in their brain tissue. Ruth, David's daughter, was one of the lucky few who would remain alive. A second, more vital question was how the parasitic cysts altered the host's behaviour. If it was chemical, then he should be able to isolate such a compound from the brain tissue of the sacrificed children. Concentrating this chemical compound may be a valuable addition to the water supply of people prone to rebel, students, academics and alike. Control the peasants and the bourgeois middle class and control the world.

***

David felt his stomach lurch as he swallowed the last drop of cabbage soup. Following a loud rumbling sound, he regurgitated a mouthful of the vile liquid. Fearful that he would lose its little nutrition, he swallowed it again. Today the soup was worse than ever, it had fermented, and it smelled as bad as it tasted. The more times he drank the stuff, the more his stomach rebelled. David was convinced he would starve if it were not for the small amount of hard bread they had with it. Looking around, his father-in-law seemed to be having the same trouble. His pained expression told David that he, too, was fighting the urge to vomit. As the seconds passed and his grimace worsened, it foretold that Isaac would lose the battle to keep the soup down. Holding his stomach, the old man stood and staggered across the room to the open drain in the corner.

"You make a fucking mess, old man, and I'll rub your miserable face in it. Piss off outside if you're going to puke." Roared Noh Sung-Uk threateningly.

As Isaac turned to escape from Noh, he lost his struggle and brought up half a litre of pale green liquid that splashed across the bare concrete floor of what was loosely called the dining room.

Noh raced across the room towards Isaac as the old man retched repeatedly.

"You miserable bastard, you'll regret losing your dinner in my barracks."

As Noh neared the old man, he kicked him viciously in the face. Isaac fell instantly to the floor, his nose broken and his cheek split open. As blood ran freely from the unconscious man's wounds, it flowed in small rivulets that slowly merged with the vomit. At the confluence of the two liquids, one scarlet, the other green, the amalgam was black and sticky as the blood started to congeal.

Just as Noh went to hit Isaac a second time, David pushed him over. As his indigestion faded and his anger grew, David spat at the bully sprawled on the floor.

"Leave him alone, arsehole."

As Noh recovered, his face turned puce with murderous rage. "Take a look at the world around you fuck face, because it's the last you'll see of it."

Once he had regained his feet, Noh grabbed David by the throat. "I'm going to choke the life out of you, you little shit." He snarled. As David ineffectively grabbed the squad leader's wrists, he could smell his putrid-smelling breath. With his face almost purple and the blood vessels at his temples engorged and pulsating, Noh looked like he was about to have a heart attack. David was helpless. Then, just as he was about to lose consciousness, with the blood pounding in his head, Noh suddenly released him. As David fell to his knees, gasping for breath, he stared into the eyes of his nemesis and witnessed a screen of agony slowly replacing the rage he'd seen only moments earlier.

As he watched Noh curl into a foetal position on the floor, his face twisted in pain, David looked up at his saviour, Kwang-Ho. Slowly recovering with each new breath, David took the proffered hand of his friend and rose to his feet.

"What happened? What did you do?" he asked.

"Oh, nothing really," Kwang-Ho said nonchalantly, "I just gave Noh Sung-Uk a less than gentle reminder that he should keep away from my squad. A good punch in the kidneys, he'll be pissing blood for a while; that should remind him till the next time we meet."

Paul was cradling Isaac's head in his lap, pinching his nose to stem the flow of blood. Although conscious, Isaac looked like he was on a different planet, completely unaware of what was happening around him.

"We should get out of here while we still can," said Kwang-Ho, "Noh does have friends, and we can't fight them all."

With David and Paul on either side of the helpless Isaac, the men withdrew to their dormitory.

***

"He'll need stitches in his face; that wound's too wide to heal properly on its own." Said Jang-Ho, the talkative and ever-friendly squad member who idolised Kwang-Ho. "I've got a needle and thread in my sleeping mat. I'll go and get it, but you'll have to stitch it yourself because I get queasy at the sight of other people's blood."

"Thanks, I can do it," said Paul, "If I can darn my socks, I can certainly darn your face, Isaac."

Isaac could barely smile without his face rippling with pain and grunted through clenched teeth at the joke. Although his nose had stopped bleeding on the outside, fluid was still moving into his face on the inside. Black rings had started to form around his eyes as his face started to swell. If his eyes swelled too much and his eyes closed, he wouldn't be able to work, and then they would all be in trouble.

"Here you are then," said Jang-Ho, offering Paul his rather rusty needle and a ten-centimetre piece of black thread."

"I suppose you haven't got a cleaner one to have you Jang-Ho?" inquired Paul.

"Sorry, I'm fresh out of suturing needles. Besides, it's not all rust; some of its blood from the last poor sod who got stitched up."

"Well, thank you, nurse, that's gratifying to know. I don't suppose you have any alcohol to clean it or lidocaine to numb the pain." Replied Paul.

"No, but I have tea and cakes later if you'd like."

"Tea and cakes," mumbled Isaac, "now that sounds better than lidocaine." Wincing as he tried to smile.

Although the wound on his face was not very long, it was ragged and deep. As Paul pulled the pieces of skin apart, David carefully poured a little water into the wound before wiping as much dirt from it, using the inside edge of his tunic. It was the cleanest cloth they had and much more aseptic than the toe of Noh Sung-Uk's boot.

"Now, Isaac, do you want a blanket stitch or a nice running stitch?"

"Get on with it, you silly old bugger." Mumbled Isaac. "And don't make me laugh anymore. It hurts too much."

"Stop winging and turn your face to the light. If I can't see, I might do us all a favour and sew your bloody mouth shut."

That brought a laugh from the audience as Paul started his first stitch. It took another five stitches and fifteen minutes to finish the job. They had nothing to cover it with, so it oozed blood for ten minutes longer before it eventually stopped.

"You look like a bloody pirate now, Isaac," said Jang-Ho as he took back his needle. "I won't bother wiping the blood off it," he said, retreating to his bed, "it'll just add a little more character to our only piece of first-aid equipment. Besides, if it was nice and shiny, someone else might see it and steal it, then we'd leak blood all over the place."

After David retrieved some ice from outside to stop the swelling, Isaac closed his eyes and tried to shut out the pain he still felt across his face.

"We can't continue like this." Whispered David to his father. "It won't be much longer before one or all of us starve to death or die at the hands of that murderous bastard, Noh."

"Sadly, that's the fact of the matter, but what do you suggest? There are no free rides out of this place."

"No, I realise that." He paused. "We'll just have to make our way out."

"Escape? How the hell are we going to do that? We're watched constantly, and we're either down the mine or sleeping. I don't see any easy opportunities to walk out of here. In any case, where the hell would we go? We're in the mountains, miles from home and anyone who knows us. The sea is too far south to get there on foot. We're stuffed, completely stuffed."

"I know all that, but we have to leave somehow. If we stay here any longer, we won't have the energy to escape. If I can think of a way out, will you come? We'll stand a better chance if we're all together."

"It's the middle of winter; we won't survive in the open dressed in these clothes; we'll freeze to death before we get half a mile away. It's madness to think we can escape, sheer folly."

"Perhaps we can steal a truck. We have to try; we have no choice."

"Or die trying; I don't think it's possible. Besides, how far will Isaac get? He was so weak before he got this beating; he has no chance now."

David looked at his father, his eyes pleading with him for support. "I'll find a way, trust me, I'll find some way of getting us away from here. You wait and see."

***

Mine safety was non-existent at Chungbong except for the issue of a type of Davy Safety Lamp issued to each squad leader. Devised in 1815 by Humphry Davy, the lamp was created for use in deep mines to allow coal seams to be mined despite the presence of flammable gases called firedamp. Consisting of a candle surrounded by metal gauze, it prevents the ignition of firedamp by preventing the gases from reaching their ignition temperature and causing an explosion. A bonus is that the lamp also provides a crude test for the presence of firedamp, as the flame enlarges and has a blue tint if any flammable gases are present. However, their effectiveness is reduced if the wire gauze is rusty or punctured. The men press-ganged into working in the mine, had scant knowledge of mine safety and had little idea how to maintain the lamps.

Late in December, tragedy struck the Chungbong mine when the men of the second shift breached a pocket of the insidious firedamp, and a faulty safety lamp caused an explosion. The explosion was so powerful that the earth rocked, and the ladder roads collapsed. One hundred and twenty men perished in the blast that ripped through the lower levels of the mine, either torn apart by the pressure wave or crushed by falling debris. A further sixty were trapped behind rock falls, many succumbing to afterdamp, the toxic mixture of carbon monoxide gases left behind after a firedamp explosion. Three hundred others were also trapped, as the cage jammed in the shaft, and the ladder roads was impassable.

The men of the first shift, awakened by the blast, were rounded up and sent to the pithead to act as work parties underground and on the surface. The engineers took four hours to free the jammed cage and evacuate the men trapped below. With the injured coming up first, David and his father were selected to help Chungbong's only doctor triage the wounded. He wrote on a card what was to be done by the medical staff back at the clinic and pinned the card to their tunics. He also graded them from 1 to 3. The 'twos', who required urgent medical intervention, and stood a good chance of full recovery, were moved first. After stitches or bones being reset, these men could be returned to the workforce after a short stay in the clinic. The 'ones' were herded under their own steam to the drying room, where they received wound dressings and minor stitching. The threes remained at the pit head in three rows; these men had suffered crush injuries, fractured skulls or internal bleeding. They were left in the shadows, in agony, bleeding out or slowly choking to death. Tragically there were more threes than there should have been. If their injuries meant they would become disabled and couldn't work down the mine in future, they were useless to the mine manager and a burden to the regime. Those that didn't die quickly enough were helped by placing a polythene bag over their heads.

When the stream of injured eased and the dead started to arrive, David and Paul were told to join the gang of men tasked with removing the bodies. With one at the ankles and the other at the shoulders, David and his father carried the corpses to a skip behind the drying room. When the skip was full, they were told to climb in themselves and accompany the dead to the burial site.

It was an horrific journey, one that brought Paul to tears. Although neither man knew who the dead miners were, they were someone's father, husband or son. Covered with blood and gore, it took twenty minutes, along an unlit track, to arrive at the burial site. There they were ordered at gunpoint to carry the bodies to a grille that covered an abandoned shaft. Once the grille had been removed, they were told to throw the bodies down the shaft. It was a long way down into the abyss below, and many seconds passed before they heard the faint splash of the bodies entering the sump at the bottom of the shaft. By the smell emanating from the gaping maw, this was a well-used dumping ground for the many helpless victims of Chungbong. David wondered if this was the resting place of his wife, Rachel. Such a thought was too much to bear; he fell to his knees, his head in his hands, sobbing. Luckily Paul picked him up before the guard reached them. With the barrel of the guard's AK47 poking him in the chest, he was forced back towards the open shaft.

"Stop," shouted Paul, "how will I pick up the rest of these corpses myself? Are you going to help me?"

Instantly the guard stopped and turned to face the old man. "Shut the fuck up, you worthless piece of shit, or you'll be swallowing your own teeth." He snarled.

"Well, I can't manage this job alone, can I?"

The guard's response was swift and cruel. He swung the gun barrel around, catching Paul across the side of his face. As the pain swept over him, Paul's legs turned to jelly, and he collapsed.

"What the fuck are you doing, you stupid sod." Shouted the second guard as he rushed over to the group. "Have you no brains? Are you going to lug the rest of the dead over here yourself because you can count me out, you moron? We need them both, so lay off."

"Pick him up, you whimpering, sissy." Shouted the first guard to David. "Get the rest down the hole and be quick about it."

David picked up his father and wiped the blood and dirt from his face. As Paul got to his feet, the first guard spat at them.

"I'll remember you two. You won't escape me again, be assured of that." He snarled.

As David caught hold of the ankle of the next body off the skip, it was still warm. "This one's still alive." He said to his father.

"He can't be; he's only got one arm."

As Paul grasped the man by one arm and the collar of his tunic, he heard an almost inaudible moan.

"You're right, David; he is alive. Put him down, and let me see if I can hear what he's saying."

Once on the ground, the man's eyes opened, and he grasped Paul's leg with his remaining hand. Paul knelt and stooped to hear what the miner was saying.

"Help me. Help me, please." He gasped

"What the fuck are you doing, kissing the dead?" Screamed the more aggressive guard. "Get up, you queer bastard, pick him up and chuck him in the hole."

"But he's still alive." Responded David.

"I don't give a fuck. Chuck him in the hole, or you'll go instead."

"What's the matter now?" Asked the second guard.

"This man's alive. He can be saved." Pleaded Paul

"He's got a three on his tunic, hasn't he?" Snarled the first guard. "That means he's dead, so chuck him in the fucking hole."

David looked up towards the second guard, his eyes pleading for mercy.

"Throw him down the shaft and let's get out of here; I'm cold, tired and pissed off. Do as your told." Confirmed the second guard.

When David and his father picked up the man, too weak to fight back, he pleaded with them to stop.

"Please don't, let me be. Please, I beg of you, stop."

Although his voice was only just above a whisper, the two men heard him, still pleading for them to stop, as he dropped into oblivion. It was a nightmare that would haunt David for the rest of his life.

Thankfully the rest of the victims were all dead, and it took them less than ten minutes to finish emptying the skip. Once they were finished, they wondered if they would be following them down the shaft.

"Close the grille and get back in the skip." Ordered the second guard, staring at his comrade, willing him to forget his hatred of the two prisoners.

Quickly, before the guard changed his mind David and his father slammed the grille shut and then climbed back into the skip, trying in vain to avoid the patches of congealed blood that now covered the steel floor of the skip. Soon the truck was bouncing along the trail back to the Chungbong pithead. It was a journey of silence as both men recalled the face of the man begging for his life. A life that they had cut short. Neither man reconciled themselves with the thought that he may have died later of his injuries. They both just stared at their bloodstained hands, the hands that had just killed another human being, both haunted by the fading echoes of his screams as he fell backwards to his death.

5. Escape is Moot

It took a whole week to rebuild the ladder roads and a further week to clear the debris from the explosion before mining could resume in the unaffected panels. The lighting, ventilation, and pumping systems all had to be restored in the most damaged areas before mining the coal could begin in those areas again. It was a sombre time for most miners, who were still finding parts of their comrades' days after resuming activities in the mine. The smell of putrefaction or a rat dragging away a piece of flesh led them to the final remains.

Somehow Kwang-Ho had made a deal with one of the shift supervisors because even though his panel was located in one of the unaffected areas of the mine, his squad had been allocated duties on the surface. There was a lot of timber and steel that could be recycled, and one of their tasks had been to sort through the piles of debris by hand and retrieve anything useful. During this time Kwang-Ho had managed to scrounge another set of work clothes for David and his father, to replace their others, which were stiff with dried blood. They had to get the numbers of their original owners obliterated and their original numbers stencilled on the replacement tunics. It was a task that must have cost Kwang-Ho something, but what, he never said.

Under normal circumstances, David and the others were either working below ground or sleeping, having little time to peruse the daily comings and goings at Chungbong. But now, in those short weeks after the explosion, working above ground, David could observe what went on over much of the site. All that time, he was taking note of everything that might offer him the opportunity to escape. Out in the open, it was cold, so cold that they were issued with overcoats, a minor miracle. Even so, their hands and feet began to suffer from the continual freezing temperatures. If David hadn't been so keen to find an escape route, he might have wished he was back in the mine. In the mine, it might be dangerous, backbreaking work, but it was warm.

As if Isaac hadn't suffered enough, he began to get frostnip on the ends of his fingers. If Kwang-Ho hadn't spotted them, he might have lost the ends of his fingers. Once again Kwang-Ho must have called in a favour from the shift supervisor because Isaac was given a job in the drying room. Now David had eyes all over the site. He had tasked them all to keep their eyes open for opportunities to exploit, to make their bid to escape successful. The mine was ten kilometres from the nearest habitation, so any escape needed wheels, a truck or a car, anything to get some distance between them and the guards before they were missed. However, as the days rolled by, there didn't seem to be any way they could steal, hijack, or hide inside anything that would get them away from the posse of guards that would pursue them once their absence was noticed.

Then, just after Kwang-Ho had told them they had just two days of work left above ground, David saw a flatbed truck that appeared out of the blue, delivering crates of vegetables to the cookhouse near the dormitories. A truckload of, amongst a few other things, cabbages, the bane of their lives in Chungbong. As the truck backed towards the cookhouse, David could see that the driver was another prisoner and, as far as he could see, an unaccompanied prisoner. That was it, they would hijack the vegetable truck, and if they could persuade the prisoner driver to go with them, they could be gone hours before they would be missed.

David could hardly conceal his happiness, seeing, at last, their road to freedom.

***

That evening in the dormitory, after their cabbage soup and hard bread, David gathered his men folk around him to discuss what he had seen.

"Every third day, a truck from the vegetable farm at Camp 22 arrives at the mine. As far as I can determine, it's driven by an unaccompanied prisoner from the farm. And what's even better, he stays overnight when the weather is bad. This is what we've been waiting for, our ticket out of here."

"How do you know all this, where the truck is from, and that the driver travels without a guard?" Asked Isaac, cradling his frostbitten fingers in a blanket.

"I asked Kwang-Ho; I asked him how the driver got such a cushy number."

"How does he know all that?" Persisted the old man.

"He's been here long enough to know some of the things that go on here. I trust him, don't you?"

"Yes, I trust him; he fought for me. I owe him my life, but this will not be any picnic outing. This is life or death; we can't make any mistakes; we must be sure."

"I have no reason to believe what he tells me is made up. He has survived here against all odds for over two years; you don't do that without being savvy. Look how he got us to work above ground; he knows people and how things go on here. Have you noticed how the guards leave him alone? They don't harass him like they do some of the other squad leaders. He's one of the good guys."

"I'm sorry to be devil's advocate here, but we must be sure. What do the rest of you think?"

Luke looked at his father, Paul, as if asking for permission to speak. "We have no reason to doubt what Kwang-Ho tells us, we owe him a lot, and loyalty has to be top of the list."

"I agree. But tell me, how do we get rid of the driver?" Asked Paul.

"I thought we should ask him if he wants to come with us." Replied David hesitantly, his brain working just microseconds in front of his mouth.

"And if he doesn't?" asked Isaac.

"Well, we'll take him with us. We'll tie him up when we have to abandon the truck."

"I don't think swanning around the countryside in a stolen truck will get us very far. Military patrols are all over these areas to stop the bloody Chinese from crossing the border. How will we get past them?"

"I don't know about that, Isaac. I hadn't considered that. How do you know about the army patrols anyway?"

"Because before I was dumped in this shithole, I worked for the company that supplied the army with uniforms, including greatcoats and cold weather gear. We shipped trainloads to Ch'ŏngjin and from there to the Musan Plateau, Hoeryŏng and even further north to

Onsŏng. The border is crawling with patrols, believe me."

"I'm surprised you haven't talked about this before, Isaac. It might have been useful to know these things before now." Said Paul, admonishing his senior.

"I didn't know you were thinking of stealing a truck and driving us to our deaths before now." Replied Isaac raising his voice a little too much.

"Shhh, you silly old fool. If someone hears us, we're dead." Said Paul.

"Don't talk to me like that. You're not much younger than me, you stupid old fart."

"Whoa, boys," laughed David, "you'll be hitting each other with handbags in a minute. We're all family, and in the same shit, and if we don't do something about it soon, we will all die. So please, gentlemen, a little decorum, please."

It was all that was needed to break the tension that had developed. They all saw the funny side of their spat, and a peal of laughter echoed around the concrete walls of the dormitory. They were all so relaxed that they never saw someone else's approach until he spoke.

"If you continue to shout your intentions aloud, you'll all dance to the hangman's rhythm soon."

The laughter stopped immediately. Shocked at their stupidity, no one spoke until Kwang-Ho spoke again.

"I've warned you before, David, about loose lips. They'll get you all killed. Noh's always hanging around, listening for the exact conversation you've just had. He will report you. You will die, and he will be rolling drunk, toasting your mistake as his reward."

Once again, they were all silent. David, realising their mistake, turned red with embarrassment. Eventually, it was he who spoke first.

"We're sorry, Kwang…"

"Don't be sorry, be careful." Interrupted Kwang-Ho. "If you aren't, we'll all be dead."

"We can't stay here any longer Kwang-Ho. This place is slowly killing us anyway. We have to leave."

Kwang-Ho put his hand on David's head and rubbed it playfully. "Well, you won't do it with the vegetable truck. It's been tried before. It's a trap to catch the desperate. Bait, put there to tempt us all. The moment you drive down the track, thinking you've finally made it out of here, they'll stop you at the outer marker of the camp. And when you're caught, they'll torture you to find out who helped you before executing you publicly. They will force us all to kill you by stoning, just as the Jews did in our Lord's time.

Believe me; you don't want to touch the vegetable truck."

"I don't believe you." It was Isaac again. "You don't want us to try because of what might happen to you if we make it out of here."

Saying nothing, Kwang-Ho turned to leave.

"Stop." cried David, "Ignore him; he doesn't know who to believe."

Kwang-Ho turned slowly to face the group. "If I were worried about my own skin, I'd dob you into the guards right now. That's if you don't betray your own intentions by making so much noise."

As Kwang Ho turned to the door again, David jumped up to try and stop his friend. "Kwang-Ho, wait. We've been rude and foolish. Don't go. We need your help."

"Yes, you do, but I'll not give it tonight. You all need to sleep, or the next voice you'll hear will be Noh Sung-Uk and his S.S. friends, the guards, coming to drag you off to the detention centre. Get to your beds and get some sleep."

***

Over the following days, the men were too ashamed to ask Kwang-Ho to help them. They had insulted him, and time gave them space. Oddly it was Isaac who spoke first. As the men emerged from the changing room after another brutal shift underground, Isaac stood before Kwang-Ho and bowed respectfully.

"I insulted you, Kwang-Ho, by doubting your loyalty to us." Said Isaac, his eyes cast to the ground. "I, more than any of the others, have no right to do so. You saved me from Noh Sung-Uk. Without your intervention, at worst, I would surely have died; at best, I would have been seriously injured. Please forgive the foolishness of this old man. I am truly sorry."

"Stand up, my friend," said Kwang-Ho softly, gently touching the repentant man's shoulder, "Stand up before we draw attention to ourselves. Perhaps we can talk after our soup."

That night there was more than cabbage soup and bread for dinner. For some unexplained reason, the broth had peas and small shredded pieces of meat. It must have been someone's birthday. Following dinner, everyone in the barracks had a smile on their face. As David and the others retired to the dormitory, they were followed by Noh Sung-Uk. As he slammed the door shut behind him, he rushed at David, pinning him against the far wall.

"You're up to something, aren't you, you slimy bastard. Well, whatever it is, I'm making it my personal crusade to find out what it is and take you down." He snarled, spittle spraying from his mouth with each emphasised plosive. His hot breath was rank with fermented cabbage. "You won't always have your saviour Sohn Kwang-Ho watching your back. He's being transferred back to Camp 22 next week, and when he's gone, I'll squash you like a bug. Have you got the message, you little shit?"

As the last syllable left his lips, Noh head-butted David on the bridge of his nose. There was a crunching sound, and hot blood quickly poured from both nostrils. Noh shoved him violently against the wall, lifting David off his feet and banging his head against the bare concrete. At that exact moment, a 30 mm square piece of pine hit Noh Sung-Uk behind his left ear. It hit him hard enough to release his grip on David but not hard enough to do any real damage. Enraged by the blow, he spun around to see who his attacker was; it was Isaac.

Standing in front of Noh Sung-Uk, with the wooden door prop in his hand, his whole body was shaking with fear.

"Leave him alone." He stammered.

"Well, look what we've got here, the tough assassin sticking up for his kinfolk. I'm shaking in my boots. Please don't hit me." He mocked.

"He won't hit you again, but we will." It was Paul fronting up to the bully, and beside him was Luke, both men stepping forward to emphasise that they meant business.

"Arseholes, I could take you all on with one hand tied behind my back if I chose to. You'll all get what's coming to you soon, mark my words."

Mumbling empty threats, Noh Sung-Uk quickly retreated to the door. As he emerged into the corridor, he bumped into Kwang-Ho.

"When you leave, your little bum boys will be mine. They won't last long doing real work. Tosser."

Kwang-Ho pushed Noh Sung-Uk out of the way yet said nothing. Shouting more insults, Noh walked off down the corridor towards the canteen.

"Wow, I'm impressed. You got him to back off yourselves. Well done, all of you. It's not often that he's forced to withdraw." Said Kwang-Ho congratulating his friends. "How's your nose, David? It looks like you need some ice."

"No, I'll be OK." He mumbled, pinching off the flow of blood. "What's all this we hear about you leaving Chungbong?"

"That's what I came to tell you. I've been trying to manoeuvre myself out of here for some time. One of the clerks in the management office is a Christian, and he's been waiting for the right opportunity to get me out of here long before you arrived. Well, I just heard he'd pulled it off. Which is good for me, but not, I'm afraid good for you." Kwang looked at them all apologetically. "Noh's got the mine supervisor to transfer you all to his squad when I leave. It goes without saying that once he's got you underground, he'll have you at his mercy."

"Oh God, it gets worse." Mumbled Isaac.

"Well, that's the bad news. The good news is I got us a job above ground tomorrow, a real peach." He might well have been playing the trumpet for all the attention he was getting. All the men, including David, were downcast, too shocked and depressed to know what Kwang-Ho was saying.

"Listen up, folks." He shouted, clapping his hands at the same time. "This is important. Sit down and listen."

Robotically the men obeyed him, though still not looking up.

"Look at me, all of you." He said, squatting at the edge of the group. "Tomorrow, we drive out of here, legitimately."

That certainly got their attention.

"One truck you've not seen is the logging truck that comes down from the forests north of Chongsŏng. That's where all the roof props come from. The normal driver is sick, so my friend, the clerk, got me the job. I've driven heavy trucks before when I was a student, so it raised no concern when my name was put forward. Better still, I've got jobs for the four of you, loading the truck up at the logging camp."

David and the others looked at Kwang-Ho in amazement.

"As the crow flies, the Chinese border is just twenty-five kilometres from the camp. I thought you might want to hike the border with me."

"Shit, when did you work this out?" Said Luke.

"I've been planning for this opportunity since I came here. It's just taken a long time, that's all. Thank God it's come before my transfer to Camp 22."

"All your blessings coming at the same time." Said David.

"Well, yes, but the moment I came here, I realised, like you, that survival in this camp would be a miracle for any length of time. So, getting out of here has been my focus all the time. Now, with you to help, we can make it happen."

"Surely they'll send armed guards with us." Asked Paul.

"Yes, two in the truck and one in the back with you lot. I think loading the truck at the camp will work and then jumping them on the way back. The truck often breaks down; it's as old as the hills, so it won't be missed, possibly till the following morning when they will send someone to fix it."

There were smiles all around; unified in a single purpose, the men were hopeful for the first time since they had arrived at Chungbong.

"This is how I see it," said Kwang-Ho conspiratorially, "once we leave the camp fully loaded, you guys will have to jump the guard in the back with you. You're pretty useful with a piece of timber in your hand Isaac; I'm sure you'll be up to that. It's bloody cold up there, and it will be an uncomfortable journey. The guards they use on the truck are old guys who've done the trip a thousand times. They'll drop off to sleep soon as we leave; clobbering them will be child's play."

"What about the two in the cab with you?"

"Once they've nodded off, I'll jam the brakes on, then take them out as they bounce off the windscreen."

"Sounds too easy." Said Isaac.

"Well, that's the easy part. The hard part comes after that." Suddenly concern appeared on the faces of all four men as they wondered what hard meant.

"Firstly, we can't drive the truck up to the border. There are few roads, and those that are will be patrolled. So, we will have to hike cross-country through snow that may be waist-deep. It'll be a long, tough journey. You'll feel it the most, Isaac, because we can't dawdle about it. We have to get to the border before it gets dark. We'll cross during the night and get as far away from it before morning. The Chinese people along the border are wary of Korean refugees; they inform the police and get them sent back. Koreans stand out like sore thumbs, so they'll spot us immediately. We'll have to be vigilant during daylight hours and be careful not to be seen."

"What the hell will we do then?" inquired David.

"I have a contact in Yanji; she's part of the Christian Underground Railroad, the Seoul Train, organised to help North Korean refugees escape to the South. She'll help us. It's more than 1600 dangerous kilometres to the Laotian border and our freedom. All it takes is a miracle and a lot of money; then we'll be safe."

"We can get money. I have a son in the South, Peter; he owns and runs a large chain of vegetable shops; he'll send us money."

"I hope he doesn't sell cabbages; I've had enough to last a lifetime." Said Luke.

A quiet ripple of laughter rose amongst the friends, buoyed by the thought of escape. Isaac, though was the exception. He was worried at the thought of one whole day and night racing through the mountains, snowdrifts, and rivers. His hands were already frostbitten. He was weak and not up to the journey. He realised that speed during those early hours of their escape was essential if the group were to stand any chance of success. He had no money, no relatives in the South, and the fading memory of his wife and son were all that kept him going.

"I will have to stay." Mumbled Isaac.

"What? What did you say, Isaac?" asked David of his father-in-law.

"I can't make such a journey. I'll only slow you down. With me dragging you back, you'll be caught for certain. I can't allow that; you must leave me behind."

"If you stay, Noh Sung-Uk will kill you. I can't allow that." Stated Kwang-Ho emphatically.

"There's no way we will leave you behind, you silly old fart." Echoed David.

"Less of the old, my boy." Said Isaac, slapping his son-in-law on the shoulder. Isaac bit his tongue as another peal of muted laughter circulated the group. He wouldn't argue with them tonight; there was no point. He'd make sure, though, in the morning, that they left without him.

***

The following morning a freezing wind was blasting down from the north. Isaac needed no further confirmation that his decision not to go with them was sound. On the way over to the pithead, the group were in an ebullient mood, which Isaac had to fake. As he smiled and joked with the others, he thought of his wife Kun-Sun, hoping beyond hope that she was still alive. He remembered his beautiful daughter, Na-Young and his dead son-in-law, Simon. He looked back to their marriage, the happiness and laughter of Kun-Sun crying with joy as her daughter took her vows. He recalled the joy at the birth of their first child, the puffy-faced little girl that had melted his heart. Those were the times he now held close; they were the treasure no one could take away from him, not even the brutal Noh Sung-Uk.

"Come on, old man," said David, slapping him on the back, "put some spring in those steps; this is a great day, a day we will celebrate for the rest of our lives."

"Yes, you're right. One we'll remember for a long time." Replied Isaac hiding his bleeding heart.

Once they reached the changing room, Kwang-Ho approached them with a broad smile. "Good news, my friends. We're to be issued with cold-weather clothing for our journey. I think that mine-supervisor, Shim, must be going soft. He said you'd be useless to anyone at the lumber camp if you were frozen to death by the journey. That could prove to be a lifesaver later on. What do you say, Isaac?"

"That's good fortune." He replied.

"Shit, I thought you'd be a little more enthusiastic than that."

"Yes, you're right. I'm sorry, that's brilliant news."

At the equipment store, each of them was issued with a set of grubby cold weather clothes, a pair of quilted breeches and anorak that were a reasonable fit, a pair of mittens and padded boots, and most important of all, a sheepskin hat.

"What the fuck are you doing with those, you lazy bastards?" Standing in the doorway was Noh, silhouetted against the floodlights surrounding the pithead.

David and the others ignored him as they struggled into their new gear, stiff with dried sweat and whatever else the previous owners had left behind.

"I said what are you doing with those clothes? Didn't you hear me?" He said, striding across the changing room, his fists clenched and ready to pound one of them.

"They're going with me." Replied Kwang-Ho from behind him. "If you've got a problem with that, argue with me."

"I might have fucking known they'd be skiving off with you. Never mind, they'll be mine soon. You won't be able to protect them then, arsehole." Hissed Noh escaping through the far door.

"Come on guys, chop, chop. Your chariot awaits; I'll wait for you behind the pithead.

David and his father were ready and were about to follow Kwang-Ho out when they stopped to see Isaac struggling with the buttons of his tunic.

"Can we help, Isaac?" Said his son-in-law.

"No, it's OK. My frostbitten fingers aren't cooperating as they should. I'll be out soon."

"I'll stay with him, David," said his brother, "just in case Noh comes back."

Luke waited patiently as Isaac finished buttoning up his tunic and then accompanied him outside.
Thankfully Noh Sung-Uk was nowhere to be seen. As the two men stepped into the shadows cast by a large generator just metres from the pithead, Isaac stopped in his tracks, patting his pockets as if looking for his wallet or car keys.

"Sorry, Luke, I forgot my mittens. Wait here; I won't be a second."

"OK, be quick, though. Just in case you know who returns."

"I'll be as quick as I can." Replied Isaac as he walked off towards the changing room. However, once out of sight, he doubled around the generator and went to the ladder roads.

As Isaac reached the first landing, he turned round to check that Luke hadn't followed him. He hadn't. Standing there alone, he remembered once more Kun-Sun, his daughter Na-Young and his dead son-in-law Simon. Deep down, he knew he was doing the right thing. He stepped forward onto the first rung of the first ladder, then deftly swivelled sideways into the abyss below. He never uttered a sound.

6. The Journey North

"Looking for your old friend?" It was Noh Sung-Uk again, but this time he had a sickly grin on his face. "The silly twat's just stepped off the ladder roads. Nearly killed two blokes, doing some repairs on the second landing. They said they heard him bouncing off the walls, all the way down to the sump at the bottom. It seems he couldn't face the prospect of joining my squad." He was gloating, believing he had that much power over Isaac.

Luke moved as if to hit the bully, but by the time he had taken just two steps, Noh had disappeared into the shadows. Probably with a piece of timber or a wrench in his hand, ready to kill anyone who might think of following him.

"Stop, Luke; he's probably gone already. Wait here while I check on his story." Commanded Kwang-Ho, and he quickly disappeared, taking a different route to the pithead. The rest of the men waited beside the logging truck in stunned silence.

Although called a logging truck, it was not one in the conventional sense. Certainly, it carried logs, but it would more accurately be called a flatbed truck with a tilting bed.

As Kwang-Ho passed the men of the first shift, waiting to descend in the cage to their day's labour, there was no hint of what had happened to Isaac. However, as he approached the ladder roads from behind the generator, Kwang-Ho saw Supervisor Shim standing on the first landing, shaking his head. That was all the confirmation he needed. As he turned, the mine supervisor shouted across to him.

"Looks like you've lost your first squad member to suicide Sohn Kwang-Ho. Who was it?"

"Ha Dong-Min, Sir. An old guy, he couldn't keep up with the rest of the squad, Sir."

"That's unusual for you to lose one like this. Had he got some other problems?" Said Shim as he crossed over to where Kwang-Ho was standing.

"He feared Noh Sung-Uk, and couldn't face the prospect of being in his squad next week, sir."

"That man's a fucking menace. Why didn't the old guy want a holiday jaunt to the lumber camp then?"

"He'd already suffered from a little frostnip to his fingers, so I suppose he was wary of a long cold journey."

"Oh well, can't be helped. You'll want a replacement, I suppose."

"No, I got a good bunch of hard workers waiting by the truck. Ha, wouldn't have been that useful anyway."

"Well, why the fuck did you pick him?"

Kwang-Ho shrugged and replied. "I felt sorry for him, I suppose. I didn't want Noh beating on him while I was away. It's still my squad until next week."

"There's no room for sentiment up here, Sohn. Now fuck off and do your job properly this time. And bring them all back as well. Any more suicides, and you'll be in Noh's squad as a labourer till they carry you out of that bloody mine feet first."

"Yes, Sir. Already gone."

***

On the journey north, the men in the back of the logging truck hardly spoke. Sitting on cardboard to protect themselves from the truck's steel bed, they huddled together against the freezing wind. As they bounced along the unsealed road, the men bobbed up and down in concert with the truck. If they were cold, the guard, sitting alone, must have been freezing. Half an hour out of Chungbong, before the sun rose in the east, the guard could stand it no longer. He banged his AK47 on the cab's roof, signalling them to stop. Rather than the guards swapping over, all three crammed into the front cab. If they were all in the cab on the way back, they might be unable to overcome them and escape.

The logging camp was deep in the pine forests that covered the southern bank of the Tumen River. It would have been picturesque in another lifetime as the snow-covered trees wouldn't have looked out of place on a Christmas card. The pit props were stacked in a clearing shared by the logger's hut and a plastic Portaloo.

Loading the truck could have been done more quickly if the loggers had used their front-end loader. However, the loggers all watched from the comfort of their hut while the Chungbong prisoners toiled away unassisted. Even though the air temperature was below zero, the surrounding forest protected them from the cruel wind blowing from the north. Kwang-Ho had advised them to look busy but not build up a sweat, as this could freeze close to their bodies on their journey out of captivity.

It took them four and a half hours to load the truck and chain the load down. They had then put their cardboard sheets on a smaller stack of poles between the cab and the main load. David was worried that if Kwang-Ho used his brakes too fiercely, the load might shift and crush them against the cab.

"You ready to leave now?" Asked the logging camp supervisor.

"Yes, we should; it's getting late." Answered the guard in charge of the prisoners.

"OK then, I'll radio the mine to tell them you're on your way. See you next time."

It was just after 5.00 pm when they left, and it was already getting dark. Half an hour after they left the camp, David got to his feet and staggered over to the side where the guard sat with his back to the cab.

"Where the fuck are you going." He shouted above the engine noise, pointing his rifle straight at David's chest.

"I need a piss." He shouted back.

"You should have thought about that back at the camp. Hold on to that stanchion, and don't piss on me; otherwise, I'll shoot your dick off."

David had thought about peeing at the camp but purposefully hung on to it all to get close to the guard. As David sprayed urine all over the place, the guard looked away so that none might be blown into his face. That was all the time and space David needed. As he lurched towards the inattentive guard, he picked up a carefully hidden stick, and Paul started to get to his feet. As the guard opened his mouth to speak, David hit him across the side of the head with such force the guard's hat flew off and into the snowy wake of the truck. He was unconscious before his body hit the truck bed. As the men braced themselves, David hit the cab with his stick. One of the guards in the cab was already asleep, but the other was distracted by the banging and turned to look out of the small window at the back of the cab to see what all the fuss was about.

Kwang-Ho slammed on the brakes, and both guards in the cab hit the windscreen with sickening force. Both were instantly knocked unconscious. As the truck careened off the road, one of the pit props rocketed forward and narrowly missed Luke's head; if it had made contact, it would have instantly crushed his skull. As it was, it smashed into the cab, almost puncturing the thin steel and killing Kwang-Ho.

As the truck bounced to a halt, the men in the rear were catapulted into a heap. Laughing heartily, it was a few minutes before they realised the truck had stopped. As they unwound themselves and stood up, they were joined by Kwang-Ho. The release of tension was palpable; they had made it, overcome three guards and were now free. They celebrated with a series of high-fives before hugging one another. There was more laughter and then tears. Tears of joy that they had been successful and mournful tears for those who hadn't made it; Isaac, Rachel, and Simon. But the glad thoughts that they were still alive gradually turned sour to feelings of guilt that some were still living the nightmare of Camp 22.

The temperature dropped as the light quickly faded, and fresh snow started to fall. Kwang-Ho found a good section of rope in the toolbox behind the driver's seat and expertly bound the still unconscious guards together in the front cab. As Kwang-Ho finished, David searched their pockets and retrieved anything that might be useful to them on their trek to the border. As he slammed the door shut and turned his back to the truck, he was pierced by the paradox of conflicting emotions; the relief of leaving this hellhole behind and grieving the abandonment of his son and daughter in Camp 22. Overcome by guilt, David sank to his knees and wept. Thoughts that he might have saved them were too distressful to contemplate, so there, in the snow, he mourned them as if they too were dead. There would forever be an open wound in his heart, occupied by the malignancy of doubt.

***

During a complete search of the truck, Kwang-Ho found a large groundsheet, an entrenching tool, a can of petrol, a small bottle of water, a large empty coffee tin, a torch and a first aid kit. From the guards, David gathered two boxes of matches, a penknife, three identity cards, 128 wŏn (the equivalent of $58 USD), an apple, two small bars of chocolate and a bag of peanuts. Being able to start a fire might be crucial to their survival, so finding the matches was a minor miracle. David believed finding water would not be a problem, so he emptied the water bottle and refilled it with petrol. Using some cord, Luke bundled their items into the groundsheet, then folded it to form a crude rucksack.

"Shall we take the AK47s?" Asked David.

"Might as well; I'd rather die fighting than being stoned to death back in Camp 22." Replied Paul.

They had to get as far away from the truck as possible, just in case the truck was discovered sooner than they expected. Kwang-Ho led the way north, followed by David, then his father, before Luke, carrying his improvised rucksack, took up the rear. The forest was an eerie place at dusk, a monochromatic landscape, with the almost black trunks of the pine trees contrasting entirely with the brilliance of the snow-covered ground. Although darkness was fast approaching, route finding was easy as the snow effectively reflected what little light was left. The only sound in this vast wilderness was their boots making a crumpling sound as the snow beneath each step was compressed.

They marched between the trees for three hours before emerging into a small clearing. By this time, it was quite dark. With the aid of the torch, Kwang-Ho looked at his companions, checking for fatigue. Even walking in the snow, ten to twenty centimetres deep, was easier than the work back in Chungbong.

"Should we press on?" Asked Kwang-Ho.

"As long as we can see where we are going, yes," replied Paul. "I think we need to put a few more kilometres between us and the road before we stop."

They agreed to press on and started across the clearing to a small track that led roughly north. With the way on bathed in moonlight, the going was easy, and with the snow on the trail not much deeper than before, they made good progress.

As dawn approached, they were still a reasonable distance from the border and travelling by day, even in this wilderness, might end tragically with their discovery.

"We are still a long way from the border, so we have no choice but to rest up during the day. Once it gets dark again, we'll press on." Said Kwang-Ho once the men gathered around him.

"How far have we left to go?" asked Paul.

"I'm guessing about five kilometres. Resting up during the day will be safer for us, not to mention warmer. Unpack the groundsheet Luke, and I'll dig us some shelter.

It took just five minutes for Kwang-Ho to find a small hollow on the east side of the track and only twenty minutes to excavate a substantial hole where they could rest up for the day. Helped by David, he first lined it with the groundsheet and then overlaid it with branches before finally covering them with snow. Using the cardboard, they had each carried with them to sit on, their hideout was snug and warm. Best of all, from the track, the bivouac was invisible.

"We obviously can't have a fire, so we should huddle together and keep warm." Said Kwang-Ho, still the natural leader of the group.

"Won't they be looking for us now it's daylight?" Enquired Luke.

"Maybe, maybe not."

"If they are, they'll surely find us by following our trail in the snow."

"Yes, they will," he admitted, "but we have no choice. If we blunder into a border patrol, then what will happen to us next is too awful to contemplate. We should rest; we still have a long way to go."

With each man imagining the horrors of what awaited them if they were captured, they were initially too tense to sleep. However, exhausted by their nocturnal march through the forest, the men eventually dropped into a fitful sleep.

With the wind howling and rattling their shelter, the four escapees awoke with a start just after midday.

David crawled out of the shelter and looked at the sky between the treetops. Large baleful clouds, laden with snow, hurried across the gap to the south. They were in for a storm. Swirling vortices of wind, carrying razor-sharp spicules of ice, peppered his face. They were going nowhere. Even if they wanted to, walking into the teeth of a blizzard would be tantamount to suicide. As David climbed back into the hollow, he didn't need to say anything; the wind said it all.

***

For thirty-six hours, the men were subjected to the most violent storm any of them could remember. It started with a sharp temperature decrease, and even though it was daytime, the light faded ominously. As it began to snow, the wind picked up. Although the forest largely protected them from the northerly gale, the power of the icy blasts was awesome. With gusts of over fifty kilometres per hour buffeting their shelter, they were thankful the entrance faced south. Very soon, a blizzard, carrying blinding wind-driven snow, whirled around the trees and caused an enormous drift to close the entrance completely. Before long, their snow shelter became a snow cave. Once the snow fully enclosed them, the temperature inside rose above the freezing conditions outside.

Shivering and shaking from the cold, the four men huddled together to conserve heat. Although they knew that falling asleep might kill them, their efforts to remain awake were in vain. Their fitful sleep, broken by nightmares of imagined suffocation, was far from restful. As the hours passed, they each awoke occasionally, and each of them would rouse their companions. Listening to the raging storm outside made them grateful they had stopped when they did and built such an effective shelter.

***

When the wind died down after a day and a half, David awoke first. Sitting upright in the dark, the eerie silence outside seemed strange. Just a short time ago, the storm had been deafening; now it was done, there was silence. David felt cheated by its absence. Taking the entrenching tool, he jabbed it into the shelter's roof, twisted it, and then withdrew it. He expected to see the stars yet saw nothing. How deep was the snow about them? David, starting to panic, rose to his knees and pushed the steel shovel further into the hole he had made. He pushed harder and harder until his whole arm was buried in the drift. Now he could hardly twist the shovel at all. It was apparent to him that he had not breached the wall of snow. Why hadn't they suffocated, he wondered? He pushed and shoved his companions on the edge of hysteria until they were all awake.

"We're trapped." He screeched. "We're completely buried in this tomb. We'll suffocate. What shall we do?"

Paul and Luke were still stupefied by sleep and completely disorientated to be of any use to David. As Kwang-Ho tried to embrace him, David pushed him away.

"Calm yourself, David; we're not trapped."

"Yes, we are; we're going to die. I have to get out of here." Grabbing the entrenching tool again, he hurled himself at the drift.

"Stop. David stop. If you don't, we'll be buried alive if this shelter collapses." Shouted Kwang-Ho.

It made no difference; David continued attacking the snow in front of him.

"He's claustrophobic Kwang-Ho." Said Paul, now fully awake.

"Stop him, or he'll kill us all. I've already made a hole. The drift can only be half a metre thick beside me. I've kept it open all the time we've been in here."

While Paul, joined by Luke, grabbed David and pulled him back from the wall of the shelter, Kwang-Ho grabbed the entrenching tool. As the panic-stricken David was wrestled to the ground, Kwang-Ho enlarged the breathing hole until it was large enough to crawl through. As he emerged into the cold night beyond, the undulating, snow-covered landscape beyond was intimidating. If the snow carpet was too deep, they would quickly become exhausted before they walked half the distance left to the border.

Soon joined by the others, Kwang-Ho turned to David and put his arm around him once more.

"You OK now?"

"Yes," he stammered, "now I'm outside; I'm fine, thanks. What do you reckon, are we going to get out of here?"

"I'm worried about the depth of the snow. If it's too deep, we're stuffed."

"Perhaps we can make some snowshoes. We've got enough gear." Said Paul.

"What?" laughed Luke smugly. "How the hell are we going to do that?"

"Simple, if you'll pay attention for a second." Replied Paul scolding his son. "First, we need two long green sticks each. We'll have the frames if we bend them into a loop and bind them with some cord. Then we cut up the groundsheet, using the frame as a pattern, and bind it to the frame using more cord. If we stiffen the frame with a couple of cross braces, we can tie them to our boots. I'm convinced they'll be effective. What the hell? We have nothing to lose by trying."

The others were stunned at the simplicity of his idea and equally convinced they could make it work. Working only by moonlight, it took over two hours to fashion the sticks and pieces of groundsheet into serviceable snowshoes. Once the task was complete, they were ready to move on. However, they became reluctant to leave their shelter.

"Perhaps we should eat something first." Said David.

After cutting up the apple and one of the chocolate bars, their feast looked no more than a snack. It might not have been much, but none of them complained. It had been so long since they had eaten anything but stale bread and cabbage soup; this was a feast, and the four friends savoured each mouthful. A mcal that should normally have taken them only two minutes to eat took fifteen.

And so, it was nearly midnight before the small group set off for the border.

"At least our tracks from the truck will have been obliterated." Remarked Luke. "They'll never be able to follow us now."

"True, we may not have the danger of being pursued, but the border guards will have been alerted to our escape for a long time now. We'll have to be very careful." Replied Kwang-Ho probing the depth of snow in front of him with a long straight stick he had found.

Although their improvised snowshoes looked frail, they were remarkably robust and worked flawlessly. It was a simple solution that, without doubt, had saved their lives.

They reached the edge of the forest at around 4 am. Beyond them lay the Tumen River and the border of North Korea with China. Guarding the 1360-kilometre border, North Korea has over 100 000 soldiers, effectively one man every fourteen metres. With guard posts every 250 metres, it is one of the most heavily guarded borders in the world. With very few areas where clandestine border crossings are possible, corrupt border guards charge a small fortune to look the other way while refugees escape the oppressive regime of the Democratic People's Republic of Korea.

The Tumen River and its flood plain form a barren no man's land that must be crossed invisibly before freedom can be attained. It is a natural killing zone with open fields of fire for the border guards equipped with AK58s and 68s. Lying in the snow, it was possible to see that they were equidistant from two guard posts, one to the east and the other along the river to the west.

"Can you see the river, Kwang-Ho?" Enquired Paul.

"No, but I'm sure it's frozen over at this time of the year; it doesn't melt till March."

"So, what now?"

"It's too late to cross now. We'll have to wait till it gets dark again this evening. Move back into the forest and find somewhere to hide, and I'll stay here to watch what happens as dawn comes." David led the other two back into the trees before all three looked around for some hollow in which they could lay up safely till the day was through. After only a few minutes, they found what they were looking for, and within a short time, they had excavated the snow to form another snow shelter. Looking back towards the river, David worried about the trail they had left that led from the forest's edge directly to their hiding place; it was something that didn't allow him to relax and rest up.

Kwang-Ho found them just after seven in the morning. As he approached, David saw his friend brushing away the trail they had left with the pine fronds of a fallen branch.

"What did you see?" Asked David.

"Once it was light, I saw two guards patrol the area between the towers every hour. Amazingly, I saw none before dawn. It seems lackadaisical to me; I can only suppose it's too cold for them to be more effective than that. This is astonishing because they must know we're out here."

"Are there any patrols closer to the tree line?"

"I doubt it; if they're not even patrolling the warmer, more open spaces, they won't be coming up here in the shadows."

"What now?"

"Try and get some sleep. We've got a dangerous journey tonight."

"I'll take the first watch in case they change their mind about coming into the trees."

"OK, David, wake me up in a few hours, and I'll take over."

As the hours of daylight dragged on, none of the men could relax completely. All imagined the horrors of being discovered. They were oblivious to the possible problems that lay before them across the border in China, for they paled into insignificance compared with what lay behind them.

***

They waited two hours after darkness fell before returning to the forest's edge. Luckily it was a cloudy night. As a result, it was so much darker than it had been on the previous few night. They waited an hour to ensure the border guards had finished their daylight vigilance. The friends would have to cross an almost flat plain with almost nothing to hide behind for nearly a kilometre between where they lay and a similar forest on the other side of the river. When the time to move could not be put off any longer, they slid on their bellies down the steep bank before them to the flood plain below. They might have crawled the whole way if that had been possible. However, it was too far and would have taken all night.

Walking at a stoop, they slowly and carefully approached the river. They stopped every hundred metres to rest and ensure they were alone. It took forever to get to a boundary they believed was the riverbank. Now thcy lay down again and edged forward across the ice. To their astonishment, the river was not completely frozen. Where they were, there was a gap of three to four metres. In despair, they looked up and down the fast-flowing river for a narrower gap. As far as they could see, there wasn't, both upstream and downstream; the gap became wider.

"What shall we do now?" Asked Luke.

"Let's crawl further upstream and see if the gap narrows." Replied Kwang-Ho.

After one hundred metres and one hundred and fifty metres closer to the guard post, they saw something that might help them. The gap between the two icy edges had widened to twenty metres, but in the middle was an island, and between them and the southern edge of the island, the gap was just two metres. There was no time to debate their next move. Kwang-Ho immediately stood up, then after backing up a few paces, he ran towards the gap before launching himself over the frigid waters of the Tumen River. One after the other, they all successfully followed Kwang-Ho onto the island. Crawling to the gap on the island's northern side necessitated moving around a rock the size of their abandoned truck. Luckily it meant there was a blind spot between them and the nearest guard post. Any hope of jumping across the northern shore was dashed when they reached the river's edge; it was over three metres away, too far to jump. They lay in the snow staring at the gap, hoping that it would miraculously narrow.

"Dam and blast it." Exclaimed Paul banging his fist on the ice. "We're stuffed now; we'll have to go back."

"Whoa, slow down a bit." Said Kwang-Ho. "The gap may be bigger, but we can still make it if we jump from a height, like from the top of this bloody rock."

The answer was obvious to them now that Kwang-Ho had pointed it out. The trouble was that standing on top of the rock would expose them to the nearest upstream guard post and possibly the downstream one as well. While the others watched and waited for their turn, Kwang-Ho went first. He was on the rock for seconds and quickly leapt across the remaining gap. Luke was next, and he, too, promptly made the far side. Before David got up, he looked into his father's terrified eyes.

"I don't think I can make it, David. What if I fall in, I can't swim. I'll have to go back." He stammered.

"Crap," responded David, "you're as fit as I am. You'll easily make it. You go next, and then I'll follow."

"No." He said emphatically. "You go first, and then I'll follow you."

David looked into his father's eyes again, searching for the truth. His father grabbed his shoulders and then hugged him fiercely.

"Go on, David, I'll follow, I promise."

David kissed his father on the cheek. "You can make it, Dad; really, you can."

Paul tenderly stroked the side of David's head before pushing him towards the rock. David jumped the gap with almost a metre to spare before rolling to a stop on the far side. Paul seemed to take forever climbing the rock. Then as he looked at the black, roiling waters of the river below, he froze.

"Come on Paul." Kwang-Ho hissed.

After a little more hesitation, Paul readied himself, and then with his eyes tightly closed, he jumped across the gap. He made it easily, but as he picked himself up, a sickening crack caused them all to hold their breath. As Paul stepped away from the river, the ice gave way, and he fell backwards into the freezing water and disappeared from sight.

Part II

China

7. Manchuria

As they watched Paul fall backwards into the river, time seemed to slow down, with each passing second captured in a series of still frames. They were paralysed by the horror of what was unfolding before them. Like the gaping maw of a monstrous leviathan, a huge splash erupted from the surface before the dark waters swallowed Paul completely. Stunned, the men stared in disbelief at the surface of the frigid water, fully expecting him to reappear immediately. He didn't.

"Oh, my God!" Exclaimed David, throwing himself to the ground.

In a futile attempt to save his father, David pulled himself up to the edge of the ice and thrust his arm into the water. It was far too late, and his flailing hand touched nothing. He was as good as dead if the current had forced Paul under the ice. With his eyes brimming with tears, David turned onto his back, tugging at his hair with both hands as he uttered a muted scream. Luke immediately knelt beside him, cradling him like a child, muffling David's sobs against his chest. Kwang-Ho stood beside them, staring at the distant watchtower hoping their activities had not drawn the attention of the border guards. Luckily, they had remained undiscovered, but knowing that might change at any moment, he urged David and his brother to be quiet.

"Get up, both of you; he may have surfaced downstream, we may still have a chance to save him."

Keeping as low as possible, they crabbed along the edge of the ice, each mumbling a prayer that they might find Paul alive. Yet with each additional step, their hopes slowly faded. Suddenly a faint and distant sparkle on the river's surface caught Luke's attention. It was his father holding onto a log that was wedged against the ice, the water churning all around him as he grimly hung on with his last remaining strength.

"He's here; quick, help me get him out of the water." Urged Luke.

Having grabbed the old man by the collar, Kwang-Ho, with a single colossal effort, he hauled Paul's almost lifeless body across the log, so the others could help pull him out of the water. Once he was back on the ice, Kwang-Ho felt for a carotid pulse. The pulsating artery beneath his fingers could hardly be detected; although it was weak, it was there.

"We need to get him away from here as quickly as possible. Help me drag him to the far bank; we can pick him up properly then and rush for the tree line."

Paul probably weighed only sixty-five kilograms, but he was closer to ninety with his padded suit full of water. However, the three men got him into the trees beside the river in under a minute. As Kwang-Ho checked to see if they had been discovered, the two brothers stripped their father of his sodden clothing and started to rub his pale flesh to encourage the return of some circulation. Without hesitation, Kwang-Ho stripped off his tunic and gathered Paul's torpid body to his own warm flesh. With David and his brother continuing to massage their father's body vigorously, the three-person team was eventually rewarded by the groans and moans of a man they thought was dead. Although semiconscious, with his body warming slowly, Paul's survival was still not assured. With each of them taking turns to press their warm bodies against Paul, while the others continued the massage, it took them nearly three hours to warm him sufficiently enough to stand. With Paul dressed in David's tunic and Luke's padded trousers, they pooled their underclothes so the two brothers had no exposed flesh. It was bitterly cold, and they desperately needed to light a fire to regain the warmth they had lost over the last few hours. But to light one this close to the border would be tantamount to suicide. To survive, they had to distance themselves from the border and find shelter quickly before the weather worsened.

With Kwang-Ho leading the way, the two brothers put their arms around their father and half-carried him along a well-worn track through the trees. Using such a pathway was risky, but they desperately needed to distance themselves from the border. Even though they were exhausted, they kept going through the dawn hours until Kwang-Ho felt they could no longer use the track safely. When they came to a frozen stream, they branched off the track and kept to the icy surface for a full hour before setting off again in a northerly direction.

Just after ten in the morning, they found the way blocked by a steep limestone precipice. Having travelled northwest along the base of the cliff for nearly an hour, they eventually came to the entrance of a small cave. It was a minor miracle, shelter at last.

Using the torch, Kwang-Ho explored a short way into the cave. From the entrance, the roof of the cave dipped towards the floor until it formed a short, narrow passage. After just two metres of crawling on his hands and knees, Kwang-Ho emerged into a large chamber that resembled an upturned saucer. At the rear of this first chamber, a shaft of light penetrated the darkness from a small opening in the roof. As Kwang-Ho neared the hole in the ceiling, he spotted a circle of stones previously used as a rudimentary fireplace. Scattered around the rocks were half a dozen wooden staves with the charred remains of linen; they had previously been used as torches. A smell of ammonia in the chamber confirmed what Kwang-Ho had already surmised; the cave held a colony of bats, and the fireplace and torches belonged to the local peasants who harvested them. While the temperature outside was minus two degrees Celsius or less, inside the cave, it was a balmy ten degrees – the ideal sanctuary for hibernating bats and hypothermic North Korean fugitives.

Finding dry wood wasn't as onerous a task as Kwang-Ho might have thought because the bat catchers had left plenty of wood just inside the mouth of the cave. Dry wood should minimise any smoke produced by fire and hopefully not attract the unwanted attention of any Chinese or North Korean pursuers.

They were all warming themselves around a large fire in the first chamber within half an hour. As Paul gradually recovered from his ordeal, the damage to the ends of his toes soon became evident. The tips were numb and had turned purple. They would have to wait to see how bad the long-term damage would be. If severe, the toes may eventually turn black and become gangrenous, and then they would have no choice but amputate them with the penknife – something Paul wanted to avoid as he could not walk properly till the stumps had healed. An air of depression settled over the group; they were exhausted and starving.

"What about some nice bat soup then, boys?" Asked Kwang-Ho trying to lift the mood.

"I'll eat anything given the chance. Can I have mine with fries?" Joked Luke.

Laughter was the best medicine to lift their spirits because their moods lifted instantly. After a few nuts and a mouthful of chocolate over the last few days, even bat soup sounded appetising.

While Kwang-Ho looked for the bats, David melted snow in the coffee tin over the fire. At the rear of the chamber, a short climb up an inclined rift led to another small chamber. The smell of bat guano was oppressive, and the chamber floor heaved with insect life living in the bat excrement. When Kwang-Ho shone the torch on the inverted animals, he expected them to wake up but they remained in their hibernating torpor. All he had to do was pick them off the cave roof. Before they woke up from the heat of his hands, Kwang-Ho decapitated them with the penknife. The bats were the size of large sparrows, so he thought they would need quite a few. He took sixteen back to his companions in the first chamber.

"So, what now," he asked, "should we skin and gut them first?"

"I'll do that," volunteered David, "it can't be any more difficult than cleaning a rat."

"Be quick, my boy, or I'll eat mine raw." Remarked Paul smiling.

"Yes, bat sushi, my favourite." Added Luke.

"I thought I would select a few leg chops, a la bat, and roast them over the fire."

Once again, a chorus of laughter spread around the companions. It was the first time since his arrest that David felt normal. Although he had lost his wife and children, a wound that would forever be raw, at that moment, in a Chinese cave, in the middle of a frozen wilderness, there was a tiny seed of happiness deep within his soul.

Boiled bat may not be a recipe in the latest cookbooks, but every mouthful to the fugitives from Camp 22 was as satisfying as fillet steak, although four bats each was hardly enough to quash months of near starvation.

"Well, that was a nice aperitif; when do we get the main course?" announced Paul.

Another peal of laughter coursed around the group, borne of food in their bellies, a warm, open fire and a release from the stress of captivity.

"I'd like a nice bottle of burgundy with my next course." Replied David, prompting fresh laughter.

"A cup of tea would satisfy me." Said Luke innocently.

There was a sudden silence as the others turned and stared at the younger man. When Luke naively shrugged his shoulders, they all burst into hysterical laughter again.

Outside the cave, the muffled laughter of those inside halted the searchers in their tracks. With their AK-47s pointing towards the inner recesses of the cave, they anticipated having a fight on their hands.

***

An Sang-Ho turned away from the window and addressed his son directly.

"Sang-Ki, I have read your testimonials from the 6B project leader; they are excellent. You have worked well since you came to Camp 22. I am pleased that you are to be part of this project."

Sang-Ki smiled at his father, whom he idolised. An Sang-Ho had graduated from Pyongyang Medical University – PMU as the top science student of 1951, after a fashion Sang-Ki achieved the same in 1975. Throughout his childhood and studentship, he strived to emulate his father. Sang-Ki may have succeeded academically, but in his personal life, he had failed. Sang-Ki had few friends, for he was brash and arrogant. He had been privileged throughout his life by being the son of one of the most respected scientists in the Democratic People's Republic of Korea. A fact that he reminded people of repeatedly. When disciplined at school, he played the famous father card and frequently escaped punishment. Although his father's research involved the sacrifice of political prisoners, he was not overtly cruel. Sang-Ki, though had no morals at all. As a child, he had experimented on neighbourhood pets he had stolen and had taken great satisfaction in observing the agony he had metered out on his animal victims. He was cruel and heartless. He gained his academic credits by blackmail, plagiarism and cheating in exams. A sociopath, if he had not been licensed to kill by the state, he would have done so anyway in his spare time and in his final year at PMU Sang-Ki had married impetuously. She was a talented science student that had helped him with his assignments. When his father reprimanded him for his foolishness, he abandoned the girl. Pregnant and ostracised by her parents, she had begged Sang-Ki to take her back. He spat in her face and called her a whore. When her naked body was found in the basement flat, she had once shared with Sang-Ki, no one questioned the suspicious circumstances surrounding her death. Questions of why she had cut her own throat and yet not left a suicide note, why there were bloody claw marks on the inside of the bathroom door, or why she had left a part-eaten meal before killing herself were never asked. No one bothered to interview her closest friend, whom she had arranged to meet later that evening, or Sang-Ki after a neighbour stated that she had seen him earlier run from the flat. Who would care that some hysterical girl had taken her own life for no apparent reason, no one?

Although An Sang-Ho loved his son, he did not like him very much. He knew nothing of his dishonesty or cruelty because he had not shared a close relationship with him. His wife Eun-Hee, had brought him up almost single-handedly. He had been too busy to play with his son, take him fishing, or get to know him. Sang-Ki attended boarding school from age four until he went to university at eighteen. Eun-Hee had spared her husband of the poor reports, the complaints, and the recommendations that he move schools. When she threatened to vilify the school, the poor reports ceased. When Sang-Ki became older, he was clever enough to pass his exams and ruthless enough to keep his teachers and principal fearful of the consequences if they ever wrote anything negative about him.

"Thank you, Father; I am proud to be part of your illustrious project."

"Yes, yes," Sang-Ho replied, dismissively sweeping his hand through the air; he had no time for sentimentality.

"I want you to concentrate on identifying the compound or compounds released by the *Toxoplasma gondii* cysts into the brains of the principal host – the rat – that cause the behavioural changes. It must be chemical; there is no other explanation. If we can isolate such a compound, we can begin synthesising it ourselves. It will be a breakthrough in social control. If we can enhance its effects, we can either reduce the concentrations needed to induce satisfactory behavioural changes or develop a dosage dependant range of effects, from slight to severe."

"Thank you, I am honoured, Sir, that you think I am worthy to lead such an important part of this project. What, may I ask, will you be investigating from now on?"

"I will continue looking at the behavioural changes in humans. I will try to identify what part of the brain is affected by parasitic cysts and the cause of the behavioural changes. Once you have identified and isolated the chemical compounds responsible, I will try to identify the receptors in the brain that trigger the behavioural responses and see if we can develop a chemical agent that can block those receptors."

"A sort of antidote?"

"Yes. If we can develop this into a biochemical weapon, everyone working in the infected area after the attack must be protected."

"This could take years to complete." Said Sang-Ki. "Will the government continue to support our research for that amount of time?"

"I have the ear of no less than Paek Hak-Mi, the Director of the Ministry of Public Security. He has assured me that this project is of the utmost importance to the government and vital for the future stability of this country. With such a weapon, we can easily subdue the rise of dissidents within the general population and, in particular, their breeding ground, our universities. I see no reason to doubt such an important member of our country's intelligence community."

"That is good news, Sir. On another note, will I have access to the human testing programme?"

An Sang-Ho looked at his son and wondered why he should ask such an obvious question. Sang-Ki must have anticipated the question behind his father's searching gaze.

"I just wondered because I will have to test the compounds I isolate to measure their physiological and psychological effect. Particularly if we are to quantify their potency."

Sang-Ho sensed some other motivation behind his enquiry, one he couldn't yet explain.

"Yes, of course, you do when the time comes. But I want you to work on the rats, to begin with. The turnaround is much quicker with such experimental animals. It will allow you to identify the compounds responsible for the behavioural changes much quicker than with humans. Once you have isolated a compound with a measurable effect in rats, the obvious follow-on would be to test its potency on humans."

"Yes, of course, I fully understand. So where do I start?"

"Song Min-Su has all the data from our initial experiments. He will show you around the animal testing lab, the rat room – so to speak – and then the molecular bioscience lab that will be your home for a while."

Sang-Ho pressed a button on his desk intercom. "Min-Su, you can come in now."

As the office door opened, Sang-Ho turned once more to his son and asked:

"OK Sang-Ki, have you any questions?" Yet, before he could answer Sang-Ho looked towards his assistant, Min-Su, who had just entered the room. "Min-Su, take An Sang-Ki and show him around our facilities before introducing him to his lab assistant in the molecular bioscience lab."

Addressing his son again, he concluded: "I have asked Min-Su to work with you for the first week or so, as he knows the most about our initial experiments. Once you have settled in, he will leave you to it and return to me in the main lab." Before Sang-Ki could answer, Sang-Ho turned his attention to an open file on his desk. "OK, off you go. I'll catch up with you both later, I'm sure." He said without looking up.

Sang-Ki was used to his father's dismissive attitude; it didn't affect him anymore. As he got up from his chair, he bowed his head in deference to his father before turning to Min-Su.

"This way, please, Sir." Said Min-Su, as he held open the door to his master's son, a man he would soon come to hate.

***

As suddenly as their flickering silhouettes appeared on the cave wall, the four refugees from Camp 22 knew they were in trouble. As they turned to face the intruders, three AK-47s were cocked and aimed at their chests. By the light of a flaming torch one of the intruders held, the escapees saw five figures on the far side of the chamber. Three carried the rifles and were kneeling whilst two others stood beside them holding flaming torches. The two rifles Paul and David had brought were out of reach; they were trapped.

The fifth intruder spoke first in a language the fugitives could not understand. Getting no response, he repeated what he had said. As Kwang-Ho stood up, two rifles immediately zeroed in on him. The fifth man bellowed something that warned him not to move again.

"Excuse me, please; my friends and I are merely travellers sheltering from the storm outside. We wish you no harm." Said Kwang-Ho, in textbook Mandarin Chinese.

"You are Korean." The fifth man replied as a statement rather than a question.

"Yes." Replied Kwang-Ho.

"What are you doing here?"

"We have all escaped from the mine at Chungbong. We're political prisoners, not criminals. If we'd stayed at the mine, my friends and I would be dead. We had to escape. Can you help us?"

The fifth man turned to a sixth person who had just entered the chamber. It was a woman. The two conferred for a few minutes, again in a language none of the escapees recognised.

"Where did you get those guns?" Said the woman.

"We were returning from the lumber camp across the Tumen River to the Chungbong mine when we managed to overpower our guards. We left them tied up in the truck and escaped into the forest. The guns were just two of the numerous items we salvaged from the truck. We took them for our safety because we would certainly have been tortured and executed if we had been recaptured. We would rather die at our own hands than return to Chungbong."

The woman came forward and picked up the two rifles before returning to the others in her party. She handed them to the fifth man, who sniffed at the open breaches of both rifles after first checking to see if they were loaded.

"These have not been fired recently; you are lying. Perhaps you are intelligence officers sent to spy on us."

"No, we're not spies. I crashed the truck that we were travelling in, incapacitating the guards. We are alone, and as far as we are aware, we weren't followed. We had no reason to fire the guns; it would have drawn attention to ourselves."

"How did you cross the border without being seen?"

"We crossed at night. Just before the recent storm."

"The river isn't frozen completely; it cannot be crossed at the moment."

"We crossed to a small island between two of the guard posts. My friend here, Paul, fell in. We sheltered in this cave because we had to light a fire; he was still in danger of becoming hypothermic."

"I know this island." Said the woman. "Perhaps you are telling the truth. How did you get from there to this cave? The snow is very deep in places, impossible without snowshoes?"

"We made some from green sticks, cord and pieces of a groundsheet. They're over there to your left."

The woman took the flaming torch from her confederate and retrieved one of the snowshoes. Once again, she and the fifth man conferred in the strange language.

"These are very good," she said, addressing Kwang-Ho again, "you're very enterprising. What else did you take from this truck?"

"It is all here on what remains of the groundsheet."

"Show me." Commanded the woman.

While Kwang-Ho showed the woman their belongings, the other five men remained on guard, unwilling to trust them. When satisfied, the woman spoke over her shoulder to the others in her party before returning to the escapees.

"I think you may be telling the truth." She said in perfect Korean. "Who fell in the river?"

"I did." Stated Paul.

"Are you OK now, warm enough, I mean?"

"Yes, I'm good."

She picked up David's tunic. "This is surely what saved you from drowning. You were lucky."

"Yes, praise the Lord; it certainly did."

"You are Christians?" She asked harshly.

Paul and the others looked at each other, silently debating whether it was safe to admit their belief or dangerous. When they all nodded, he replied, "Yes, we are. Does that matter?"

"Yes, it does." She said, almost whispering.

Again, the woman and the fifth man debated this new fact. While those aiming their rifles at the four friends never wavered.

"What precedes the book of Romans?" She asked.

"The Book of Acts." Replied Kwang-Ho immediately.

The man and the woman whispered again before she returned to the group.

"We have to be very cautious, I'm afraid. We must be sure you are genuine refugees, or we'd all end up dead." She said, opening her arms submissively. "Please forgive me. My name is Sūn Li Ming; this is Wú Kuan-Yin we live in a small village just north of here. We regularly come to this cave and others in the area to harvest the bats. I can smell that you have eaten some. Did you enjoy them?"

"Li Ming, we would have eaten anything," Luke said, pointing at the coffee tin they had boiled the bats in. "This is the first meal containing meat protein we've had for months."

"I'll have to get the recipe." Li Ming joked. With a wave of her hand, the three men holding them at gunpoint shouldered their arms and exited the chamber. "We will collect some of the bats first and then stay in the cave until morning. Then if you wish we will take you to our village, we have many friends there who can help. What were you planning to do; this part of China is dangerous.

"Well, we hadn't thought about that in any detail. We had to escape when we did and hoped that whatever village we found in China would help us escape to South Korea." Replied Kwang-Ho

"Whoa, that's pretty naïve." She exclaimed. "This area is very dangerous. There are gangs who traffic North Korean women into slavery. There are Chinese security police that round up North Koreans and send them back to their deaths. These police think nothing of torturing their victims to extract any knowledge they may have of anyone who helped them. Some villagers would gladly give you up to the security police for a few Yuan. Those caught helping refugees may be fined 30 000 Yuan or face lengthy prison

147

sentences. There are posters everywhere saying that it's the duty of all Chinese people to arrest and denounce North Korean refugees."

As Li Ming spoke of the difficulty they faced, an air of despair spread amongst the group.

"We had no idea; we naturally thought people would help us." Said David.

"Well, it's a good thing we found you first." Replied Li Ming. "Because if you had blundered your way into any of the villages around here, you would have found yourselves being arrested very quickly. There is no love for refugees, like yourselves, on this side of the border. Our peoples are oppressed just as much as yours, and people live in fear of being arrested by the security police."

The more David and his friends heard, the worse they felt. *Out of the pan and into the fire* was an English saying that came to mind.

When the three riflemen reappeared, they spoke to Wú Kuan-Yin, who then talked to Li Ming.

"Our friends say that you are alone." She said, pointing to the three riflemen hauling several baskets. "With the weather as it is outside, no police would be waiting to ambush you or us. They would be frozen solid. Perhaps we can trust you after all."

148

8. Nanyangcun

As the small party set out for the village David and his friends helped to carry the baskets of bats harvested from the cave. Although they were treated respectfully, their two AK-47s were not returned to them.

"What language do you speak; it's a dialect I can't recognise." Asked Kwang-Ho of Li Ming.

"Manchu, it's a Tungusic language that used to be the language of the Manchu people, spoken here in Northeast China. Most Manchus speak Mandarin these days, and Manchu is nearly extinct. There are nearly 10 million ethnic Manchus, yet fewer than 100 native speakers of the language; that's the official story, anyway. All our group speak it. It's the language of our forefathers, and something we believe should be preserved. It's a secure tongue that helps our group remain below the radar."

"What is your group? What do you do that requires a secret language?"

"I've said enough for the moment. Our leader will answer all your questions when we reach the village."

As Li Ming increased her pace and joined the others in her group, Kwang-Ho and the other fugitives felt more than a little wary of their new friends. Who were they, and why all the subterfuge? David was utterly mystified. He thought the initial questions about their Christian beliefs might provide a clue. Christianity was outlawed here in China, just as much as in North Korea. Perhaps, he thought, they were some Christian fundamentalist group that wanted the return of self-government in Manchuria. Despite the mystery, he didn't believe these people would betray them to the Chinese authorities.

Although it was very cold, the air was crisp, and the visibility was clear, one of those winter mornings that made everyone feel happy. The snow crunched beneath their feet with each step, making that satisfying sound that every child remembers. Kwang-Ho's long stick indicated that the snow was 800 mm deep in some places. Without their improvised snowshoes, they would be effectively stranded and unable to progress through the drifts.

Picking up a handful of snow Kwang-Ho tasted it; it was pure, cool and fresh to his tongue, just as he remembered from his childhood. Without thinking, he balled it in his hands and threw it at David. It hit him squarely on the back of his neck. At first, David thought it had perhaps fallen from a tree and, apart from brushing it from his collar, took no notice. When the second hit him harder and in the same place, he knew exactly what had happened and quickly dodged behind a large tree. All he could hear was Kwang-Ho laughing. Before he could retaliate, he was hit again, this time in the middle of his back. Behind him, Paul was in stitches with laughter. Scooping up a large amount of snow, he quickly made his own snowball and threw it at his father. Another snowball hit him on the side of his head, and Luke laughed. With snow flying in all directions, any tension between the refugees borne of the mystery surrounding their new friends soon disappeared.

Once the Manchus realised their Korean friends had stopped, they stood open-mouthed and shaking their heads at the sight of grown men in a snowball fight. But when a snowball hit Li Ming just behind her ear, it signalled all-out warfare. There were no sides; everyone was vulnerable to everyone else. It was anarchy.

With fingers starting to hurt with the cold, only the hardiest continued, and then, as suddenly as it started, it ended. As they all sank to their knees, exhausted, laughter spread around the group, Manchus and Koreans alike. It was a poignant moment in the thawing of relations between the two groups and the seed from which trust would grow.

***

It was late in the afternoon when the party arrived at the village of Nanyangcun. There was no welcome, no fanfare for the returning hunters. Once the baskets had been handed over to the riflemen, Li Ming showed David and the others to a hut on the outskirts of the village. It was warm inside, with a fire at its centre and sleeping mats around its periphery. All the men were exhausted and needed no invitation to curl up under a blanket and immediately fall asleep.

Kwang-Ho was first to awake as Li Ming carried in a meal of boiled chicken, lentils and rice. Before she could ladle out a second bowl, three other pairs of hands wanted her to feed them next. It was food they could only have imagined just days before. The men from Chungbong would have killed for less.

"Any more?" She said once the first bowl had been consumed. "Perhaps I should leave the pot here, and you can help yourself."

"Thank you." Was all that was said.

"Look, once you've finished your meal, I'll be back with the leader of our group. He will tell you what will happen next and answer all those questions you have been bursting to ask. I'll be about an hour, OK?"

"Thank you." Was, again, the collective reply.

***

As promised, Li Ming returned just before the hour was up. A tall, thin man with her carried a large teapot and six cups.

"Gentlemen, let me introduce our leader, Wú Kuan-Yin. He will tell you about our group and our plans for your escape from China."

David and the others didn't know what to say, still not knowing whether they had been rescued or betrayed. He addressed them in perfect Korean as they transferred their gaze from Li Ming to Kuan-Yin.

"Forgive all the cloak and dagger business, but we have to be sure you are bona fide refugees and not government Quislings who would destroy our group. This village is one of the few inhabited by persons of similar beliefs. Not only are we all Christians, but we all believe that the regime in North Korea is just as evil as ours here in China. Neither country is renowned for its civil rights, both now and in history. We are just a few ethnic Manchus that care about what is happening on both sides of the border. You mentioned earlier that you were from the mine at Chungbong, so I presume you and perhaps your families started in Camp 22."

The four men were surprised by what they had just been told. So, when Kwang-Ho spoke for them, his voice was no more than a squeak.

"Yes, Kuan-Yin, you're right on both counts. We were from Camp 22, and yes, our wives and children may still be there."

"That's very sad." He replied, his voice heavy with emotion. "My father strayed across the border ten years ago; we haven't seen him since. We have been told, by other refugees we have helped, what Camp 22 is like, so we can surmise what eventually happened to him." Kuan-Yin paused momentarily as his mind returned to his father, waving goodbye on the day he disappeared. It was a sad memory etched on his heart. He had shed many tears reliving that moment over the years; he would shed many more over time. When Li Ming touched his arm, he continued without looking at her.

"We can help you escape from China, for our group has links with the underground railway that assists people like yourselves. Koreans living in South Korea, Japan and the US have provided money to establish such an underground railroad, enabling thousands of refugees to reach South Korea via nations bordering our country, such as Russia, Mongolia, Burma and Laos." Kuan-Yin poured them all tea whilst watching the faces of the Koreans as if he was not entirely convinced of their authenticity.

"Beijing has offered big rewards to hand in refugees like you." He continued. "This has made everyone involved with aiding refugees suspicious, always vigilant for those who would betray us. We have heard on the short-wave radio that troops from Chungbong have been searching for you, although they gave up after the storm hit. You must thank the Lord for not wandering into any other village seeking help because you would surely have perished." Once again Kuan-Yin paused as he sipped his tea.

"Our job now is to pass you along the line until you are free. We don't know much about what happens down the line, for the less each section knows about another, the more secure the whole 'railway' becomes. Now we will let you rest tonight; in the morning, we will feed and clothe you and transport you to the next rendezvous, where another group will be responsible for you. What we demand of you is complete secrecy. You must never reveal any details regarding the railway to anyone, including your relatives. Is that understood?"

"Yes." Was the unanimous reply.

"Now, about your relatives, we cannot fish around on the other side of the border for information regarding your loved ones. That would draw attention to ourselves and secure the deaths of those we sought. Believe me, when I say there is little we can do, I'm sorry."

"We've already heard of the deaths of a few." Admitted David. "My wife was killed in some bizarre medical experiment; my brother died after a beating...." Suddenly David choked on his words as

155

his heart began to break. He had given little thought to the death of his wife since he had been told; such were the inhumane conditions at Chungbong that he had needed to concentrate solely on staying alive. Now with freedom within his grasp, the emotional barrier, built so high at the mining camp, burst. His body shook uncontrollably as the tears began to flow, and he gasped for each breath as he broke down. Li Ming was the first to reach him, and his head fell against her shoulder as she embraced David. David was drowning in the sorrow he had not allowed himself to feel in captivity. As the faces of those left behind grew in his consciousness, one amongst all the others cut him the most; it was Ruth, his daughter. As the guilt of abandoning her consumed him, the bitter taste of bile rose into his mouth. Turning his head away from Li Ming, he retched. With the vile fluid pooling in his cupped hands, David got up and rushed out of the hut. Once outside, he sank to his knees and then onto all fours. With his hands pressed against the snow, he lost control, vomiting and sobbing simultaneously. Strong hands on his shoulders brought him back to the world of the living, and the petulant ghosts of his lost family began to recede.

"David," said his father, "don't let the dead consume you. Empty your heart of the pain you now feel, release it all, leave nothing behind and fill that space with the good times you shared with them, the birthdays, the Christmases, the firsts. They would not want you torturing yourself over that you had no control over. You must fill your heart with all the good times you shared with them."

As David turned his face toward his father, Paul's words began to echo in his ears as meaningless vibrations merged with the white noise that filled his reality. Words alone could not help him, yet with each involuntary contraction of his stomach; he exorcised the mystic demons that haunted him. As he fell upon the snow, physical and emotional exhaustion swept over him, diminishing his pain and leaving only the sadness.

When Paul knelt beside his son, holding him in his arms, he looked upon his tortured face and began to cry. Although he had long since purged himself of the same ghosts that David mourned, the emotional turmoil associated with the torture and death of so many of his own family was still just below the surface of his own cognition. In their grief, David and his father rocked gently backwards and forwards, oblivious of the frozen ground until Luke and Li Ming found them.

"Come on now, both of you," commanded Li Ming, "let's get you inside before you both freeze to death."

Having helped his father and brother up, Luke embraced them both. "Enough now," he whispered, "we've nothing to blame ourselves for. The dead can help themselves; we must look after the living now."

At first, David was stunned by his brother's words, believing them insensitive, yet as he looked into Luke's tear-stained face, he quickly realised that he had made sense.

He did not resist as he was ushered back into the Manchu hut.

"Have some tea, both of you," said Kuan-Yin as he gave them a cup. "It has magical restorative powers, and even if you don't believe me, it will warm you up from the inside."

David barely smiled at the Manchu leader's light-hearted comment; it would be a while before his humour returned.

***

The tea did have magical restorative powers, as all four refugees felt much better as the evening wore on and the fifth pot of tea was consumed. It would take a long time to recover physically and mentally from the privations of Chungbong, but emotionally they were on a high.

"What's in this brew, opium?" enquired Paul jokingly.

"No, we don't use any opioids here, though we do use many herbs, which stimulate the brain to release endorphins, which in turn help to relieve stress. One of the ingredients in the tea is *yuan zhi* to quiet the heart and help you relax. It also contains *he huan* to soothe the emotions. It's obviously working, as you're all smiling."

"I think, for the moment, we have patched over those raw areas of grief that surfaced earlier. They will always be there, but perhaps with time, we will learn to cope with them a little better than we did."

"I'll drink to that." Said Luke downing another cup of tea.

"What is that awful smell?" Enquired David turning to Paul as he removed one of his socks.

"I think it's my toes, they've split, and some foul-smelling gunk is oozing out of them."

"Oh, my goodness." Exclaimed Li Ming. "They're badly frostbitten. We need to get those seen to straight away. I'll get our doctor immediately."

Within ten minutes, Li Ming returned with another Manchu. He was a short, lean, old man, in his sixties, with his hair tied in a braid, which stretched down his back.

"This is Dr Teng Cheng-Gong; I'm afraid he only speaks Manchu, so I'll have to translate for you."

Dr Teng stooped to look more closely and sniff the black putrefying stumps of flesh that had once been Paul's toes. After addressing Li Ming, she translated his question.

"How long have you had feet like this?"

"I suppose since we sheltered from the storm late last week. Falling in the river didn't help much either."

After another round of comments, Li Ming replied;

"You are a silly man." She said, blushing. "Haven't you been in pain?"

"They were at first, and then they just went numb. They've just started to hurt now. Why are they bad?"

"Dr Teng says they are beyond saving; they smell because the flesh has died; it may be the start of gangrene. He will have to amputate them. I'm sorry, Paul, that's what he's just said."

"Oh well, what're a few toes," Paul replied nonchalantly. "I've always had a problem with ingrowing toenails; I suppose cutting them off will cure that problem."

"He says this is no joke; you may lose your feet or die if the tissue is already infected."

Paul was stunned into silence.

"It may take minutes to cut them off, but it will take months before you can walk again. He will start by giving you *zhi shi*; you may know it as bitter orange, which will help the circulation in the surrounding tissues. However, he will have to cut them off tonight if he is to save your feet."

"But, a few months? He…" Started David.

"Dr Teng says there can be no argument. Your father's life is at stake. They must be removed immediately."

The refugees stood silently, looking at the doctor as he disappeared from the hut. As they stared at one another, not knowing what to say or do, the doctor returned with a bowl full of snow. They all looked on in amazement as he bound up Paul's feet in snow-packed bandages.

"The ice is to stop the spread of infection into the live tissue. Help him up and follow me," said Li Ming.

With Paul hobbling between David and Kwang-Ho, the motley group trudged across the unlit village to another small house on the northern edge of the Nanyangcun. They were told it was the surgery after carrying Paul into a small, well-lit room. They were all ushered back into the night by a stern-faced lady, whom Li Ming said was the doctor's wife.

"It's best to return to your hut and rest. Paul will be operated on using acupuncture; he'll be in no distress. Dr Teng says you can't help him anymore and that you may come back in the morning."

"Can't we stay here?" Objected Luke.

"No, you must leave him now. He will be well looked after; Dr Teng was a surgeon in a major teaching hospital in Yanji just a few years ago. When he retired, he returned to the village of his birth to serve the few remaining Manchu people. Dr Teng is an excellent surgeon; Paul will be fine."

"But we can't stay here, in Nanyangcun, for months while Paul convalesces, can we?" Said David.

"No, that won't be possible; we never know when the authorities will drop on us and search the village. They don't know that we are involved with the refugee conduit. Still, as we are one of the few remaining Manchu-speaking villages, they are paranoid that we may become seditious, fighting for the independence of Manchuria. So, it's unsafe for you to be here without proper identity papers. Please follow me back to your hut."

The men were no longer in a jovial mood as they re-entered their hut. Fortune may favour the brave, but it surely didn't favour them. Few of them got much sleep that night.

***

The following morning Li Ming came to the hut with their breakfast and news of Paul.

"I have some good news," she said as she placed the tray of food on a low wooden table just inside the door. "Dr Teng believes that he managed to catch the infection just in time. Although Paul has lost his toes, he still has his feet, and a course of amoxicillin should ensure that he remains free of further infection. He will be back with you before lunch."

"Thanks, Li Ming, that's great news. But how can he stay here when you said it isn't safe, if he can't continue with us?"

"Well, we have a few forged documents that previously belonged to villagers that have died here. We have adapted them by altering the dates of birth, which is simple but effective. One or two new faces in the village will go unnoticed, but four is too many. If the People's Armed Police (PAP) have recently been informed, by the North Koreans, that some prisoners have made it across the border, this will be one of the first villages to be searched."

The three refugees looked at Li Ming with concern. The thought that they would be arrested and returned to Chungbong was too horrific to consider. They all knew that before they died, by stoning, they would be tortured to give up the names of those who helped them escape, both in Korea and in China.

"If the Koreans found no evidence that you survived the storm, we may have more time. However, we can't assume that, so we must get you out of here as soon as possible."

"But what about Paul?" enquired David.

"What about Paul." Came a voice from behind them. As the men turned, they saw Paul on crutches in the doorway. "Come on then, you lazy sods, don't just gawp at me; come and help me."

All three men, and Li Ming, jumped up immediately to assist him in getting through the door without falling flat on his face.

Li Ming hugged Paul and then disappeared to get some more herbal tea.

"You look great, Paul." Said Kwang-Ho. "You certainly don't look like someone who has just undergone a major operation."

"There was nothing major about it." He replied. "After sticking a few needles in me, the doc snipped off the dead toes with a pair of shears. I watched him do it; it was incredible, I felt no pain, and there was little blood. Then the skilful stuff started; I was fascinated to watch. He pared back the skin, removed all the dead tissue, and sewed me back together. Without general anaesthetic, my recovery was instantaneous. I wanted to return last night, but the doc said the acupuncture needles had to stay longer to relieve the pain. I must have dropped off to sleep when he jabbed me again with a couple more."

"How do you feel now?" Asked David.

"Great, my feet are sore, but I'm OK.

Paul felt embarrassed with the three men fussing around him, plumping up cushions, and offering a blanket and a pillow.

"Look, guys, I'm sorry I stuffed up. They say I won't be able to walk for a while yet, which means staying in the village a little longer. I'm sorry; I know you want to get out of here as quickly as possible, but it's better than Chungbong."

The others remained silent with downcast eyes, with no one willing to tell him the bad news.

"What's the matter, cat got your tongues or something?" He asked, perplexed by their reaction.

"We've been told we'll have to leave you here while you convalesce." Said Kwang-Ho apologetically. "We have to leave soon, as it's not safe for four strangers to appear in the village so suddenly."

Paul slumped onto his cushions as if punched in the stomach. He couldn't believe that he was to be separated from the others.

"Well, what's going to happen to me then?" He asked, almost childlike.

"We don't know. You barged in before Li Ming could tell us." Luke joked. "We'll have to wait till she gets back."

David sat next to his father with his arm around him.

"You'll be OK; we will all be back together in just a few weeks. After Chungbong, this place is paradise."

Paul looked at his son, not knowing quite what to say. Surely, they were kidding.

"Look, you guys, stop pulling my leg and tell me what we will do.

Just then, Li Ming arrived in time with a tray of food and a large pot of tea.

"Li Ming, tell these silly sods to stop kidding and tell me the truth," Paul asked, his voice trembling with each syllable.

"They're telling the truth, Paul; it's not safe for all of you to stay here in Nanyangcun. Four strange faces are too many. The PAP are always searching for North Korean refugees, offering rewards to people willing to turn them in and arresting those who assist them." She looked at Paul and felt some of his pain as he contemplated being separated from the rest of them.

"I'm so sorry, Paul," she continued, "if they stay, we could all end up in prison."

Logical arguments were worthless comfort to how Paul felt at that moment. They had survived the privations of Chungbong together; they had survived all that nature could throw at them, and now that he thought they were safe, he would be separated from them all. It was a bitter pill to swallow.

9. The Underground Railway

"Why is Nanyangcun such a PAP target?" Asked David.

Li Ming paused for a moment before answering her friend. "What, besides the fact that we're all revolutionary Manchu's, with a mission to depose Beijing." She joked ironically. "Well, apart from that, the village has a bit of history. When Manchuria was annexed by Japan before World War II, Japanese troops and police sympathisers descended upon the village, and, without reason, slaughtered our people and razed the village to the ground. Much later when the village was re-inhabited, the young people forged swords and spears so they could capture guns and rifles from their oppressors. Soon after that twenty young men of Nanyangcun ambushed a small unit of the puppet Manchukuo army, which was moving from Yanji to Jiulongping. They killed them all and captured many weapons. It was using these captured weapons that the young Manchu's waged a guerrilla war against the Japanese for the rest of the occupation. It was in villages like this one, that the revolutionary spirit of self-reliance was born. The PAP has never forgotten Nanyangcun, and as I said last night, they are paranoid that we will rise up once more to fight for Manchurian independence."

168

"And are they right to believe this?" Asked Kwang-Ho.

"In some ways, yes, but they're far too strong for us to battle with head-on, even using guerrilla tactics. They are cruel and savage, I'm sure they would willingly extinguish all life in this village if they could."

"So, what's stopping them then?" Added Luke.

"Well, we are a more subtle people now. We have high ranking sympathisers installed in the People's Congress, people who work very discretely to divert more authority to the Manchu people. We do not fight with guns anymore; we fight with our brains because destabilisation can be achieved by slowly undermining the mechanisms of power in Manchuria. *One wasp sting cannot kill a tiger, but many wasps, stinging repeatedly can.*"

"Sounds like my sort of battle." Said, Paul.

"Yes, we have the help of many non-Manchu people, including Koreans."

"Well sign me up sister," quipped Paul, "if I have to stay here, I might as well help out. Just point me in the right direction and give me a shove and I'm your man."

"Never a truer word said in jest." Said Li Ming. Helping North Korean refugees can help us too, for they also bring pressure to bear outside China. They raise awareness of our cause, both in the US, and the United Nations; they bring the world's attention to breaches in human rights through Amnesty International, the list of what you can achieve for both your people in North Korea and ours in Manchuria, is endless."

As Li Ming finished speaking there was an audible silence. Li Ming had very succinctly and very eloquently drawn their attention to the fact that it wasn't just North Koreans that were oppressed. These people in Nanyangcun and other Manchu villages struggled against a totalitarian regime that did not recognise the individual, their needs or their different cultural roots. In a way, they were shamed by the fact that they were not the only victims of tyranny.

***

When the time came to say goodbye, everyone had tears in their eyes. David and Luke hugged their father fiercely, unwilling to let him go, lest they would never see him again. As Li Ming hustled the three refugees into the back of a small box truck, they waved and shouted to Paul until the very last moment and the rear doors were closed. Hidden amongst sheaves of rice straw in the rear of the truck, they settled in for a long hard journey. Also sharing the same space were four small, but very noisy pigs, held in bamboo crates closer to the rear door. As the truck bounced along the unsealed tracks from the village the men were jostled and bumped so frequently, they thought they would surely break a bone.

They had been given very little detail of their journey except to say that their next stop would be another village closer to Yanji. The ruse was for Wu Kuan-Yin and Li Ming to pose as farmers, transporting stock to the rail yard just beyond Yanji. There, dressed as farmers themselves, they would be put aboard a goods train that carried stock to Harbin. As only Kwang-Ho could speak Mandarin well enough, Li Ming would travel with them all the way. This leg of the journey alone was over 500 kilometres and would take two days. The men lay in the dark, listening to the contented grunts of their animal companions until mercifully, they all fell asleep.

At Tangjin they climbed out of their transport, blinking in the remaining sunlight, and rubbing their eyes of sleep. They were hastily shepherded into a small farmhouse and in front of a welcome wood stove. Besides their bruises, they were cold and hungry.

"Why haven't we met anyone else except yourself, Wu Kuan-Yin, Dr Teng and his wife?" Enquired Luke.

"Simple, the fewer the number who see of you, the fewer loose tongues we have to worry about. You must remember this isn't a sightseeing trip, we're having to smuggle you across the country as if you were illicit goods. Everyone wants to earn a quick buck if they can, and you guys represent the cost of a new TV or fridge. The reward monies for turning you in are substantial for someone who has nothing. Added to which we may be able to dress you up, but we can't disguise your faces, you are Korean and that raises suspicions everywhere you go in China."

All three men looked at Li Ming searching her eyes for any humour, there was none, and they felt as if they had been chastised.

"That's a little harsh Li Ming." Came a voice from behind them.

At the entrance to the farmhouse stood a tall man whose short grey hair made him look more like an academic professor than a farmer.

"I'm sorry guys, yes I was a little harsh, I'll blame it on the stress of our journey if you'll let me. I get grumpy when I'm worried. Anyway, this is a good friend of ours Wu Zongxian, he will fix you up with clothes the natives wear hereabouts and issue you with the basic documentation you will need for the rest of the journey. From now on you will be riding upfront as it were, no more hiding in the back of a farm truck with the pigs, I promise.

At last, she made a joke. Although none of the Koreans laughed, they all breathed a sigh of relief.

"First some food, then the new clothes and finally a better-looking face." When a look of puzzlement flashed across Kwang-Ho's face, Li Ming caught on immediately. "Zongxian's wife is our make-up artist, we may not make you Chinese, but we may be able to lessen your racial features.

***

After dinner, David and his brother volunteered to clear away the dinner things and wash the dishes. Although Zongxian's wife, Fei Yen, insisted that she would do it, a compromise was finally reached and the task was undertaken by all three. When Li Ming said that she needed some fresh air Kwang-Ho asked if she would object to some company.

"No, by all means, I'd be glad of some company. But I hope you realise that it's probably freezing, now that the sun has gone down." She said smiling at Kwang-Ho.

"I suppose I'll need a coat then?" He replied in jest.

A full moon had already risen, and moonlight bathed the landscape in a cold light that reflected off the fallen snow. For such a late hour it was amazingly bright. Long shadows, cast by the boundary fence, produced an unusual chequered effect on the snow of harshly contrasting blacks and whites. Although there was no chill wind, Li Ming had been right, it was cold, well below zero.

At the rear of the house, tied to the high bough of a Manchurian cork tree, was a swing, made from stout rope and a seat fabricated from an old tyre. Wrapping her arms around each rope, Li Ming sat on the tyre, and leaning back she quickly flipped her legs up to start a swinging motion.

"Give me a push, please, Kwang-Ho."

"Certainly madam, and how high would you like to go?"

"To the moon and back please."

"Sorry, you'll never achieve escape velocity on this old thing." He quipped.

"Then just get me closer."

Kwang-Ho obliged by pushing her with all his might, timing his efforts perfectly so that each push gradually increased her momentum till she could go no higher. On each downward swing, the sisal rope squeaked and a smell of turpentine caught the air from the bruised bark of the horizontal limb. With each pendulous swing, the shadow of Li Ming danced across the sparkling snow, in a continuous cycle of lengthening and shortening. Keeping perfect time with the oscillation of the swing, the old cork tree groaned under the constantly changing strain.

"I love it out here." She said dreamily. "From the top of each arc, I catch a glimpse of the lake, away down the valley. Moonbeams shine off its surface like the twinkling stars above. I spent my childhood in this village and on this swing, Fei Yen is my aunt."

"Where are your parents now Li Ming?"

"Oh, they're not around anymore, they died when I was ten."

"Gosh, I'm sorry, I shouldn't have asked."

"That was a long time ago; I'm a big girl now. Yes, it's a wound, but I'm OK with it now."

"How did you lose them?" He enquired tentatively.

"I didn't lose them, they were murdered." She said bluntly.

Kwang-Ho felt the sting of her anger and thought he should be quiet. He pushed her a little harder and then stepped to the side. A silence grew between them, neither of them sure how to continue a conversation.

"I'm sorry Kwang-Ho; perhaps I'm not such a big girl after all."

"It's tough when someone close is snatched from us by violence, my father was hanged in front of me in Camp 22. He was hardly recognisable as they dragged him to the gallows, I'm sure that he welcomed death when it came."

Li Ming dragged her feet along the ground and quickly stopped swinging. She turned to face him and saw the raw emotion in his eyes. "Now I have to be sorry, I'm sure you've witnessed more tragedy than I. I should have guessed."

"It's OK. That was then, and this is now." He said lightly.

"Push me again, please, Kwang-Ho."

Pushing her quickly took away the image of his father on the gallows and the horror of his twitching legs, as he slowly suffocated under his own weight, the same image that plagued him in his dreams.

"In 1966, at the beginning of the *Cultural Revolution*, my brother was being beaten in the streets by the Red Guards. When my mother stepped off her bus after work, she screamed at them to stop and began to beat one of them with her fists. My father was a doctor, a local GP, and when some of his patients saw what was happening, they got him out of his surgery, to prevent a tragedy happening. As my father began to remonstrate with them, the leader of the Red Guards, pulled out his pistol and shot my father in the head. When my hysterical mother attacked his killer, she too was shot. They even kicked and spat on her lifeless body. Then they dragged my brother away; I haven't seen him since that day fourteen years ago." Li Ming paused as the pain from that day began to fade. "At eight I didn't fully realise what had happened. Although I had witnessed the brutality, I don't think I really knew how final death was at the age. Fei Yen hastily carried away and shielded me from witnessing the gore that streamed from their bodies. The following morning, I fully expected them to be at breakfast, as they always had been. I don't think I gave up that hope until I was much older."

As Kwang-Ho was behind Li Ming he couldn't see her tears, but her voice, thick with emotion, couldn't hide them. He stopped pushing and stood aside until she finally came to rest. When he gently placed a hand on her shoulder, Li Ming seized it fiercely, as if somehow it would save her from the agony she now relived. As her hot tears scolded the back of his hand, he was filled with remorse for causing her such pain. And when he hugged her, she sobbed violently, just as she must have done as a child.

***

177

Later that evening Zongxian, Li Ming and the others sat around an open fire in the kitchen sipping *baijiu*, a white liquor distilled from sorghum. Served warm, this potent and potentially dangerous spirit, flavoured with rose essence and crystal sugar, had an alcohol content over 55%.

"If you don't like this stuff," joked Zongxian, "don't throw it away, because I always add a little to the gas tank of my truck."

"I'm sure it would make good rocket fuel too." Gasped David, as the sweet spirit burned his throat.

"Not bad is it Kwang-Ho, you must have tasted this before?"

"Well, yes I have, how did you know that?"

"You speak perfect Mandarin and your face is not pure Korean, you have some Chinese blood in you I think?"

"Yes, I do, my mother was Chinese. She grew up near Yanji and then migrated south to Chongjin, just after World War II. There she met and married my father." He paused for a moment, looking straight at Li Ming. Seeing no sign of disapproval, for not telling her earlier, he continued. "My mum could only speak Korean poorly, so at home, we spoke both Korean and Mandarin, sometimes changing from one to the other mid-sentence." Said Kwang-Ho, smiling at the old man. "You are very astute Zongxian how did you guess I was of mixed parentage?"

David and others sat open-mouthed at this admission; they had never thought that Kwang-Ho was part Chinese.

Zongxian smiled at his guests, purposefully delaying answering the question for effect.

"Because he was a professor of anthropology at Yanbian University, in Yanji, before the cultural revolution." Stated Li Ming, before her uncle could interject. "He always does something like this when he has guests. Always analysing them, their faces and their speech, he can be downright embarrassing sometimes."

"Oh, Li Ming you speak so harshly of me, how can you deny your old uncle such a simple pleasure? It's been a lifetime since my studies at Yanbian"

"Because, my love, not everyone likes to bare their soul, involuntarily and in public. You should warn them of your party tricks first."

Fearing Li Ming had overstepped the mark, chastising her uncle, the group dared not breathe, fully expecting Zongxian to rage at his niece for her disrespectful behaviour.

"She has always been outspoken, it's part of her charm, I suppose." Said Fei Yen as she emerged from the pantry. We still love her, just the same as our own children, don't we Zongxian? Children are what their parents make them?"

"Yes, my love, that's what you keep telling me. That it's my own fault that Li Ming is a rebel."

At that moment Li Ming got up and crossing over to her uncle's chair she ruffled his hair and kissed his brow.

"He's lovely really when you get to know him. You're just a frustrated old professor yearning for his past academic life, aren't you uncle'?"

"How many years have I had to put up with you child? Too long, I can tell you."

Li Ming kissed her uncle once again before offering more *baijiu* to everyone. The tension eased, and laughter became as plentiful as the *baijiu*.

"What will happen to us now Zongxian?" Enquired Luke.

"OK, in the morning, we will fit you out with apparel worn by all the most fashionable agricultural stock managers of Jilin Province. We will also equip you with the very best documentation forgeries we can muster and put you on a train to Harbin. As only

Kwang-Ho speaks Mandarin we'll loan you Li Ming, though I have to sympathise with you there, as I wouldn't wish her on my worst enemy."

It was payback time for Zongxian and as he smiled at his niece, she bobbed her tongue out at him, demonstrating there was no ill-feeling between them.

"At Harbin, you will meet another friend of ours who will drive you to Changchun and then put you on a train to Beijing, via Shenyang and Tangshan. By that time, you will have evolved into farm managers attending a conference that is taking place in the capital, quite coincidently, this time next week. I hope you've all brushed up on modern agricultural management techniques because your attendance at the conference is vital for your cover. You see they will stamp your attendance certificates and these will form part of your cover identities. From there I don't have a clue, that will be the responsibility of someone else."

"I just so happen to be an expert in stock to pasture ratios." Declared Luke.

"Yes, and I have a master's degree in bull shit." Countered David.

As the *baijiu* flowed freely, laughter and jollity echoed around the kitchen until the small hours of the following morning.

Fine crystals of snow skittered across the platform in gentle vortices, as the breeze began to freshen from the north. It was bitterly cold. Cold or not, standing on the platform, at Yanji station, waiting for the 19:56 train to Harbin made them all sweat. The longer they waited, the greater their paranoia. To them, it seemed as though everyone else on the platform was watching them. Tense and poised to run somewhere, – they didn't know where – they continually watched for any sign of alarm amongst the other Chinese passengers. By the time the train arrived the men were completely exhausted. After they all reached their seats, only Li Ming was able to speak.

"You guys will get us all shot. Relax for goodness' sake, this is the easy bit."

"Sorry Li Ming." Squeaked David. "It's a bit like waiting to get a tooth pulled, anticipating the pain is worse than the actual extraction."

"Yes, we'll be better now, but if I smile, I'm sure my face will crack." Remarked Kwang-Ho.

"For goodness' sake lighten up and chew some of this," commanded Li Ming, as she passed around a bag containing what looked like small pieces of cake, "it contains some of the ingredients in the tea you had the

182

other night in Nanyangcun. It will help you to relax. So, get chewing."

"Pass me some quick before I shit myself." Declared Luke. He could always see the funny side of things, whether it was deep in the mine in Chungbong or up to his waist in snow on their way north from the logging camp.

At 20:00 the train was still stationary and David began to worry again, wondering if the train had been held back by the PAP. Edging forward from his seat he craned his neck, looking first in one direction and then the other. Li Ming swatted him with her hat.

"Stop it. What's your problem? Sit down and relax."

"But we should have left already. Why aren't we moving?"

"That's why you berk. They're loading someone, in a wheelchair, into the next carriage. Ease off, and sit back in your seat." Li Ming commanded.

David did as he was told and forced himself back in his seat. Closing his eyes, he tried to think of something else. Instantly the voice of his daughter echoed in his ears, urging him to be calm. Startled by its realism, he quickly opened his eyes and the voice stopped. Confused that she was not sitting beside him, he felt cheated that he could not see her. Re-closing his eyes, he fully expected the voice to return, but it didn't; only the crashing of carriage doors entered his reverie. Then the sudden jolt of the carriage couplings taking up slack signalled that they were now, at last, on their way. It was going to be a long night; they would not arrive at Harbin until 06:22 the following morning.

"At least it's warm in here, better than being in the back of the stock truck." Stated Luke.

It was indeed warm, and combined with the monotonous clackety-clack of the train's wheels, all except Li Ming, fell asleep.

***

When the clatter of the wheels, crossing a series of points, signalled the trains approach to Harbin only then did Li Ming wake her sleeping companions.

"Are we there yet?" Enquired Luke, feeling foolish the instant he finished the final syllable.

"Yes, my boy," joked Li Ming, "we're there."

Chuckling at Luke's reddening face his companions were glad they hadn't asked the same question.

Long before the train came to a halt, other passengers gathered their belongings from the overhead racks and made for the door. Li Ming and her fellow travellers, however were not as keen to leave the warm confines of the carriage for the freezing morning, that awaited them outside.

"What happened during the night, did the guard come round to inspect our tickets?" Asked David.

"Yes, while you were asleep. I told him that you'd all worked a full day before getting on the train." Li Ming replied as she got up from her seat. "He saw nothing unusual in that, he just smiled and punched the tickets, then moved on down the carriage. No drama, we're still safe."

As the others got up from their seats, she said they should follow the crowd out of the station to avoid any unwarranted attention by the PAP who would be standing at the station exit.

Although getting out of the station wasn't a problem, finding their next contact was. Li Ming admitted she didn't know who was going to meet them and instructed them to move along the pavement towards the bus stop. As they waited several, taxi drivers asked if they needed transport. As neither of the brothers could speak Mandarin they loitered behind Li Ming and Kwang-Ho. Then, just as one of the policemen near the exit, started to take an interest in the small band of travellers, a tall man emerged from the group of taxi drivers and swept Li Ming off her feet.

"Li Ming my love, how are you." He said in a loud voice. "Did you and the others have a good trip? Sorry, I'm a little late but the traffic was awful."

Li Ming realised immediately what was happening and hugged the stranger, then kissed him on either cheek. As the small group of taxi drivers dispersed, the policeman – luckily – seemed to change his mind about checking the four strangers and turned back to a new stream of passengers, that had just got off the latest train arriving at the station.

Still hugging Li Ming –who barely reached the tall stranger's shoulder – he pounded the others on the back welcoming them all to Harbin.

"Come with me, I have the van parked just around the corner. Chilly isn't it," he continued, "I'll bet you're feeling the cold after the warmth of the train. Come on Wei Lie, don't dawdle. I have a flask of tea in the van, that'll warm you all up."

It took a second before Luke realised that the man was referring to him, using his forged identity. Of all the Mandarin words that Kwang-Ho and Li Ming had schooled him in, OK, was the one he felt most confident with, but when he raised his arm to acknowledge the tall man, all that emerged from his mouth was a grunt. It was enough though, and he quickly followed Li Ming.

The van was a Dongfeng panel truck. Inside, it had been lined with plywood and had two bench seats screwed to the floor on either side of the cargo space.

"OK, hop aboard and I'll tell you what happens next." Said the tall stranger.

Once they had all taken their seats their guide jumped into the driver's seat and started the old diesel motor. It took a couple of attempts but eventually, the old engine coughed and spluttered into life, discharging a large cloud of black smoke that nearly gassed them all.

"It's a little gem this truck," said the driver, waving his arm out of the window, "I've disguised it as a beaten-up wreck, but in reality, it's a Ferrari."

All of the Koreans looked at each other wondering if this guy was a comedian or a reliable guide. Inside the cargo space, the noise from the engine was deafening, so none but Li Ming heard the drivers attempt at humour. Without looking behind, the driver pulled away from the curb and almost collided with a passing car. Amidst the honking of horns and expressive arm movements, the van eventually, merged with the other vehicles leaving the station car park.

"I'll take you for some breakfast down at the market, you're probably starving, you won't have to wait much longer." He shouted over his shoulder.

Again, he waved his arm out of the window, as if it gave him license to alter course without looking. As he turned left and cut across the path of other vehicles, there was once again a chorus horns objecting to the antics of the mad van driver. Travelling west on Tiandi Street, they had just passed the Linyuan Hotel, when their driver started to make a series of right turns that brought them round in a large circle.

"Just in case you're worried," shouted Mao over his shoulder, "I'm driving in a circle to ensure we're not being followed. I saw James Bond do it in *Goldfinger*.

Soon they were travelling along Xidazhi St, past the Heilongjiang International Exhibition Centre, until once more he turned across the path of oncoming traffic and pulled into a small car park. and switched off the engine.

"Right, who's for nosh?" The driver inquired, still shouting, even though there was no need for he had already switched off the engine.

"Come on, jump to it." He commanded as he swung his door open. "I have a mate that's a street vendor just up there." He said pointing to a narrow street at the other end of the car park.

Having parked too close to another vehicle on his side, he found, much to his disgust, that he couldn't get out.

"I'll have to get out your side Luv." He declared to Li Ming.

As they all followed in the wake of the stranger he suddenly stopped and turned to face them.

"By the way, you can all call me Mao," he whispered, "it's not my real name you understand. I couldn't live with a name like that of our great revolutionary leader, he was a Marxist wanker and personally, I didn't like the guy." He said conspiratorially, looking over his shoulder to see if anyone was listening.

"I have to be careful who I say that to these days, people soon forget all bad things he did, the genocide etcetera, etcetera, some people even see him as some kind of bloody hero. Not me though, he was responsible for killing both my father and grandfather."

Without further explanation, Mao turned and continued his march up the alley. Luke put his hand on David's arm and looked him in the face.

"Is this guy for real? Are we going to trust our lives to him, he's nuts?"

189

"Li Ming," said David, "do you know this guy? Is he reliable?"

"Never met him before. She said nonchalantly as she followed Mao. Then, almost as a postscript, she added; But, if Zongxian trusts him, so will I."

10. Mad Mao

Unbeknownst to the travellers from Nanyangcun, their time in Harbin was to be longer than they had anticipated. The special train that would take them from Changchun to Beijing, and the agricultural conference, was not due to leave for another twenty-four hours. They would have to wait in a safe house in Harbin until it was time to make the four-hour, three-hundred-and-fifty-kilometre drive to the station at Changchun. From the rear of Mao's panel truck, the travellers saw very little of Harbin. However, what they missed was described by Mao, who gave them a continuous travelogue of the city as they made their erratic, sometimes terrifying, way through the great provincial city.

"Often called the oriental St Petersburg, Harbin is renowned for its Russian and European-influenced architecture," Mao said in his best tourist guide's voice. "Harbin is also famous for its local cuisine, influenced by our past connections with Russia. Tonight, you will savour *lie-ba*, Russian bread, and *qiu-lin hong-chang*, Harbin's European sausages."

He described the taste of the sausages so well that the ever-hungry refugees found their mouths watering as they thought of them.

"Harbin was once under Russian rule," he continued, "and being at the end of an extension to the Trans-Siberian Railway, the city is now a centre of international trade with Russia. The city is also infamous for Unit 731, where Japanese military doctors tortured and experimented on Chinese prisoners during World War II. Today the Unit 731 museum is a novel tourist attraction." Mao said bitterly.

Talking of Unit 731 focussed the refugee's attention on their own plight and that of the loved ones they left behind in Camp 22. Mao recognised the effect of what he had said and remained quiet for the rest of the journey.

The safe house turned out to be no more than a secure warehouse. Used to store old bicycles destined to be recycled, it was a two-storey building on the southwestern edge of Harbin close to the Songhua River. At the rear of the building was a small apartment, which had originally been accommodation for the warehouse caretaker. Though a little Spartan, it was a functional place to stay for a few hours until they continued their journey to Changchun.

As promised, Mao served them the famous Harbin bread and sausages, followed by copious quantities of tea. There was little conversation during the meal, and soon after they had all finished, they each found a comfortable place to sleep and nodded off before their long journey recommenced. Unlike the others Kwang-

Ho was far from sleepy; he watched Mao from his leather lounge chair as Mao lit a cigarette and went outside. Kwang-Ho was fascinated by the enigmatic guide and, after a few minutes, followed him out onto the back porch.

Mao was a tall, lithe man with an oval face pockmarked with acne scars. His small head, topped by a mop of unkempt, grey hair, seemed unnatural on such a tall frame. When he spoke, which he did incessantly, the glint of a gold-capped incisor forever caught your eye and ensnared one's gaze. Perpetually smiling, his jovial mood belied the serious nature of his work, for if he was caught, he would surely end his days imprisoned somewhere in one of the toughest prisons in the world. At first, Kwang-Ho thought that he was mentally incapacitated, one sandwich short of a picnic, he had said to David. But the longer he was with the man, the more he thought Mao's simplistic behaviour was just an act. There was an underlying intelligence in the way he described things, and his vocabulary was more like that of a crossword puzzle expert than someone intellectually handicapped. Mao reminded him of *The Scarlet Pimpernel* from the adventure novel set during the French Revolution by Baroness Emmuska Orczy. Kwang-Ho wondered how many other characters their enigmatic guide could impersonate.

As Kwang-Ho approached, Mao turned and stared at him for a few seconds before turning back and resuming his gaze upon the frozen river.

"You should grab some sleep while you can. I'll wake you when it's time to go."

"Thanks," replied Kwang-Ho, "but I'm not very tired, not after being shaken up in the back of your truck for the best part of an hour."

"Yes, sorry about that. I have to keep up appearances." Mao replied curiously.

"What do you mean by keeping up appearances?" Asked Kwang-Ho.

Mao didn't reply immediately, which made Kwang-Ho unsure if he had heard him correctly. But when he was considering repeating the question, Mao flicked the ash from his cigarette and turned his head to face him. It was as if Mao was searching his soul, looking for clues that he could trust the Korean.

"Appearances, yes, that's a fair question." He said in a voice much different to Mao, the travel guide. "Strangely, the crazier I appear, the less attention I get from bystanders in the street and the authorities. I don't know whether it's because they are tolerant of those with an intellectual handicap or fear that craziness is contagious. In any case, I don't care; it works, so I play my part."

"So, who is Mao, really?"

Once more, there was a pause before he replied.

"My real name is Tien Chang-Lin, though I used to be called David Tien. Although both my parents are Chinese, I am a New Zealander. Troubled by what they saw as being the future of China, they emigrated to New Zealand just after the second world war. There they set up a clothing manufacturing business in Auckland before owning a string of Chinese takeaways. They were already New Zealand citizens when I was born, so I automatically became a naturalised New Zealander."

"Oh," replied Kwang-Ho, "I would never have guessed that you weren't a native Chinese."

"Well, there you go; appearances can be deceiving, can't they? The whole point of my alter ego is to be seen but not seen."

"Well, you certainly fooled me."

Mao laughed. "Well, that's to be expected; you're only half-Chinese."

"Ah, someone's been telling tales; that was quick."

"When your life is on the line, it pays to know who you are taking risks for."

Kwang-Ho wondered if Mao's reply was a hint to keep quiet, but his fascination with the man had increased exponentially and only fuelled his curiosity even more.

"So, how did you end up here, in Harbin?"

"It's a long story. I'm pretty sure it would only bore you to death."

"No, I'm fascinated. Please go on."

"OK. When I grew up, my parents constantly told me stories about our family, originating from Harbin. We were a bilingual family, speaking English at work, in school, and in Mandarin at home. I was told of the horror of life under the Japanese, of my grandfather who survived Unit 731, and my grandmother digging up roots to feed the family. I listened to my mother describing how she nearly died after my sister was born because there were no antibiotics. My father described being imprisoned because one of his workmates, a political commissar, was jealous of his achievements. In those days, life was really tough just after the war." Mao flicked his cigarette away as if he were exorcising himself of those terrible stories.

"When my mum reported that the same commissar had raped her, he was locked up, and my father was set free. That was the end for them in China, so they, and my sister, escaped to Korea before ending up in New Zealand.

In New Zealand, I studied politics at Auckland University, principally Chinese political history. At university, I thought of myself as becoming a political crusader, fighting for justice, liberating the victims of tyranny and restoring democracy to the oppressed. I couldn't wait to save the world. I was incensed by China's subjugation of Tibet and the suppression of fundamental human rights there. I was appalled at the horrific rumours coming from North Korea of concentration camps and human experimentation; it was just as my parents had told me, a repetition of Unit 731. I had to do something." Mao paused, swallowing hard to quell his anger before he continued.

"As a naïve student, I really did believe I could make a difference. But I eventually realised that life isn't a textbook but much more complex than that. Life is about people, their needs and emotions. Life under tyranny becomes a compromise between what is right and what is possible. I learned that lesson the hard way. In Auckland, I belonged to a Christian church that sent missionaries to China to help those escaping from North Korea to a better life in the South. That's why I came back to China."

"Do you have family here now?"

Once again, Mao looked at Kwang-Ho to reassure himself that this stranger could be trusted.

"When I first came to China, I lived, just over the border from North Korea, near Yanji. I met my wife, Wu Chien-Shiung, there. We set up a corridor, for want of a better word, to channel Korean refugees along to others all across the country, like my wife and I, so that with sponsorship from our worldwide church, they could settle wherever they wanted. My 'cover' was being a farm machinery salesman; it allowed me to wander around the countryside adjacent to the border relatively freely. Not long afterwards, I learned that crusaders can't save everyone; though they may survive, their families may not."

As Mao's voice faltered with emotion, he paused momentarily before continuing.

"Some corrupt police in Yanji thought I was running a black-market scam, and while I was away, they arrested my wife. Although she was pregnant with our first child, they stuck knitting needles in her and put a blowtorch on her feet. They became worried when she went into labour and took her to a local hospital. We had contacts there, and one night she was smuggled out right in front of their corrupt, rapacious noses. Since then, we have lived well away from the border and helping refugees like you directly."

"How many children have you got now?"

"Two, a boy and a girl."

'Do you get to see them much?"

Mao smiled; there were some questions he thought were best unanswered.

"From time to time."

Kwang-Ho put his hand on Mao's shoulder.

"You're a good man Mao; I pray that God will look after you and your family."

"Thanks, Kwang-Ho; I appreciate that." He replied, smiling once again. It was as if he had just replaced his mask. Once again, he was the Mao everyone else saw.

***

Back inside the warehouse, Kwang-Ho recalled what Mao had told him. He thought about his own lost family. He wondered what he would be doing in the next year or so. No matter how hard he tried, he couldn't see himself living a normal life again. The nine-to-five, coming home to the wife and 2.4 kids. He reeled at the thought of becoming a couch potato, stuck for hours in front of the television, with the only exercise being washing the family car on the weekend. The more he thought about it, the more he believed he would hate such a life in the South.

Then he thought of Li Ming and the life that she led. How could she face danger every day and keep smiling? He felt a sharp pain in his chest when he remembered what she had told him about her parent's death and her brother's disappearance. Then came thoughts of his own family, he, Mao, and Li Ming had all shared the anguish of losing loved ones to violence. It was then he realised that he could not live the life of an architect again, being an employee, a business executive with a lovely house and a nice car. He almost retched at the thought of it. He had seen too much suffering to return to that clinical existence again.

He remembered Isaac's supreme sacrifice so he and his companions could live. He remembered the countless deaths he had witnessed at the mine and Camp 22, the nameless victims of brutality. Like the one-armed man, David had been told to throw down the old mine shaft; the live one that would join the countless others who had fallen before him. No, no, no, the word echoed in his mind repeatedly. His life must mean something else, something good must come from all that, and it didn't lie in South Korea. He was sure of that.

Wiping away the tears, he thought once again of Li Ming, the way her nose wiggled when she laughed, and her sparkling eyes that shone when she smiled. She was, he realised, very special to him, he couldn't let her go. Life for him lay along the path he was now treading in China, helping others like himself. He could pass as Chinese; he spoke the language, surely there was something he could do to help keep the underground railway running.

***

Harbin to Changchun took the ever-smiling, crazy Mao just over four hours. They made it with time to spare for a meal on the shores of Nanhu, and to watch the ice skaters. It was a cold evening, but none of them felt the chill. It was another exciting leg of their exodus from captivity. Kwang-Ho, though was deep in thought.

What's the matter Kwang-Ho?" Asked David.

Kwang-Ho hadn't heard his friend's question and remained isolated in his revere.

"Kwang-Ho," repeated David, shaking his friend's shoulder, "whatever is the matter?"

"Oh, nothing," lied Kwang-Ho. "just a few thoughts about those we've left behind. I'll be OK. I'll be better when we get on the train; I'll tell you then."

Just as if Kwang-Ho had flicked a switch, his mood changed dramatically; he was his old self once more. Helped by a little *baijiu*, those last few hours beside the lake were full of laughter and merriment. It was the closure of another phase of their journey and the start of a new one.

Just after 10 pm, they arrived at the station, and as they shuffled along the platform towards the Z62, overnight sleeper to Beijing, there was a little sadness amongst them when they realised, they would not see the personable, but crazy Mao again. With waves and a few kisses from Li Ming, they said their goodbyes to Mao and boarded the train.

Their sleeping compartment had four makeshift beds; the two on the bottom were formed from the upholstered bench seats on either side of the window, whilst the other two folded down overhead, like those that hid Cary Grant, in the classic Hitchcock movie *North by Northwest*. David and his brother took the upper beds leaving Kwang-Ho and Li Ming the lower ones.

Unlike on the previous train journey from Yanji to Harbin, all were relaxed. Yet although they were now experienced travellers, used to moving amongst strangers and through ticket checks, there was still, occasionally, that slight nagging worry that their real identities might be discovered. Li Ming seemed unaffected by it all, though she could have been faking it.

"OK, mystery man, tell me what was bothering you at the lakeside?" demanded David.

Kwang-Ho was hoping that his friend might have forgotten the concern he had for him at the lake. Now he was no more prepared, to tell the truth than he had been then. David and the others deserved the truth, for his decision would affect them all. He took a large gulp of air, praying that what he was about to say would make sense.

"I don't know how to put this," he said as the trapped air rushed from his lungs. "But I've decided not to carry on to South Korea."

There was a stunned silence, as no one knew what to say in reply to such a bombshell. Li Ming was the first to speak.

"Wow, what's brought this on?" She asked, smiling at Kwang-Ho.

Kwang-Ho felt like a small boy telling his friends he wasn't coming out to play.

"Well," he stuttered, "having spoken to Zongxiàn and mad Mao, I believe I can be of greater use to other people, like us, escaping from the DPRK if I stay here in China."

Again, there was silence as what Kwang-Ho had said sank in.

"Err, what do you mean, you spoke to mad Mao?" Enquired Luke. He's as crazy as a rat in a tin shithouse. Sorry Li Ming, you know what I mean."

Li Ming acknowledged his apology with a smile. She had never heard such an expression before, and it certainly didn't offend her.

"Mao is no crazier than I am. It's just a…."

"You've got to be crazy if you want to stay here." Interrupted Luke.

"Mao's craziness is just a disguise. Underneath it all, he's a sensitive and clever man. We're only here because of people like him, Li Ming and all the others that have helped us. I speak both Korean and Mandarin; I almost look Chinese. I can help others cross the border because I've already been there and done that."

Kwang-Ho paused for a moment, looking across at Li Ming. Her face was bright, and her eyes shone once again as she smiled at him; it was then that he knew he'd made the right decision.

"That's good Kwang-Ho, my friend. I've only known you briefly, but my life and the others have been in your hands more than enough times for me to know that you're sincere. I believe you; you will be a great asset to the underground railway and…to Li Ming." Said David.

"What? What about Li Ming?" Said Luke quizzically.

"Grow up, little brother; can't you see what has been in front of you for the past week?"

"What have I missed? I don't understand you, and don't call me little brother either; I'm much bigger than you, since you've been on the cabbage soup diet."

Always the comedian, Luke had made them all laugh once more.

Then grabbing Kwang-Ho by the hand, Li Ming led him out of the compartment and into the passageway beyond.

"Oooooh," quipped Luke behind them, in his best schoolboy voice, "we know what you're doing."

"Shut up, you silly sod." Commanded his brother as Kwang-Ho closed the compartment door behind him.

As he turned to face Li Ming, she threw her arms around his neck and kissed him, gently at first and then more passionately. As he responded to the touch of her lips; it was electrifying. As she moved closer to him, and her lips parted slightly under his own, Kwang-Ho's head began to spin; it was like being kissed by an angel, he thought. In that precious moment, as they embraced, the world about them disappeared. All the pain and suffering they had both experienced in their lives slowly drained away. It was just the two of them.

"Excuse me said the guard; you need a license to do that on my train." He joked. "Have you got your tickets?"

"Umm, yes, I have." Said Li Ming laughing. We also have two companions in this compartment; I have their tickets too."

"Well, I'll also have to see them, my dear. I hope they're not "*in flagrante delicto*." He replied, quoting the euphemism for being caught in the act.

"No, no, they're two brothers; they're good boys. Here are the tickets."

"Thank you." He said, and as he checked and punched the tickets, Li Ming knocked on the compartment door and quickly opened it before either David or his brother could reply.

"Just the guard checking the tickets; come on, boys, show your ugly faces to the guard and then get back to sleep." She commanded.

Both brothers looked above their pillows and peered at the inquisitive guard as he quickly looked about the compartment.

"Good evening to both of you." He said casually. "If you sleep now, we'll be pulling into Beijing just as you wake up tomorrow morning."

"Thanks, goodnight." Said David, in textbook Mandarin.

The guard doffed his cap at Li Ming and moved on down the corridor to the next compartment. Giggling together like naughty children after being caught kissing for the first time, both Kwang-Ho and Li Ming jumped back into the sleeping compartment and simultaneously collapsed on their beds.

Now they all laughed with joy.

"I suppose we should celebrate the happy couple, don't you think, Luke?" Said David as he removed a whole bottle of *baijiu* from his bag. "Now I know why Mao gave me this bottle; he knew about you two, didn't he? Even before either of you did, didn't he?"

"I suppose that's why he's crazy. He can see the future before the rest of us mortals." Another chorus of laughter followed as they passed around the bottle of undiluted spirit.

"Whoa, that's good stuff." Wheezed Luke. It would burn holes in your stomach if that were any stronger."

***

Paul made his first faltering steps just one week after his toes were amputated. Helped by acupuncture, Paul felt little pain, but it did very little to stop the phantom itching on toes he no longer had. The doctor's wife was lovely and sympathetic in those early days following his operation. However, once he was on his feet, she became her old self again, stern-faced and humourless. She had devised a brutal rehabilitation regime that lasted two hours every day, two hours that Paul hated with a passion. Looking back, though, they were nothing compared to what he, and the others, had to endure at the mine. In hindsight, he wondered how they had lasted as long as they did, being overworked and so close to starvation.

Nanyangcun was a small village nestled in a deep valley between rolling hills covered in pine forests. On the sunny afternoons, Paul would sit on the back porch thinking about the past, the present and trying to anticipate his future. He wondered what he would do in South Korea. Would he have a place in his son's food products factory? Would Peter and his wife, Young-Ya, tolerate him and his idiosyncratic rituals? Perhaps they would insist he move away from them; after all, they hadn't seen him for twenty years. It was so easy to become pessimistic and melancholic about the unknown. Dr Teng had told him he might become depressed in those early days after his operation, he was right, as usual, but Paul was sick of needles, and his morbidity was the necessary penance for those he had abandoned back in Camp 22.

As the sun sank low on the horizon, it bathed the village in golden orange, reflected by the snow and gave a spiritual tranquillity to the end of each day. Coupled with the billowing smoke from every home that slowly dissipated in the frosty air, the aroma of burning cedar logs was a feast to the senses. After the privations of Chungbong, life in Nanyangcun was a veritable paradise. More than anything, the slower pace of life surprised Paul the most. No more guards screaming to double up, to run here and there; the people of the village just glided by without a worry in the world. He knew this would not be the case in Wŏnju, where his son's factory was established. Perhaps he could stay here, he wondered.

"Paul," called Wu Kuan-Yin, "I've just heard from Li Ming."

"Excellent; how are they?"

"They made it to Beijing just after 7.00 am yesterday and went immediately to the agricultural show at the National Agricultural Exhibition Centre. They stayed there for the rest of the day, learning all about feeding pigs whey powder protein and the fungal diseases of rice; Brown Spot, Sheath Blight, Bakanae and alike. Li Ming says they've gained expertise in a multitude of agricultural sciences she can't even pronounce. She had to drag Luke away by the ear; he was fascinated by everything he saw."

"Well, that's a turn-up for the books. I never thought he'd become a farmer. I suppose we've all had our perspective on life changed by Chungbong. What are they doing now?"

"They caught the overnight train to Zhengzhou and got there at ten past seven this morning. Then they caught another train at eleven to Xian and arrived at quarter to seven just a few minutes ago. They have rooms booked at the Silkroad Hotel. It's large enough to be anonymous and cheap enough to stay a few nights."

"Sounds good; what will they be doing tomorrow?"

"They're going to become tourists. She said they would start with a visit to the Terracotta Army, then the Wild Goose Pagodas and finish with the Huaqing Hot Springs."

"I wish I was there with them."

"You'll soon be with them once you can walk unaided. We won't insist you do the Beijing marathon, but you'll have to walk some fair distances under your own steam."

Deep in thought, Paul didn't reply. Choked with emotion, he imagined being there with the boys.

"They'll catch the train to Chengdu the day after tomorrow."

"Gosh, all this train travel must be costing you dearly."

"We have some very generous benefactors who support what we do; without them, we'd be hamstrung. It isn't just the travelling expenses that cost us; we have to grease a few palms here and there to ensure a blind eye, or two is shown along the way."

Paul was again silent for a moment while he considered what Kuan-Yin had told him.

"I can see my future now." He said hesitantly, dreamily staring off into the distance as the last of the sunlight disappeared below the horizon.

11. South to the Border

From Chengdu, David and the others caught the late train to Kunming. It was yet another sleeper and a journey that took them nearly twenty hours. They were exhausted when they got off the train just after eleven in the morning. Tired of train travel, they all agreed that it would be too soon if they ever saw a train again. Outside the station, they caught a taxi to the Kunming Hotel on East Dong Feng Road; it was expensive but anonymous. At the grand entrance, the concierge looked at them as if they had just crawled out from under a rock.

"What's his problem?" Said Luke, jerking his finger over his shoulder towards the glorified porter.

"Have you seen yourself in the mirror lately, little brother? You're hardly respectable custom."

Once the dishevelled travellers got to their room on the seventh floor, they showered, dressed smartly and went to lunch in the hotel restaurant. Although they were all exhausted, they were also famished. It was also the meeting place for their final travel guide on the Chinese side of the Laotian border. Halfway through their meal, the waiter approached Li Ming with a bottle of Choujiu rice wine.

"From the gentleman on table three, madam. He says he remembers you from the agricultural conference."

"Tell him thanks, and if he wishes, he may join us." Replied Li Ming.

"Yes, madam, certainly."

In his early forties, the man was short and stocky, with black hair that was greying at the temples. Although ruggedly handsome, he had the appearance of a boxer, as his nose had obviously been broken at some time and poorly straightened. As he approached their table, he proffered his hand to Li Ming, which she accepted and shook warmly.

"Yang Wenyuan, isn't it?" Asked Li Ming confidently.

"You have a good memory, Ching Shih. Have I remembered your name correctly?"

Li Ming smiled at the alias he had used for her; Ching Shih was a famous Chinese woman, a pirate from the early 1800s. Li Ming thought of herself as more of a patriot rather than a pirate.

"Please sit with us." She invited.

"No, I won't impose if you don't mind, but please accept my card. I run a travel company on the city's south side; if you and your friends wish, I could show you around our fair city."

"Thank you, that would be nice; we'll certainly give you a call later."

"Excellent; I offer very competitive rates." His smile was broad and disarming; Li Ming almost laughed at his aplomb. "Good day to all; I look forward to meeting you less formally."

As the man turned to leave, he almost knocked over a waitress serving the table behind. The man was nearly as funny as Mad Mao.

"Oh, sorry, my dear." He said, patting her bottom as he passed.

"Another bloody comedian." Retorted Luke. "I hope he drives better than the last one." This time no one laughed, and Luke caught a frosty look from David.

"What, what have I said wrong now? Mao couldn't drive a nail."

"Eat your lunch Luke and leave the jokes to me." Said David.

That was funny and brought a muted laugh from them all, for David was always too serious to be funny.

***

"Hi, got all you need? This will be a very long journey." Said their new travel companion.

"Yes, I'm sure. It took us long enough to pack this morning so I certainly hope we have." Said Li Ming as she heaved her heavy holdall into the back of the Nissan Safari.

"Excellent. Gentlemen, please get your stuff in the back. If you can all sit in the rear seats, I'll look after the fair maiden, in the front, with me."

They all did as they were told, though from Luke's face, it was plain that he didn't like being ordered around. It was bad enough getting up and out of the hotel at this unearthly hour, besides being patronised by this slimy toad, he thought to himself. He had quickly forgotten Chungbong, where getting up before dawn and constantly being shouted at was the norm.

As the four-wheel-drive Safari pulled away from the hotel, the thought that this was the last leg of their trans-China journey brought a collective sigh of relief.

"OK, some introductions are perhaps in order first. My name is Jason Tan; I'm an American ex-pat living here in Kunming. I run a legitimate travel business from an office I share with a few other small businesses, just off Xingyuan Road, close to the lake. I have four employees, and four of these marvellous 4 x 4's, and we take visitors to this area, to all the top spots, whether it be a day trip around Lake Dianchi or a two-day jaunt to Jinghong and Mengla just like this one."

Tan looked closely at Li Ming, prompting her to continue the introductions.

"OK," she said, "I'm Sun Li Ming, and in the back, we have David and his brother Luke and behind you is Sohn Kwang-Ho; they are…."

North Koreans, from Chungbong," Interrupted Tan, "yes, I know that much; where are you from, my love?"

"Me?" Hesitated Li Ming, perturbed by Tan's interruption. "I come from Wulan, a small village near Jilin." She lied. There was something about this smooth-talking American that she didn't like very much. She couldn't pinpoint what it was but felt uncomfortable revealing too many details about herself. She certainly didn't want her bottom patted by this sexist ape, that was for sure.

"Can't say that I know that part of the country, though that's hardly surprising when China's such a big place, I suppose." He laughed. "OK, today's scenic tour of Yunnan will take about fourteen hours once we've cleared Kunming. All things being equal, we should get to Jinghong about 8 pm tonight. We're booked into the Crown Hotel there."

Tan turned once more to Li Ming as if seeking approval. Once she smiled back, Tan continued with the itinerary.

"So, we'll have time to shower and eat before hitting the sack. Tomorrow, I'll get you all up at, say, 6 am, and then after breakfast, we'll drive to Mengla, which should take about four hours. We'll stay in Mengla for about 2 hours, have lunch, and then drive to the border at Mohang. I have all the docs you'll need, so don't worry; it'll be a piece of cake. I've done it a thousand times. Then once across the border, we stay overnight at the Boat Landing Guesthouse in Luang Namtha before flying you to Vientiane the next day. From there, it's up to you."

"That sounds good," remarked Kwang-Ho, "bring it on, is what I say."

"That's the spirit. However, I must warn you that the road to Jinghong is pretty bad."

Tan had understated the road quality; it was abysmal. There were countless potholes, and as the road wound through the mountains, you could never be sure that the traffic coming the opposite way would be on their own side of the road. Six hours into their journey, as David and the others in the back of the Safari lurched from one side of the vehicle to the other, Luke looked at his watch and then prodded David in the ribs.

"I take it all back," he mumbled in his brother's ear, "Mao is a much better driver. I was wrong to cast aspersions on our crazy friend; this guy's a shocker."

Another corner saw both of them collide heads before David could reply.

"Yes," he replied, rubbing his head, "he is much worse."

"And we have another eight hours of this." Grumbled Luke.

With half the journey behind them, they pulled off the road to take a break. As Jason Tan put a kettle on a crude, but functional butane gas ring, Kwang-Ho and Li Ming walked across the road and sat on a rock overlooking the valley below.

"Why did you lie about coming from Nanyangcun?"

"I don't know; as I opened my mouth, Wulan came out. It was silly of me; I wish I hadn't now."

"Don't you trust the guy?"

"Well, I suppose I do; it isn't that. He's a bit of a smooth operator, and patting the waitress' bottom in the restaurant last night put me off him completely."

"It was harmless; perhaps he's disguising the real Jason Tan like Mao was? Besides, if he is a genuine travel operator, he has to be smarmy to keep on the right side of his rich customers."

"Patting some woman's bum is never harmless." She said sternly. "I don't know; perhaps I'm being oversensitive; perhaps it's charm, not smarm."

Kwang-Ho squeezed her hand and smiled. "I would never pat any strange woman's derriere," then, after pausing for a moment, he continued, "Well, only if they asked me to."

Li Ming punched him on the arm and smiled. One thing she did know was that Kwang-Ho was light-years away from being like Jason Tan. As they laughed and joked, David brought them some tea and a couple of rice cakes.

"It's beautiful here, isn't it?" He said, looking down the valley to the stream beyond. "I'd love to live somewhere like this, tranquil, away from the incessant hum-drum of life. They say New Zealand's like this."

"I've been to New Zealand." called a voice behind them.

As they all turned, they saw Jason Tan walking up beside them. Sipping his tea, he contemplated the view in front of him.

"It's every bit as good as this, I can tell you. The west coast of the South Island is spectacular. Fiordland, Milford and Dusky Sounds must be experienced before you can call somewhere is the most beautiful place on earth."

"When were you over there then?" Asked David.

"That's where I first started in the travel business. Looking after rich Americans. Made a packet for a while."

"What made you leave then?"

"Two reasons: First, I got sick of my clients and their demeaning attitude to the place. *Oh, how quaint it all is, Chuck.*" He said in a broad Texas drawl. "Second, everybody else had the same idea, so when my profits dropped, I came here. That's when I realised that money isn't everything."

"Making money is far from what you're doing now." Remarked Li Ming.

"Yes, you're right, it is. However, I still have the business and make pots of money. But now I have a conscience and a wife as well." He confessed. "Now I have responsibility; I see the world differently, not merely as a cash cow, but as a place where my children live and an environment where others deserve the same freedoms. A trifle egalitarian perhaps, but you understand what I mean?"

"Yes, thankfully, we do. Glad to have people like you sharing our world because without the sacrifice you and others like Li Ming here, we would be back in Chungbong." Declared David.

"Look, if you've had enough of the view, we ought to be pressing on."

As they re-crossed the road, Luke was coming to meet them.

"Back in the truck, little brother." Said David.

"I felt left out; did you have a good chat with Tan?"

"Yes, I think we misjudged him; he's OK. He told us he lived in New Zealand for a while and said it was just as beautiful as this. Once I get the chance, I'm going there to check it out. If it's as good as they say, I might up-sticks and live there."

"Whoa, hang on there a minute. Live in New Zealand, what about me? What about Dad and Peter? You can't abandon us?" Luke growled.

"If I do decide to live there, New Zealand's not on the dark side of the moon. Besides, it isn't as if we'll live in each other's pockets in South Korea anyway. You'll carve out a life for yourself, find a wife, and run a business. We all need to find our niche in life. After what we've all been through, I don't think I can see myself with a normal job, living in a normal house anymore. Remember, Kwang-Ho's not going any further. He's decided to stay with Li Ming and help others like us."

"He's crazy. I want a normal life, in a normal house, with a normal job and a normal wife and kids. How can you not want normal?"

"Because I had all those once and then lost it all. I don't think I can be normal anymore. I need to be free, free to do what the hell I want to, little brother." He said, slapping Luke on the back. "Get in the truck and stop moaning."

"Hey, I told you about calling me little." He replied, smiling at David. "I suppose I can see where you're coming from, or should I say going to?"

"Get in the truck, you silly sod, before Jason drives off without us."

***

The Crown Hotel was OK, just like all the others they had stayed in. The food was excellent and the beer even better, but all the friends wanted to do was get over the border and start their new lives. Jason Tan

222

had told them that he would leave them in Luang Namtha and that their next guide would leave them contact details with the proprietor of the Boat Landing Guesthouse. With everything in place, they retired to bed early. It would be a big day tomorrow, their first semi-legitimate border crossing on their road to freedom.

Luke had been washed and dressed for over an hour and, much to the annoyance of his brother, had been pacing the room like a caged lion. When Jason Tan knocked, Luke flung open the door just after six before Tan had time to step back.

"You're late." Said Luke rushing past him and pounding down the stairs to breakfast.

"Don't mind him, Jason; he's just nervous." Said David when he saw the startled look on Jason's face.

"Well, I'd never have guessed." He said sarcastically. "Li Ming and Kwang-Ho have already gone down."

"Good, I'm starving; let's go."

At breakfast, Jason Tan passed over his few travel documents to the Koreans and told them what would happen at the border.

"OK, you haven't got passports because we can't produce fake ones that would be good enough to pass inspection. The Chinese border guards know all about

223

North Korean refugees and will turn you in for the reward without a second glance. There are mountain passes we could tramp over if you had the right gear, but that is very dangerous, and if you're caught by the army, PAP or drug smugglers, you would be shot on site by all of them. This is the only safe way to get you over the border." He said, pulling open the front of his anorak.

Inside his jacket, they could all see wads of American dollars. "Cash," he said conspiratorially, "cash speaks louder than anything else around here, and knowing when our 'friends' are on duty, at the border, on both sides, that is how we can guarantee your safe passage.

"Shit," exclaimed Luke, "are you saying that my neck depends upon the greed of a couple of border guards?"

"Greed is a powerful vice, my friend, and believe me when I say that this is the least complicated and most successful way of getting you out of China and into Laos."

"How much does getting a single person over the border cost?"

"About a thousand dollars, US. You're not cheap."

There was a chill silence as they all took in what had been said.

"Jason, I didn't know anything about the money and all. I naively thought we'd be crossing the border illicitly sometime during the night." Declared Kwang-Ho. "This has come as a bit of a shock. Look, there is no other way to say this, but I've decided to stay on this side of the border with Li Ming."

"Well, I assumed that Li Ming would go with you into Laos because she has legitimate documents and can easily pass through the border. I'm sorry, but we'll still have to pay up whether you go or not. I have had to prearrange this well ahead of time. We can't just turn up and surprise them. Many other pairs of eyes are looking on besides the greedy ones. I have to say, who's crossing the border under these arrangements. They know there will be three paying customers, so they expect three wads of cash." He explained. "You may choose to pass through with your friends or stay here, but whatever you decide will still cost us money."

"That's OK, Jason, we'll all go through, and then once Kwang-Ho sorts out genuine travel documents, he can come back legitimately. He has a Chinese mother; perhaps we can arrange a Chinese passport."

"I think that's unlikely as he'll have to declare where he was born, to whom, and ultimately why he's been entertained by the DPRK in Chungbong."

"Perhaps we could create a new identity for him?" Pleaded Li Ming.

Jason patted his anorak and the money beneath. "If you have a lot of cash, anything is possible. Have you got that sort of money?"

With tears forming in her eyes, Li Ming shook her head. "No, I haven't."

"Look, I'm sorry, this is really embarrassing. Kwang-Ho has to face up with the rest, and I have to hand over the money. He must pay more if he still wants to stay in China."

As Li Ming started to cry, Kwang-Ho put his arm around her.

"Kwang-Ho, my brother, Peter, is rich. I'm sure that he'll give us what we need. I'm also confident that we can generate the proper documentation to get Kwang-Ho back across the border, legitimately or not." Replied David.

"Do you think so, David?" Pleaded Li Ming.

"There, you see, there's nothing to worry about. It will all be sorted in a little while. We have to be patient." Said Kwang-Ho, endeavouring to pacify her.

"Right; if we've all finished breakfast, we should be off." Said Jason Tan.

Li Ming wiped her eyes and stood with the rest of them. Then flinging her arms about Kwang-Ho, she held him fiercely.

"You will come back, won't you?"

"Of course, I will; wild horses wouldn't be able to hold me back. It will just take a wee while, that's all. Can you wait for me? That's the other question?"

"Well, I can't wait too long, I'm getting older, and my suitors are already queuing outside the house."

Kwang-Ho laughed and kissed her gently.

"Come on, or we'll miss the bus."

***

The journey to Mengla took nearly four hours. Four long hours of the same bone-crunching, lurching as the previous day's journey to Jinghong. When they finally arrived, they all got out of the truck, weary and desperate for a long cold drink.

Market day in Mengla is a feast for the eyes, with every kind of produce for sale, from Ginseng to Geese and products from clothing to CDs. The smell under the covered market constantly changed from spices to drying offal. Behind the market was arguably the world's worst public toilet, which added something a little more organic to the smell of the market. Walking the maze of streets led the friends up the 200 steps to the inner mountain top, where the houses were a mixture of ancient and modern, where toothless women smiled graciously at strangers, and small children followed anyone new.

Lunch was at a kerbside café that Jason Tan recommended. It was a joyous place that conquered the market smells with freshly roasted coffee and roasted duck marinated with honey and soy. During their meal of Har Gow dumplings – smooth, almost translucent pockets of dough filled with shrimp and bamboo shoots – a young boy pestered them incessantly till he had earned his keep by polishing their shoes. Mengla certainly was a special place.

Back in the truck, it was just a short drive to Mohang and the Chinese-Laotian border. They were directed to park the vehicle behind six or so other vehicles being processed two hundred metres before the actual border. Then they were asked to take their documents into a single-storey building across the main road.

"Relax, guys, this is completely normal." Said Jason Tan reassuringly. "This process takes about twenty minutes. First, the documents are checked, and then the vehicle. They're mainly looking for heroin and weapons. Bring your bags with you. They'll want to check those too."

Humourless armed guards stood beside the vehicles and lined both sides of the road nearer to the barriers. Jason gave his passport inside the customs building to one of the customs officers, who then asked them to wait.

The monotonous hum of a ceiling fan whirling above them began to fray their nerves as each minute passed. A fellow traveller standing next to Li Ming grinned at her, his breath rank with a toxic mixture of stale cigarettes and alcohol. She returned the smile and then quickly looked away. A small girl standing behind her caught her eye as she continually picked her nose before wiping her finger on her tattered dress. Li Ming offered the girl a mint to divert her attention from her nose.

"This way, please." Said another guard, equally as stone-faced as those outside.

They were led into a large office and told to sit on chairs that lined the left-hand wall. It was a stark, featureless room with dull, whitewashed walls. Sitting behind a desk at the far end of the room was an officer of the Peoples Armed Police. When he eventually looked up from the papers in front of him, they could see that the right side of his face was scarred; the outside corner of his right eye was pulled down, giving him a lopsided appearance. His dark menacing eyes did nothing to reassure them that this interview was normal.

"You three." He commanded, waving his pencil at the three Koreans. "Stand up and face me."

Another PAP officer, a sergeant, moved towards them. As the sergeant took his swagger stick from under his arm, they had no illusion that he would hit them with it if they did not obey instantly.

"You are North Koreans. You have escaped from the DPRK recently." They were statements of known facts and required no answer.

"You must therefore be dangerous criminals who should be locked up immediately."

Kwang-Ho moved to speak but was hit in the mouth by the sergeant's swagger stick. Li Ming winced at the force of the blow and looked towards Jason Tan for reassurance that this was normal, but Jason quickly looked away, avoiding any eye contact with her.

"You will be returned to the DPRK once you've been interrogated. You entered this country illegally and have no rights here in China. Put your hands behind you, now." He commanded menacingly.

Once they had obeyed, the sergeant quickly bound their wrists with self-locking, plastic cable ties. The bindings were tight and uncomfortable.

"You." He shouted, pointing his pencil at Li Ming. "Stand up."

As Li Ming obeyed the officer, he once more consulted the paper before him.

"You are Sun Li Ming, from Wulan, it says here, but that is a lie, isn't it?"

Suddenly the penny dropped; they had been betrayed, by no less than their guide, Jason Tan. As she turned to Tan, who was still seated against the wall, he continued to look away from her. Suddenly the sergeant's stick hit her across the mouth. The pain was excruciating, and the metallic taste of blood flowed freely into her mouth.

"Look at me when I speak to you, not at that snivelling wretch who traded your lives for money."

12. Ching-wu

"You are not from Wulan; tell me the truth; where are you really from?" Shouted the officer again.

"Umm, no, I am from Wulan." Said Li Ming, spitting blood on the floor.

As the sergeant's stick flashed through the air once more, Kwang-Ho purposely stepped in front of it, catching its full force across the bridge of his nose. He instantly fell to the floor, bleeding and unconscious.

"How touching that he should sacrifice his face for yours, and they say chivalry is dead." Hissed the officer. "Perhaps I should allow the sergeant to beat your friend until you answer my question correctly."

He flicked his hand nonchalantly towards his sergeant, who promptly started kicking Kwang-Ho in the ribs.

"Stop, stop, please stop." She pleaded. "I'll tell you, I'm from Jiangzhuang."

"Oh my, how soft we are. Barely a scratch on this worthless piece of Korean trash, and you cough up the answer straight away. That's not much fun, is it, sergeant? Kick him again; I like to see the look of panic in her eyes."

"Please don't hurt him; hit me instead."

"Sergeant, the Korean first, and then the woman."

The sergeant kicked Kwang-Ho twice before turning his attention to Li Ming. He hit her across the side of her head with the stick, splitting her ear. As she fell to her knees, crying in pain, he lashed out with his boot again.

"Do I have to witness this? I've given you them, I've given you the money, what else do you want?" complained Jason Tan.

"You must do as you're told, you filthy, treacherous bastard. If you wish to cross this border in future with your wealthy American clients, you should hold your bloody tongue and sit still.

"Wake the Korean up." Ordered the officer.

A bucket of cold water brought Kwang-Ho slowly to his senses. As he writhed on the floor, trying to get to his knees, the officer got to his feet and stepped around the desk.

"So, you and the woman are in love? It's a shame she isn't pregnant; we hate Korean half-castes. We could have cut it out of her to see what sex the brat was.

Suddenly the door burst open, and two armed guards rushed in. Just as the officer was about to abuse them, a third man entered the room. The officer immediately jumped to attention and saluted the newcomer.

"Colonel, sir, we weren't expecting you till later. I..."

"What is the meaning of this, you imbecile?" Said the colonel waving his brown leather gloves at the two prisoners sprawled across the floor.

"These men are North Korean convicts that have crossed into China near Yanji. This woman is Sun Li Ming from Jiangzhuang. She has been harbouring these fugitives and has been caught attempting to smuggle them across the border into Laos."

The colonel looked down at Li Ming, trying to see her face properly.

"Get her up." He ordered.

The sergeant quickly lifted Li Ming to her feet as the colonel stared at her face. Then just as he was about to say something, he thought better of it.

"And who is that, Lieutenant?" Said the colonel referring to Tan, still sitting at the side of the office.

"That sir is Jason Tan, the conscientious citizen who has brought this crime to my attention, sir."

"And the money on the table?"

That is the money the woman carried to bribe my loyal officers. I had just confiscated it, sir."

"You lying bastard." Croaked Kwang-Ho. "Tan gave you that money so that he could carry on his business across this border."

"Tan, is it?" the colonel asked the now whimpering Chinese-American. "Explain what you have to do with this."

"Umm, I run a travel business out of Kunming." He sputtered. "I bring tourists across the border to visit Yunnan and other parts of China. I was giving these people a lift when I discovered they were fugitives, so I thought it best to report this to Lieutenant Yeh."

"Is that true?" the colonel asked Kwang-Ho.

"No, it's all a pack of lies. Tan was to smuggle us across the border by bribing guards with four thousand American dollars…"

"You lying bastard, Tan, you told me it was two thousand…" Screamed Lieutenant Yeh at Jason Tan before he realised what he had just admitted.

"Shut up, Yeh, or I'll get your sergeant to beat you. Continue, please," he said to Kwang-Ho, "I'm intrigued by this tale."

"It was all a ruse; Tan had no intention of taking us across the border. He had a deal with this man to betray us and share the money. His business depends on getting through the border quickly, and he bribes Yeh to get what he wants."

"Get yourself and your friends back on those seats and be quiet." The colonel instructed Kwang-Ho.

Then the colonel turned to the two guards, who came in with him.

"You two, bind both the sergeant and the lieutenant, then take them to the guardhouse and lock them up. I'll deal with them later. You'd better take that blubbering specimen too." He said, referring to Jason Tan. As Tan passed him, the colonel held up his hand, and the guards halted the prisoner. Without hesitation, the colonel put his hand inside the man's jacket and retrieved two more thick bundles of cash.

When Tan looked across at Li Ming, hoping for sympathy, she looked upon him with utter disgust.

"I'm so sorry, Li Ming; he's held me to ransom for a long time. He's beaten me just the same as Kwang-Ho, many times," he snivelled, "how do you think I got my nose broken."

"Get them out of here." Ordered the colonel. "And when you come back, stay outside, and guard the door. I'll shout if I need you."

***

The colonel knelt in front of Li Ming, whose head was bowed, and gently lifted her chin so he could look into her eyes.

"Li Ming, Sun Li Ming? Were your mother and father shot in Nanyangcun in 1966?"

Li Ming heard the kindness in his voice, but she couldn't register what the colonel was saying. When he repeated the question, a burning sensation flooded her chest. The timbre of his voice was somehow familiar. A distant childhood memory was rekindled as she wiped the tears from her face and focussed on the colonel. She knew this man. As the memory of her parents being slaughtered came flooding back, she suddenly recognised him. It was Ching-wu, her brother. At first, she thought her mind was playing tricks, but when he smiled at her and saw the sparkle in his eyes and that ever so familiar impish grin he always had, she knew it was Ching-wu.

Flinging her arms about her brother's neck, she hugged him fiercely, frightened that he would disappear again if she let him go. With tears streaming down her face, she sobbed on his shoulder.

"I thought that you were dead. I thought I had lost you forever. Where have you been? Why haven't you searched for me?"

"It's a long story that I will gladly tell you later. First, let's get you and your friends tidied up a bit."

Ching-wu took a clasp knife from his pocket and cut David's bonds.

"Cut the others free and clean him up if you can." He said, referring to the bloodied Kwang-Ho. "I'll get a doctor to look him over. Guard." He shouted at the closed office door, which opened instantly.

"Yes, Colonel Sun?"

"Get the doctor in here quickly, please, and tell him to bring his bag with him."

Once the guard had disappeared, Ching-wu hugged his sister once more. "I won't let you go again, Li Ming. I'll never abandon you again."

When the doctor arrived, he quickly surveyed the scene and took a sharp breath. "Oh, my goodness!" He exclaimed, "What in the name of God has gone on here?"

"Two of these folk require several stitches, doctor. Can you see to them here?"

"Yes, at once."

Li Ming required four stitches to her ear, and Kwang-Ho needed three in the wound on his nose and four more in his cheek. His broken ribs made breathing difficult, but once the doctor was satisfied they were not compromising Kwang-Ho's lungs, he bound his chest with strong adhesive tape and gave him a mild analgesic to ease the pain. Realigning his nose, though, was a little more complicated. With a few carefully placed acupuncture needles, the realignment was sickening, though achieved painlessly.

"Doctor," asked the colonel just before he left, "I've had reports that such brutality, like this, is a regular occurrence. Is that true?"

"Yes, colonel."

"Then why haven't you reported it? Why did I have to hear of it via an anonymous telephone call?"

"I did report it, sir; the anonymous call was from me."

"Why didn't you report it properly through the correct procedure?"

"Because Lieutenant Yeh would have killed me, sir, just as he did the last doctor. Lives are cheap when there is big money involved."

"Oh, I see. Can you prove what you have said?"

"To a degree, yes. I've kept a diary of all the people I have treated who came into this office under their own steam but were carried out. I have the names and addresses of the injured. I have statements regarding the exchange of money and kept the property of the dead."

"Will some of these people give evidence in a court-martial?"

"I doubt that very much, sir. They are in fear of reprisals to themselves and their families."

"I see. What about Captain Liu, the commandant of this post? Did he know about what was going on here?"

"I understand that he was forced to take monies from Lieutenant Yeh. The captain, too, fears reprisals from Yeh and his goons. This is a can of worms you may have wished you hadn't opened, sir."

"I doubt it, doctor; it's my job to find the rotten apples and get rid of them before they contaminate the rest of the barrel. Thank you for your candour, doctor.

I hope you will not be too timid to give evidence at Yeh's trial."

"I am too old to be frightened of Yeh; now you have him in custody. Yes, I will give evidence and enjoy the experience to boot."

"Thank you, doctor, that will be all for the moment. Could you please ask the guard outside to get us some tea?"

"Certainly, sir."

***

When the tea arrived, Li Ming once more flew into the arms of her brother, Ching-wu.

"Since the day the Red Guards dragged you away, I thought you were dead. Tell me what happened afterwards; why didn't you come home?"

"After I was arrested, I was taken to the military camp in Harbin. I was foolish when interrogated; I cursed and swore at them, which only worsened things. The more they hit me, the greater my resolve to resist them. I was a university student leader; I believed they wouldn't break me. But eventually, of course, they did, and I was sent to prison for life. I spent about five years in Chifeng Prison. The

241

privations of the prison regime and the so-called re-education programme broke my will but not my spirit. When they thought I was sufficiently re-educated, I was conscripted into the army."

As Ching-wu saw the pain on his sister's face, a lump rose in his throat. He loved her dearly and had always wanted to spare her the anguish of reliving that fateful day in 1966.

"All through my captivity, they told me that my past life was over and that if I ever attempted to go back to Nanyangcun or contact anyone there, I would be executed immediately, together with any of my remaining relatives. So, you see, I couldn't come back, my past life was over, but they couldn't stop me thinking of you, Li Ming, and I never did."

"So, you made a career out of the army?" Said Li Ming, wiping her tears away.

"It was the only thing I could do if I wanted a normal life. Because I was university educated, I quickly moved through the lower ranks. Then in February 1979, I was one of the 120 000 Chinese troops who crossed the border into northern Vietnam. In the battle for Lang Son in March of that year, I commanded a detachment of troops guarding a communications centre when Vietnamese troops broke through our lines. Under my command, thirty-five officers and men repulsed a Vietnamese force of over two hundred. My part in the battle was recognised, and I was

242

awarded the Order of Loyalty and Valour; after that, I could do no wrong. Now I am a colonel in charge of an anticorruption unit based in the Yunnan region. Our headquarters are in the provincial capital, Kunming."

"Have you any family yourself now?" Enquired Li Ming.

"Yes, my wife Feifei and I have a four-year-old daughter, Li Ming. Did you ever marry?"

"No, not yet, but I'm always hopeful." She replied, looking towards Kwang-Ho.

For a brief moment, no one spoke. Everyone was stunned by the events of the past hour. It was then that Ching-wu made a decision.

"As I said earlier, I had suspicions that Lieutenant Yeh was corrupt, and the events here have proved that. With the doctor's testimony, he and his sergeant will be imprisoned for a long time to be re-educated." As the last syllable left his lips, he remembered his re-education. Smiling, he relished what would happen to Yeh as the corrupt lieutenant's perspective was readjusted.

"I will take him and the sergeant back to Kunming with me, where they will disappear into the system for a while. As for Jason Tan, I think a short while behind bars would be good for him. Once he has repented for his sins and becomes, shall we say, more compliant, I will get him to sign a deposition corroborating Yeh's corruption? After that, I will see that he is deported."

Spying a bottle of *baijiu* on a table in the far corner of the room, Ching-wu poured them all a glass and passed them around. As each one of the captives drank the fiery spirit, they didn't know if it was to celebrate or commiserate, as they had little idea what would happen to them next. Sensing the sombre mood, Ching-wu told them what he had in mind for them.

"I suggest you all take Tan's Safari and drive across the border to new lives in South Korea."

He took two of the bundles of cash from the desk and passed them to Li Ming.

"This should give you a start, at least."

Li Ming hesitated before accepting it. She felt as if she were taking Judas Iscariot's blood money. Passing it on to David, she looked at Kwang-Ho's battered face before turning again to her brother.

"I don't want to leave you now or live abroad, knowing that you are still here in China. I want to meet your daughter and hug her as my niece."

"That's OK; you have your passport and can return anytime. There will be no arrest warrant for Li Ming from Nanyangcun. As I overheard it, you were from Jiangzhuang."

Feeling a little coy, Li Ming lowered her eyes to the floor. "Kwang-Ho and I want to be together. How can he come back?"

Smiling at her admission, Ching-wu pulled her towards him and hugged his little sister fiercely.

"Kwang-Ho can apply for a new passport in South Korea, and once I have Yeh and his cronies in jail, Kwang-Ho can return to this country legitimately with you."

"Will I ever see you again?"

"Of course, you will. I'm a national hero, don't forget; I can do almost anything. There are no restrictions on me anymore."

Li Ming kissed him; at last, she recovered some happiness from the trauma of that day back in 1966 when her family was so brutally snatched away from her.

Ching-wu moved to inspect Kwang-Ho's wounds. Although the bleeding had stopped, the swelling hadn't. There was an ugly bruise on either side of his nose, and his left eye was beginning to close up. His lower lip was twice the size of the other and was cut in two places. He probably needed to be hospitalised, even if it was just to check him over for any further damage caused by Yeh's pet thug.

"You are certainly in a sorry state, my friend." He said, shaking Kwang-Ho by the hand. "You'll take care of my sister, won't you?"

"Yes." Replied Kwang-Ho wincing at the pain in his face when he tried to speak.

"I don't know what the Laotian customs police will make of you two attempting to cross into their country. You both look like shit."

At that moment, as they all began to laugh, the captives began to relax. Perhaps thought Luke everything was going to be alright.

"I think I'd better write a note to the Laotian border guards, informing them that you've had a road accident on the way to Mengla, that a doctor has already checked you out and that you are fit to travel. That should do the trick; what do you think?"

"Yes, that would be very useful; thanks, Ching-wu, we owe you a lot." Said Kwang-Ho.

As Ching-wu sat at the desk writing the note, he thought about Li Ming and her role in smuggling North Koreans out of China. He had heard about the so-called underground railway because it was one of the primary reasons why so many border guards were corrupt and why his unit existed. The irony that he, and his sister, were fighting the same battle but from

246

opposite sides hadn't escaped him. It was a dangerous business, and he didn't want his sister to be re-educated, as many others had before her. Although he had much more freedom than most Chinese citizens, he wondered how he could assist her group directly. It would be something that he would discuss with her if she ever came back to China.

Having gathered all the correct documentation, Ching-wu walked his sister and her companions out to their newly acquired vehicle. It was tough saying goodbye to someone you had yearned to meet for nearly twenty years. Holding Li Ming for the final time, he wondered if he would ever see her again. Helping Kwang-Ho into the vehicle's front seat, he searched this stranger's eyes, probing, hoping to see that his sister would be happy with this man.

"I will take care of her, Ching-wu; please believe me." Whispered Kwang-Ho. "We will be back soon. You will hold her again, I promise."

Ching-wu took a business card from his tunic and gave it to the man that held his sister's future.

"Give me a call when you return. Then we can arrange for Li Ming to meet her niece."

"Thanks, Ching-wu; it was good to meet you, a miracle, in fact.

As the Nissan Safari crossed underneath the raised barriers, Ching-wu could see Li Ming waving to him through the driver's side window. As they disappeared into the distance, he was left with an empty feeling in the pit of his stomach. After all these years, he finally found his sister, and now, it felt like he had lost her again. With an ache in his heart and a tear in his eye, he returned to the main office. Although Yeh had no idea who he had brutalised and never would, he would pay dearly for laying a finger on his sister.

***

Once over the border, it took them just a short time to reach Luang Namtha and the Boat Landing Guesthouse. The proprietor was a short fair-skinned lady in her mid-sixties. Warm and friendly, she was very concerned about the injuries to Kwang-Ho and Li Ming and asked them if they needed a doctor. What they needed was a bed, as they were all exhausted. As they turned to go to their rooms, Li Ming turned back to their host and asked if there were any messages for them.

"No, my dear, I'm afraid not. Were you expecting any?"

"Yes, we were. That's a little worrying."

"I have a telephone if you need to contact someone."

"That's OK for the moment; I'll have to consult my friends first. Thanks though."

In Li Ming's room, they all sat on the bed and discussed what they should do next.

"That rotten bastard didn't arrange for us to be met here. He was going to betray us to the authorities right from the very beginning." Said Luke angrily. "What the hell do we do now?"

"Well, I can telephone Wu Zongxian and tell him what's happened. If he doesn't know who our contact here should have been, he will know someone who does. I'll go and ring now."

Li Ming was away for the best part of half an hour before she returned, smiling.

"I think the old lady downstairs was going to have kittens because I was on the phone for so long. But when I gave her twenty US dollars, her face lit up as if it was Christmas."

"Forget about her. Tell us what Zongxian said." Asked Luke impatiently.

"Zongxian was so pleased to hear from me. Word had already got back to him that we'd been arrested. Everything's in hand now, though. Our contact is a guy called Tim Peters; he's another American. He was expecting us until Tan telephoned him yesterday, telling him we'd been arrested. He still has all our documents and will be here tomorrow."

"Can we trust this one?" Asked Luke sceptically. "After Mad Mao and Treacherous Tan, we need someone normal. I don't think I can face any more weird ones."

"Well, I can tell you that he was a Christian missionary that lived in South Korea in the 1970s. He was blacklisted by the government for handing out anti-government leaflets, criticising the regime of President Chun Doo-hwan and was deported. He's been trying to get back into the country ever since."

"That doesn't fill me with much confidence." Said Luke.

"Ease up, brother," said David, putting his hand on his brother's arm, "we're free now."

Part III

Camp 22

13. The Breakthrough

"It's a prion." Declared An Sang-Ki, as he burst through his father's laboratory door.

"What's a prion, Sang-Ki?" Replied his father, looking up from the microscope.

"The agent for behaviour control, in latent toxoplasmosis. The chemical transmitter that alters the behaviour of the secondary host."

"Are you sure? Prions are a pretty obscure group of infectious proteins.

"I'm almost positive." Replied Sang-Ki, so excited he was almost out of breath.

The idea that some diseases, particularly fatal infections of the brain – such as in Creutzfeldt-Jakob disease – were caused by an infectious agent composed solely of protein was first proposed by Tikvah Alper in the 1960s. Until then, it was thought all known pathogens reproduce using nucleic acids, such as DNA or RNA. Although their potency may be reduced, prions are generally resistant to denaturation by normal digestive enzymes, high temperatures, and radiation. In nearly all cases, prion-propagated diseases are incurable and fatal.

"This is excellent news; how did you identify such a compound, so little is known about them?"

"Well, from the beginning, I realised that the cysts found in the brains of infected animals must hold the key. The chemical agent responsible for the onset of the symptoms of toxoplasmosis must be the same regardless of the infected species. I thought that this substance, whatever it was, affected rats differently from other animals, including humans, because of differences in the neural structures, not the chemical itself. Chemical receptors on the neurons of rats and humans are known to be different.

"Yes, yes, I know all this." Said his father impatiently.

"Well, anyway, I concluded that if these compounds bind to the neurons of humans, they may well stimulate a different response. So, whatever I was looking for must be common to all species and must be acting locally, close to the cysts themselves. It took a while, but I have managed to separate a compound from homogenised cysts that are immunologically identical to compounds I found binding to neurons close to the cysts themselves. I've done all sorts of analysis on this material and have found that it is a pure protein with a complex misfolded structure that remains active even when subjected to digestive enzymes and heat. QED, it's a prion."

"Well, you'll have to do a bit more to convince me that your conclusion is correct, but you may be on to something. Do you know much about the protein structure itself?"

"Not at the moment; I don't even know the amino acid sequence because it is so resistant to digestion."

"Many proteins resistant to digestive enzymes can be digested by hydrolysis using acids and high temperature. Try 50% hydrochloric acid and heat it, under a vacuum, for 24 hours, then run it through the amino acid analyser. As for the structure itself, have you got enough of the material to do x-ray crystallography?"

"No, not yet; its potency must be immense because it constitutes a tiny fraction of the total cyst tissue."

"Okay, separate as much as you can and then give it to Min-Su; tell him to crystallise it and do an x-ray analysis of its structure. The sooner we characterise it, the quicker we can theorise how to synthesise it. Because we'll need to mass-produce the stuff if we are to use it as a weapon of social control."

"Yes, I'll see to it straight away." Replied Sang-Ki, thoughtfully. Min-Su was his father's technician, and giving him the prion to crystallise and x-ray its structure was tantamount to giving his discovery away. His father should give him the glory of deciphering its structure, not Min-Su.

Sang-Ki turned towards the door, determined to keep the prion under wraps until he had time to research its structure.

"Oh, by the way, your mum and I are going to take a holiday, a cruise somewhere. I need a rest, and it's been a long time since our last holiday."

"Good, you need a break. So, I'll be in charge of the lab while you're away?" Said Sang-Ki, already assuming that his temporary promotion was a certainty.

"No, I don't think so. You have too much work to do with this prion thing. No, I'll leave Min-Su in charge. He's more than capable; giving his ego a little boost will be good."

The lab door closed with a bang as Sang-Ki retreated to his own laboratory.

***

Sang-Ki looked through the one-way mirror at the young girl on the other side. She was beautiful. Her eyes were large and mysterious; she was taller than the other girls, and her breasts were more prominent. Sang-Ki had watched her before when she showered and toileted in the apartment that was part of the experimental block, where the lives of those infected with toxoplasmosis could be observed 24/7.

The young girl's number was F18473; she was eighteen and so stunningly good-looking that Sang-Ki had looked up her real name in the camp records. Her name was Ruth, the daughter of F18472, Rachel, a prisoner who had died during the final phase of the nerve agent project. She was also the daughter of M16284, David, a prisoner who had escaped from the mine at Chungbong with three others eight years ago. Sang-Ki stared at the girl again, wondering if her mother had been as beautiful as her. Probably not; she would have been weak and emaciated if she had been still alive and working in the pharmaceutical factory or the vegetable farm. Sang-Ki had separated Ruth out for special privileges, special food, medicines when she was sick and clothes to please his eye. Once, when one of the other girls in the experiment complained that her clothes were not as lovely as Ruth's, he saw that she had been euthanised next so that her brain cysts could be homogenised and studied for the mysterious infectious agent.

As he saw Ruth undress, he could feel his arousal. When she pulled on her pyjamas and combed her raven-black hair, he thought he could resist her no longer. She would be his tonight, willingly or not.

"Do you need me anymore this evening, sir?"

It was Min-Su, who he had asked to prepare the brains of two other girls, from whom Sang-Ki would extract the cysts that contained the precious prion proteins.

"No, that's all. Thanks for your help this afternoon." Said Sang-Ki distractedly. "Can you come by tomorrow and finish off the cyst extractions?"

"Not a problem; see you tomorrow then." Min-Su bowed to his superior and left.

Sang-Ki rubbed the bulge in his trousers; he could feel his powerful erection through his clothing. Smiling at her eroticism, the imagined touch of her hand on his naked body consumed him. He could smell her, even taste her. He wanted to expose himself to her, to see her reaction when he released his erection.

Feeling the key to the experimental apartment in his lab coat pocket, he could resist her no more.

***

Just as Min-Su pressed the button for the ground floor, the elevator doors began to close. They were almost shut when a hand reached through the gap to force them to retreat.

"Good evening, Min-Su." Said An Sang-Ho as he bundled himself into the lift. "Home so soon; I thought you usually stayed much later than this. It's only eight o'clock. Are you having a half day?"

Min-Su knew that his boss was only joking because he was usually pushing him through the door at night, telling him to go back to his wife and children.

"I was working with your son, sir. We have just euthanised two more of the toxoplasmosis patients, and we needed to extract as many cysts as we can, preferably within minutes of death, as once the brain is starved of oxygen, the cysts begin to shrivel up and become very difficult to see."

"Excellent. I'm glad I've got you on your own because I wanted to tell you some good news. My wife and I are going on holiday for three or four months. I haven't had a holiday since…well, for a long time anyway…."

"I've been working for you for ten years, sir, and I've never known you take anything but a couple of weekends off in all that time." Interrupted Min-Su, smiling at his boss.

"Yes, well, I am not getting any younger, and everything is okay here; I thought I'd better have at least one holiday before I die."

"Any idea where you'll be going?"

"Well, quite a few places, I hope. But one thing is certain: part of our time out will be on a cruise, visiting a few Pacific islands, watching a few hula girls waggle their hips, I hope."

Min-Su smiled, he had never met Sang-Ho's wife, but he knew hula girls would be on the banned list if she were anything like his own wife.

"Anyway, I have decided to put you in charge of the lab while I'm away. The director has agreed, and you'll be paid a little extra for your troubles. You've worked with me a long time now, and I thought it was time you got a little recognition for all your hard work."

As Min-Su realised the implications of what his boss had just said, the smile slowly faded from his face.

"I know what you're going to say," Sang-Ho said, holding up the palm of his hand to stop his assistant from objecting. "I've also told Sang-Ki, I can't say he's pleased, but he'll just have to live with it. You have far more experience than he does; you're a better scientist in many respects. The director will keep Sang-Ki on a short leash. Besides, you will be in my office most of the time, dealing with all the administrative tasks."

"But…"

"No buts, you'll be the boss for a few months. Besides, it will do the young puppy a bit of good to be a little more humble."

As the lift doors opened, Min-Su patted his pockets, trying to locate his keys.

"I'm sorry, sir, I'll have to return to the lab; I've left my keys in my lab coat pocket."

"You'd forget your head if it wasn't screwed on properly. Go on; I'll see you tomorrow."

***

"Keep still, you bitch." Screamed Sang-Ki, as he lashed out with his fist.

The fierce blow struck Ruth just below her left eye, splitting her parchment-thin pale skin and propelling her head into the rock-hard laboratory floor. As the blood flowed from the wound, Ruth slowly regained her senses. With her arms held above her head and the weight of her attacker across her body, she was powerless to fight him off.

Sang-Ki reached into his jacket pocket and extracted a switchblade. He opened it in front of the girl's eyes, angling it deftly to reflect the strong overhead lights into her face.

"Struggle any more, and I'll stick you like the squealing pig you are." Hissed Sang-Ki.

As Ruth wriggled her lower body from underneath her attacker, he stuck the point of his knife into her abdomen, only a centimetre, but painful enough to prove that his threat was serious. As he struggled to release his belt, she felt the knife momentarily snag the waistband of her pants before it cut through the material and exposed the lower half of her body. She could feel his stale, fetid breath across her cheek as the knife traced the outline of her pudenda. Though her body was trapped, her mind was racing, trying to escape from what she knew was inevitable.

"Playing possum now, are you, you filthy whore. Just lie still a bit longer, and you'll get the best fuck of your miserable life."

When Sang-Ki used his hand to force his penis into the now unresisting girl, his face lowered a few centimetres towards her own. It was all she needed. As he licked her face, her mouth opened invitingly.

"So, you are warming to my attention. You're privileged to have my dick inside you and fill that tight pussy of yours."

Ruth clamped her jaws tightly shut as his tongue entered deeply into her mouth. She had him. His prick withdrew instantly from her, and his scream, muffled

261

by his trapped tongue, was weak and agonised. As blood filled her mouth, Ruth used all her strength to guide the blade of his knife between them. She was now in total control.

Then, just as suddenly as his violent attack began, it ended. Like a rag doll falling from a child's grasp, Sang-Ki's limp body rolled onto the floor beside hers. Nauseated by the blood in her mouth, she turned her head and vomited. A man she did not recognise stood above her when she opened her eyes; however, she did recognise what he was holding, a cattle prod. In that instant, her consciousness disappeared in a blitz of white noise and pain.

***

When Sang-Ki awoke, his mother's face zoomed into his vision. He attempted to say something, but his tongue was so sore and swollen it almost filled his mouth. Her face was stern, her eyes bloodshot. In one swift vicious movement, she slapped his face and retreated two steps.

"You disgusting maggot, I wish she had cut it off completely."

With that exclamation, she was gone. Sang-Ki panicked and felt below the sheets for his penis. It was heavily bandaged, so he couldn't tell what was happening down there. That bitch will pay for this, he thought. She would die a thousand painful times before she met her maker. His anger boiled over, and the blood pressure alarm began to beep incessantly. A nurse came rushing in to see if her patient was having a heart attack.

"Sir, what is wrong? Are you feeling ill?

"Thuk oth." Was all Sang-Ki could utter.

It was late in the afternoon that Sang-Ki awoke, spluttering and coughing, once his father had unclamped his fingers from his son's nose. Unable to speak Sang-Ki looked mystified at his father, wondering, after his mother's reaction, if his father was trying to kill him.

"I understand you have been rude to some of the staff here." It was a statement, not a question.

"Well, my boy, if you want to get out of this hospital alive, you had better buck your ideas up and be as nice as possible. You are not in Camp 22 now but in a public hospital. And my reputation is already damaged by your fucked-up sense of fun. So, listen carefully, my boy...."

An Sang-Ho's fingers re-clamped Sang-Ki's nostrils.

"I don't want to hear about any rudeness, insensitive or uncooperative behaviour from you. You are to be a model patient. Am I getting through to you? And, if you come back to work, and that is a big if, you will not have any access, to any prisoners, of any gender, at any time."

An Sang-Ho released his son's nose.

"I think you have got off lightly, four stitches in your tongue and four at the base of your prick. You could have lost both or bled to death. Your mother is ashamed. She had to be told why you sustained such injuries. There is no hiding from that. Not from a two-legged lab rat, eh?"

An Sang-Ho chuckled at his own joke.

"I don't think you will be welcome at home for a while, so I will arrange some accommodation for you at the camp. Perhaps in the prisoner's quarters, as you have an affinity for them?"

He had another little chuckle to himself as he made to leave.

"You'll be here for about a week until the swelling of your tongue subsides and they remove the stitches. They will feed you through that nasogastric tube if you haven't already gathered that. A bit demeaning being fed through a tube at your age, eh?"

15. The Prion Structure

While An Sang-Ki was recovering, Song Min-Su extracted excellent samples of the prion from the brain cysts of the lab rats. Using Infrared and X-ray spectroscopy and computer analysis, he and a team of skilled spectroscopists from Pyongyang University of Science & Technology had managed to determine the structure of the prion. It was 210 amino acids long and replicates exponentially in the chosen growth media of homogenised brain tissue. For An Sang-Ho, this was a significant breakthrough in his research as he now had a way of multiplying and purifying the prion. All he needed now was to weaponize it and develop an antidote. Both of these steps, he realised, might take him and his team years. Would he still get the funding, he wondered?

The answer to one of these questions came when his son returned to the lab after a month of rehabilitation. Not that such a long time was required, but his father insisted that some of the 'dust' may have settled by then.

An Sang-Ki opened his father's lab door with some trepidation. An Sang-Ho was sitting at his desk. Father and son had only spoken a dozen or so times since his return to the lab, and on half of those occasions, it was a brief and only good morning."

"What do you want?" Said his father

"Actually, I have come up with the solution to one of your big problems."

"Go on; I am all ears."

"I have solved the antidote problem."

"How?"

"I left a plate of prions out on the bench over the weekend, and when I came in on Monday, all the prions had been destroyed."

"How?"

"By a fungus, to be more specific, a membrane-bound oxidoreductase. This enzyme breaks the disulphide bonds between the amino acid chains in the prion, which consequently curls up and falls apart."

"Can you grow the fungus and extract the enzyme easily?"

"Yes, to both questions. I have a fermenter established now for growing the fungus. The extraction process can be done with a commercially available kit, or we can adapt one of those ourselves, but it would take a little longer."

"Well, I have to say that your poor chemistry hygiene has paid off, big time; well done. That bit of luck has saved us years of conventional plodding about by trial and error. Trying to find a way to break a prion is notoriously difficult, particularly enzymatically. How long till you could develop the process for commercial quantities?"

"It is a simple process, as straightforward as making proteases for soy sauce.

"That's excellent; we could get the food industry to make it then rather than bother ourselves."

"Yes, they don't need to know why we need it; it's just an enzyme."

"Excellent, excellent, my boy. Pass your notes to Min-Su, and I will get him to organise a company to make the damn stuff for us. Are you sure it works *in-vitro*?

There it was again. 'Give your notes to Min-Su'. Bloody Min-Su this; bloody Min-Su that. Sang-Ki was sick of it.

"Have you done any *in vitro* trials with the enzyme?"

"I have injected infected rats and cats in a body mass corrected dose over a week and have an 80% clearance rate. However, the enzyme was only crudely purified for those trials. I would expect the clearance rate to be much better with a purified enzyme."

"No human trials, no, of course not." His father said, answering his own question. "Okay, buy a couple of commercial enzyme extraction kits for your fermenter production, and we will try it out on some human subjects then."

"By the way, why is the cylinder of carbon monoxide in the corner of the lab?" Enquired Sang-Ki.

"Oh, you don't need to worry about that. Off you go now and get those enzyme extraction kits by express delivery."

***

Sang-Ki swiped his security card over the electronic keypad expecting it to go green. However, it beeped annoyingly and changed to red. He tried again. Same thing, beep and red. Just then, a technician emerged from the human experimental accommodation, and Sang-Ki held the door open for her. As she passed by, he went through. He was determined to get his revenge on the bitch that had cut him. She was going to pay dearly for what she had done to him. As he approached the inner door, he was confronted by two armed guards on each side of the corridor. As he approached, they moved to block his way.

"Out of the way, you imbeciles. Do you know who I am?"

The taller of the two guards, a sergeant, spoke first. "I am sorry, sir; the Director has told us not to let you through."

"Bullshit; let me pass."

"No sir, we cannot let you through. That is final."

The shorter of the two guards used his radio. "Control from 34, we have An Sang-Ki here trying to access the human experimental accommodation."

"The reply was immediate. 34 from Control. I will contact the Director immediately. He will contact An Sang-Ki himself."

Within seconds of Control answering the soldier. Sang-Ki's cell phone rang. Seconds into the call Sang-Ki's ear was burning with the rebuke his father was metering out to his son about his flagrant disobedience of trying to access the human experimental population against his express orders.

"If you don't return to your lab immediately, I will enrol you in the prison population at the Chungbong Mine this afternoon. Is that clear enough for you? So, get moving."

Bastard. Was the word that came to mind as Sang-Ki made his way back to his lab. He recalled pulling the legs off a spider in his youth and watching it trying to crawl away. He would not forgive his father for this, and just like the spider, he would relish watching Daddy as he struggled when he faced oblivion.

***

Back at his desk Sang-Ki tried to access his father's computer remotely. He tried three times with the most common password he could think of but was denied access. Any more than three times would alert security, he thought. He could try again in 24 hours. But he was too impatient. What if Song Min-Su had access? On the second attempt, Sang-Ki hacked Min-Su's computer using his wife's name. Simpleton, he thought.

As he had suspected Min-Su had access to his father's research diary and had the authority to add material to the journal, though not to edit anything. Rather than dwell on Min-Su's computer and risk possible detection, he downloaded all the relevant files to read at leisure.

One aspect of his father's research that interested Sang-Ki involved using carbon monoxide. A topic which his father had brushed aside when he had asked him about it. His research notes revealed that he and

Min-Su had been trying to develop carbon monoxide-releasing molecules, termed CORMs. Previous research had involved CORMs containing metals such as ruthenium and manganese, which could be toxic, so his father had developed a polypeptide carrier rich in cysteine, a sulphur-containing amino acid. His father had always considered using the toxoplasmosis toxin as a weapon and having an antidote for personnel entering the field of conflict after the weapon was released. So why the need for CORMs? Sang-Ho was always worried about funding, so why was he spending money on research for something Sang-Ki couldn't figure out?

Sang-Ki also found that his father had developed a blood test for the prion from the work of Dr Claudio Soto, which involved amplifying the prion first and then using western blot electrophoresis.

So many jigsaw pieces; so, what was the big picture? Sang-Ki referenced CORMs on Wikipedia and found that they had been used, despite the dangers of their toxicity, as an anti-rejection drug following the transplantation of organs. It transpires that naturally gaseous carbon monoxide within the body acts as a cellular signalling molecule and provides potent cytoprotective effects in organ transplantation. So, CORMs mirror that effect.

As Sang-Ki pondered over the puzzle pieces, a picture began to emerge. They had the weapon. They had the antidote. They had the blood test to detect who had and who had not got the toxin. Now they had the polypeptide CORM which would provide cytoprotective effects to the brains of those who had the toxin and were given the antidote. Perfect. That is if it all worked.

16. The Accident

Human testing began that summer; three males and three females were in the test group, and a similar number were in the control group. Before the test started, blood tests showed all were toxin free. MRI studies showed their brain structures were normal. During the first week, both groups were subjected to compliance tests. The tests were physical and mental, carried out in the morning and afternoon for an entire week. On analysis, the test scores for each group were statistically the same.

At the beginning of the second week, the test group were given the toxin. After a week, the blood tests revealed all the test groups were toxin positive. During the third week, the test and control groups were subjected to the same series of compliance tests. When the scores were analysed, the test group were 63% more compliant than the control group. Although they were a little 'spaced' out, perhaps, they otherwise looked quite normal. In the physical tests, however, they were only 37% as strong and agile as the control group.

During the fourth week, the test group were hospitalised and given the intravenous antidote infused with the polypeptide CORM based on their body mass. At the end of the week, the blood tests revealed that all the test groups were prion free.

273

During the fifth week, the test and control groups underwent the same compliance tests for the third time. Having analysed the scores, the two groups had no statistical difference for either the mental or physical examinations. MRI studies showed no difference between the brain patterns of the test group before or after the experiment.

***

An Sang-Ho turned to his son and Song Min-Su and smiled.

"I think we have succeeded beyond all measure. I am honoured to be the director of such an esteemed group of scientists. We have conquered a mammoth number of problems in this project in record time and with limited funds. I am convinced our party members will be very thankful. Please join me in a toast to our glorious leader."

"Kim Jong-un". They saluted in unison with their raised glasses of Pomjandi sparkling wine.

The inevitable question came after the handshakes and backslapping, more wine, smiles, and finger food.

"What next, sir?" Asked Min-Su.

"Well, we have a long way to go with this project before we hand it over to the production technicians. We have to weaponize it and design how to produce the components on an industrial scale, etcetera, etcetera. However, such a drop in physical ability, strength and agility in the test group was disappointing. Our workers at Camp 22 need to be compliant, but they must also be strong and agile to function properly in their tasks. To get the maximum output per kilo of food input, we need them to be better than 37% stronger and more agile than we found the test group to be."

"That might mean manipulating the structure of the prion, a difficult task with unpredictable outcomes, Father." Said Sang-Ki.

"We don't do random, my boy. We research what others have done; we stand on the shoulders of giants. I am sure we can find some shortcuts. That's how we found CORMs. You didn't exactly research the antidote yourself, did you? A bit of slapdash chemistry and the bloody thing fell into your lap. More luck than judgement there."

Sang-Ki felt admonished in front of Song Min-Su, and his cheeks started to colour. Bastard he thought. That word came to mind again. He saw the image of the helpless spider on his father's forehead. Bastard came to mind again.

When Sang-Ki returned to his accommodation in the officers' quarters of Camp 22 that evening, he had his meal in the canteen as usual but retired to his room very early. He was seething with anger. The hatred of his father was oozing from his pores. He sat in the dark, in his only armchair, brooding and scheming about how to get his revenge on his bastard father and that kowtowing scumbag Min-Su. He also had a score to settle with that bitch who cut him. She would pay too.

With his face contorted and his teeth grinding Sang-Ki was edging towards bursting a blood vessel. Any logical thought was impossible until a flash of genius appeared in his eyes – the writhing spider.

***

His security card opened his father's laboratory, no problem at all. There in the corner of the room, was what he wanted. He tightened the regulator diaphragm and opened the release valve so the gas could escape slowly and silently. Then turning round to the detector on the wall behind, he switched it off. The laboratory did not have air conditioning, so the gas would not escape.

On his way out of the building, he visited the deserted security office and deleted the record of his card entry to the building and the laboratory. The scene was now set for the tragedy.

***

An Sang-Ho and Song Min-Su got to work in the laboratory early the following morning. Arriving simultaneously, neither scientist noticed anything wrong with the atmosphere, composed of an odourless and tasteless killer. So saturated in carbon monoxide was the air that the symptoms progressed so quickly that neither man could react before passing into unconsciousness.

Looking through the window in the laboratory door Sang-Ki could watch the spider writhing at his desk before falling to the floor. Bastard. Suck that. As he turned away, there was an explosion as the carbon monoxide-oxygen mixture in the laboratory exploded. Sang-Ki was blown off his feet.

Wow, that was an unexpected bonus, he thought as he struggled to his feet. The fire alarm was whooping away annoyingly, and Sang-Ki could tell the laboratory sprinklers had been set off. He looked through the broken window into the laboratory and saw just a small fire by the refrigerators. Taking a carbon dioxide extinguisher from beside the door, he closed off the sprinkler valve to preserve all the data and specimens and entered the lab.

It took just two minutes to dowse the fire, and by then, help had arrived. Four paramedics attended to his father and Min-Su, while another was swabbing a cut over Sang-Ki's right eye. He couldn't have planned this any better. Both his father and Min-Su were pronounced dead. Both had blast damage to their hair and faces which camouflaged the cherry-red skin colour that signaled carbon monoxide poisoning.

Some senior staff came in as An Sang-Ho, and Song Min-Su were taken to the hospital morgue. Facing the General, Sang-Ki, with his head bandaged, tried his best to salute and briefly explained what had happened; that he was just about to enter the laboratory to see his father when the explosion occurred. He extinguished the fire and tried to render assistance, but his father and lab assistant were already dead.

"Sorry to hear that, my boy. In my eyes, you're a bit of a hero, getting in here so quickly after you were wounded yourself. The death of your father is a tremendous loss to our science division. You must step up until we get a replacement, my boy." Said the general, patting him on the shoulder.

The bastard. Thought Sang-Ki. 'My boy', he had just gotten rid of some twat that couldn't stop calling him that. Some replacement, some replacement, you patronising bastard, we'll see about that. With his mind clouded with hatred, he didn't hear what the general said next, but after the second pat on the shoulder, he and his colonel sidekick left, and he was ushered out by the forensic team of technicians and photographers.

***

Hail the conquering hero is what he felt like when he returned to the officers' quarters – lots of sorry for your loss, and lots of back-slapping too. The cook had prepared a special meal, nothing extravagant, but still delicious. People he had never spoken to wanted to talk to him. Suddenly he was the go-to guy. It didn't sit with him very well. What did they want from him?

He hadn't spoken to his mother, so he called her once he was alone in his room. She did not answer. He called his aunt, her sister.

"She doesn't want to speak to you."

"Why?"

"She says you are a maggot."

"What about the funeral?"

"What about it?"

"What about the arrangements?"

"You needn't worry about that; it will all be arranged. He will be returned to Hyesan to the family plot near the Paektu Mountains. He will lie in state for three days before being buried. You can come for the burial if you wish. I will text you the details."

"If you are sure that is not too much trouble."

The line went dead after the last syllable left his lips. Bastard.

Alone in his armchair and in the dark again, he began to think of what he would do with his future. He was not destined to be promoted to director of science at Camp 22, and he could not predict who that would be or how the next incumbent would treat him. His episode with the female prisoner was no doubt on his record and privy to the general and his lackeys, so there would be no favours given there, 'my boy'.

He fell asleep with no regrets about what he had done and with hatred still in his heart.

17. The Triads

When Sang-Ki awoke, he knew from the dream he had what he was going to do. And it was going to make him rich.

After two days of compulsory bereavement leave, he returned to his office at 8 am to find a corporal clicking his heels and coming to attention beside his locked office door.

"I have a message from the general, sir", said the corporal, handing over the envelope, "the general advises there is no need to reply, sir."

At this juncture, the corporal saluted and marched off down the corridor.

Sang-Ki waived his security card in front of the electronic keypad, which beeped and flashed green before he pushed the door open. Well, so far, so good, he thought, no arrest yet.

Leaving his briefcase on his desk, he sat on his Eames executive work chair and swung round towards the window. After lifting his feet onto the windowsill, he looked at the envelope's exterior, wondering if the contents would bite him. Only one way to find out, he thought. He clumsily ripped open the seal with his forefinger. It was one page, typed and signed by the general's lackey Colonel Kang Ja-Hoon. Looking good so far, he thought.

"An Sang-Ki, my deepest condolences on the loss of your father and work colleague Song Min-Su."

Bloody platitudes, straight in with my surname, no rank, no dear Sang-Ki. And who gives a shit about Min-Su either. His dissection of the letter, sentence by sentence continued.

"The forensic examination of the bodies revealed they died of carbon monoxide poisoning and were deceased before the explosion and fire."

Mmm, the next bit can't be bad, can it?

"Analysis of the carbon monoxide alarm in the laboratory was inconclusive as it was damaged in the fire."

Wow, that was lucky.

"The explosion was seemingly caused by the refrigerator thermostat arching when the temperature in the laboratory rose that morning, with the arrival of your father and Song Min-Su."

Gosh, it gets better and better.

"It appears the regulator diaphragm on the cylinder of carbon monoxide had not been released and that the small final release valve had negligently been left slightly open for the gas to escape into the room overnight."

Negligence, what a good word for pinning on a lab assistant.

"Only your father's fingerprints were found on the cylinder and the two valves, so one can only assume that An Sang-Ho was the last to use the cylinder."

Bugger, there was a perfect scapegoat lined up there.

"Please, can you give the forensic team a brief outline of what the carbon monoxide was used for?"

Easy to say that when working with the CORM polypeptides, they used gloves, that would let my father off the hook and line up Min-Su again for the negligent use of the gas. This is so good, thought Sang-Ki.

"I understand your father's interment will be in Hyesan in ten days once the forensic team has released the body to the undertakers. You will be allowed 21 days of leave starting tomorrow at noon and be off camp by 1400 hrs. You will be expected back at 0600 hrs on the 24 of this month."

I am sure three weeks is enough to set up my money mine. My gambling friends in Harbin will be falling over themselves to help; I can be assured of that, thought Sang-Ki.

"Until your father's replacement can be found, you have been promoted to Adjutant Director. Your pay will increase accordingly. *Kang Ja-Hoon pp* Shin Young-IL General Camp 22"

Adjutant, what bollocks is that? Bastard. No one appreciates me in this dump. After I make a few million U.S., I'll be gone.

Sang-Ki rang the forensic team and asked the Major in charge if they had his father's computer and that of Song Min-Su. They had, and they had hacked both. His father had his password on a Post-it note on the laptop cover. Min-Su had used his wife's name; he knew that. When he asked if they had finished with them, they said they had and that he didn't need to explain the use of the carbon monoxide as they had gained that information from his father's files.

"However, when preparing new batches of the CORM polypeptides, they wore gloves, so either my father or Min-Su could have touched the cylinder valves declared Sang-Ki."

"My apologies Adjutant Director but your father wrote in his notes, several times, that because of the danger of poisoning associated with the use of carbon monoxide, he forbade anyone else from touching the cylinder. He was solely responsible. It was just an accident. The regulator diaphragm valve was barely on, and the smaller release valve was always opened last to release the pressure off the regulator diaphragm. It was just a small error last thing in the evening that allowed the gas to build up during the night. We have no idea why the alarm sensor did not work. Just another sad error that led to the tragedy. As was the fridge as the room warmed with the arrival of the two researchers."

"Can you return the laptops to me as soon as possible? I have to go on leave tomorrow and would like to put them in the safe. Thank you, Major."

"I will send my sergeant with them now, Adjutant Director."

So, that's the end of stitching up Min-Su with negligence, bugger.

***

The funeral was awful, his maternal relations had ostracised him, and very few would speak to him. He was not invited to the three days lying in state, not that he cared to go anyway. His paternal relations were a little better. His two uncles and his grandfather were good people once they had a few glasses of soju inside them. After long stories of his father's childhood playing with his brothers, on the railway, being chased by police, beatings by communist soldiers and chasing girls in the dark with paper lanterns, it was off to bed; then headaches, more stories, more soju and more headaches.

After his father was interred, Sang-Ki crossed the border into China and went to Harbin and the casino, where he made money but lost a fortune. As usual, Wang Lei was behind the bar.

"Hi, Sang-Ki, come to lose some more money?"

"No, I have come to make my friends some money. That is if you can allow some of your friends to become some of my friends too."

"Fuck you, Sang-Ki. This is too cryptic for me; it is only 6 pm. Have a drink and let your tongue loosen up a bit. Then please tell me what you really want.

Wang Lei placed a long cool glass of Harbin Beer on the counter. "Here, this will relax that tongue of yours."

Sang-Ki skulled back half of the beer before coming up for breath. "Gosh, that is good, better than the crap we have."

"Now, which friends do you want to see?"

***

The two men who sat opposite him were nameless and only drank single-malt whiskey. He had been delivered to this hotel room by Wang Lei, who scuttled off before Sang-Ki was ushered into the room. He was told to sit down by a third man, about 2 metres tall and over 150 kilos in weight, who hid in the shadows by the door. The two men opposite him were sitting in front of the windows, so he could not see their faces. This was all too cloak and dagger for Sang-Ki, who assumed this would be a simple business.

"I am Adjutant Director Sang-Ki of Camp 22 in Nor…"

"We know who you are, and what you do. We know you have just come from your father's funeral in Hyesan. We know that he died from carbon monoxide poisoning from a cylinder carelessly left turned on. So, what do you want from us? What business can you put our way?

"I know you trade in human organs. I know that shipping chilled organs is time-critical. I know that shipping organs leaves a paper trail that you find difficult to deal with. I have the answer to that."

"We are listening."

I have a supply of experimental humans. I have the facilities to tissue type them to modern hospital standards. We have developed a drug that makes these people conscious but entirely compliant for transferring them across international borders. We have also developed an antidote for this drug and a supplement that, when administered, completely clears the donor's body of the initial toxin and helps suppress the body's immune response to reject their donated organ. In other words, we deliver the donor to the transplant patient. The transfer time of the organ would be minutes and not many hours the conventional way. The patient recovers in less time in their own country. And, the donor fly's away, all paperwork legitimate, no trail for any smart arse to follow."

"That all sounds very good, but we will need to discuss it with our colleagues and get back to you."

As he left the room, the giant by the door handed him a new burner phone.

"The PIN is KANG190," he mumbled as Sang-Ki slid past him.

***

When Sang-Ki returned to Camp 22, the burner phone vibrated in his pocket as he approached his office on the second day. The message contained just one word in Mandarin, yes. Later that day, it vibrated once more with an email address only accessible through the dark web. The short message accompanying the email address was just three words, input donor data.

It took eight months to set up, but thirteen donors were moved to various countries during the following three months, with a turnaround time of three weeks each. With no replacement for his father on the horizon, Sang-Ki answered to no one. He was the law in the experimental medical unit. Even as the adjutant director, when he said jump, beware those who didn't jump quick enough. The system was simple, once the donor was prepped with the toxin, one of Sang-Ki's most trusted technicians Kwon In-Ho, would take the donor across the border. At the Hanshi Hotel in the Yanbian Korean Autonomous Prefecture, the donor and the technician would be met by the triad representatives and escorted to Harbin City. With travel documents provided, the donor and technician would be transported to Shanghai and flown to the city nearest the recipient's hospital. Entry to the foreign country was covered by forged visas declaring that specialist healthcare was required by the donor, which could only be provided by specialists at the hospital cited in the visa. The compliant donor, in a wheelchair, with an intravenous drip, was more than willing to answer all the questions asked by the immigration officer, having been pre-programmed before the entire journey. In thirteen trips, there had never been a hitch.

The money involved was huge, all in U.S. dollars; it cost $180 000 per kidney; $170 000 for a part liver; $500 000 for a heart and lung transplant (a high price because of problems with the disposal of the cadaver) and $50 000 for a bone marrow stem cell transplant. Specific procedures could be undertaken in China, such as harvesting a cornea for $27 000 or unfertilised ova for $16 000 each. The most popular destination for transplant surgery was the middle east.

Sang-Ki now had an off-shore bank account with his share of the blood money. With his father's replacement due next month, he would deliver the next donor himself and not return to Camp 22 as adjutant medical director.

***

There was no guard on the door now. No one stopped him from accessing the female experimental human facilities, no technicians, no matrons, nurses, no one. When he opened cell 37, she was at his mercy.

"We meet again, you vile bitch."

Ruth was backed up against the cell wall under the high, steel-barred window. There was no escape; she had no weapons; she could not protect herself.

"You hurt me more than you can imagine, my dear. But I learn from my mistakes. Every time I bathe, I have the scar to remind me of the mistake I made with you. I have changed, you see. I am not going to rape you or beat you. I will not lower myself to such bestial levels again. What I have planned for you will hurt you much more, for you will die so that others may live. Doesn't that sound grand?"

Not understanding what Sang-Ki was saying, Ruth squirmed into the corner of the cell, fearing what he would do next. Curling into a foetal position, she tried to make her body as small as possible, her knees covering her face, her hands and forearms covering her head.

"What, cat got your tongue? Nothing to say? Nothing rebellious to say?"

"Well, I have plenty to say. You and I are going to make a little trip overseas. And you, my dear, will donate a few organs; because I have a match for your kidneys, I have someone who wants your liver, and another two people want your corneas. Because you have been undergoing hormone therapy, we will harvest your unfertilised eggs. How about that? You are going to help so many people. If I had more time, I might have been able to find a recipient for your heart and lungs somewhere too. But alas, we have to go before the month is out."

Thankfully Ruth had switched off from Sang-Ki's diatribe and had begun humming to herself silently, keeping his vitriolic words from entering her consciousness. Thankfully she knew very little of his plans for her future. That was her weapon of choice.

"I will see you in a few days; after we have prepped you for your long journey. Sleep well if you can, my lovely."

As the door of the cell slammed shut, Ruth, at last, relaxed. She was surprised that he hadn't retaliated for their previous encounter. She had lost many nights of sleep thinking of what might happen to her for attacking the science director's son. But he had done nothing. He had said he would not lower himself to such bestial levels again. He had just stood there spouting some gibberish before leaving; that was good, wasn't it?

For the first night in a long time, Ruth slept without waking till the nurse gave her the usual injection at eight the following morning.

Part IV

New Zealand

18. Auckland

It was a grey, dismal day when David parked his Mercedes in the short-stay car park at Auckland International Airport. The rain had awoken him that morning, but neither the rain nor the dark sky could dampen his excitement that morning. Now David could hardly contain his joy as he waited for his friends to reach the arrivals hall of Auckland Airport. The board above his head informed him that Air New Zealand flight NZ 288 from Shanghai to Auckland had arrived more than twenty minutes ago. Why such a long delay, he wondered.

His wife Sarah felt her husband's frustration and put her arm around his waist.

"They'll be here in a minute or two; calm down, love. Look at the board. Two flights from L.A. have arrived at the same time; they'll take a while to clear customs."

"Yes, of course, you're right." Replied David as he smiled and stroked Sarah's hair. As he looked down, his six-month-old daughter stared back at him in a sling across his wife's chest, her deep brown eyes shining with contentment. He would never have believed that he was a prisoner in North Korea just eight years ago, mourning the death of his first wife,

Rachel. Things had changed so much in such a short time it made his head spin to think about it.

After he arrived in Seoul, he was lovingly welcomed into his elder brother Peter's family. David had lived with them for his first year of freedom before moving into a small apartment close to his brother's food company. David had been appointed manager of the baby foods division of the company. He soon made his mark by the huge improvements he had overseen and the increased profits his division had made in the second year of his tenure as manager. During his third year of freedom, he directed the expansion of Peter's business into Australasia, establishing a small baby foods production plant in Auckland, New Zealand. Just two years after its launch, Auckland Organic Baby Foods had doubled in size and tripled its first year's meagre profit. David had hit a niche market, promising Peter a substantial return on his investment.

During his first year in Auckland, David joined a church on the North Shore and met Sarah Tsu, a third-generation Chinese New Zealander. Sarah was in the church choir, and every week he saw her on the small stage in front of the congregation, he sang heartily, hoping that she would notice him in the second row. When they eventually met at a friend's twenty-first birthday party in Takapuna, it was the start of a love affair that would ultimately lead to marriage, and the birth of their first baby, Rebecca.

When David turned once more to look for his friends, he saw someone he hadn't seen since leaving Nanyangcun, his father, Paul. David felt his wife's hand on his shoulder, urging him forward.

"Go on, David, go hug your Dad."

After taking his first step forward, David turned back to Sarah, who was smiling as if she had just won the lotto.

"You knew, didn't you? You knew he was coming."

"Well, a little bird did happen to mention it. Greet your father before he changes his mind and gets back on the plane."

As David approached, Paul left his luggage trolley and rushed forwards into his son's open arms. As the two men embraced each other, they were joined by Sarah and Rebecca.

"Dad, this is my wife Sarah and my lovely daughter Rebecca."

"Good to put a face to the voice on the end of the telephone line." Responded Paul, gently embracing his daughter-in-law for the first time while trying not to crush his newest grandchild.

"Sarah, how long have you been planning this?"

"Oh, about a month." She replied nonchalantly, smiling at him and someone else behind him.

"Don't we get a hug then?" Said Li Ming.

When David turned to embrace Li Ming, tears of joy ran freely down his cheeks.

"Don't forget me either, said Kwang-Ho pushing a baby buggy.

"Certainly, my friend." croaked David, hugging Li Ming and Kwang-Ho. It was one of those rare moments when the souls of lifelong friends touch and merge as one.

Though they had been separated by time and distance, the love between them was something few are lucky enough to experience. It was a love forged deep in the mines of Chungbong and the frozen wastes of North Korea. It was a love that had grown exponentially from when they had first met Li Ming and as they had shared their journey south to the Chinese-Laotian border. Though they had written to each other and telephoned, it was a love that transcended words.

David didn't know where to turn, to hug his father again or Li Ming and Kwang-Ho. Kneeling in front of the baby buggy David looked at the young two-year-old, fast asleep, unaware of the emotional meeting of his parents and two of their closest friends.

"So, this is Joshua?" Said David, his godfather, *in absentia*. "He's so big already; what are you feeding him on certainly not cabbage soup?"

"I would think he's genetically allergic to the stuff, after all the gruel we had to endure at Chungbong. No, we feed him beef steak sandwiches."

"He looks good on them; he's almost as big as me."

"Everyone's bigger than you, David." Said Kwang-Ho jokingly. "Hey, it's six-thirty in the morning. When are you going to take us home and feed us? I'm starving."

"Hark at him, he's just had a meal on the plane, and now he wants more," said Li Ming patting her husband's belly, "he's always starving."

"Chungbong has a lot to answer for."

David took over the luggage trolley and moved off towards the exit. "In forty minutes, Kwang-Ho, you can eat all you want; I have all the baby food you can eat."

Li Ming and Kwang Ho planned to tour New Zealand with David and his wife for six months. Jason Tan had said New Zealand was beautiful; David had corroborated that. Now the Chinese underground railway guides wanted to see the country for themselves.

***

Alex MacLean, part Scottish on his father's side and part New Zealander on his mother's side, had been born and raised on a farm west of Hamilton. With three brothers and two sisters, he had the freedom to choose whether to be a farmer or not. He chose not. After studying for his Batchelor of Chemistry at the University of Waikato, he enrolled in the one-year Graduate Diploma in Teaching and became a high school chemistry teacher at a girls' school on Auckland's North Shore. The introduction of NCEA put him off school life, the teaching of chemistry was the same, but its assessment, its administration and paperwork were endless tasks that took all the joy away from the chalkface.

From teaching, Alex got a job with New Zealand Customs Intelligence Section. Alex played a crucial role in discovering an elaborate drug ring during his time with Customs. At the heart of this criminal drug ring was the manufacture of Crystal Ice (methamphetamine) on a south Auckland farm near Runciman. This was a major international drug bust that involved an Auckland-based motorcycle gang called the "Skorpions" that had the distribution network necessary to sell the crystal ice in New

Zealand and their mutualistic relationship with two Croatian restaurateurs, who successfully smuggled the precursor chemicals into the country and generated vast amounts of money from this illicit trade abroad.

Since then, Alex had been headhunted by the New Zealand Secret Intelligence Service (SIS) and worked on several anti-terrorism projects following the Christchurch, March 15th 2019, terrorist attack.

Alex was late. He had promised his wife, Leanne; he would be there in the arrival hall, waiting for her when she arrived; now, he was late. Bugger. He grabbed a luggage trolley and ran across the car park with intent. He was going to make up as much time as he could. He knew his son Patrick would be a handful after the long flight from Australia. Having been woken up, held in the queue for immigration, customs and luggage, he would be as crabby as hell. Bless him.

***

David, Sarah, with daughter Rebecca and his father Paul had just waved goodbye to Li Ming, Joshua and Kwang-Ho at the departure gate after big hugs, kisses and tears. They had all promised to meet again in China or on neutral ground soon. It was tough to let them go after they had spent six months with them touring New Zealand. Showing them all those places that evoke the 'wow' and the 'that's amazing', expressions many visitors to New Zealand can't help making. They couldn't count the number of times their guests said they would love to live in New Zealand. Of course, they would; who wouldn't if they didn't have the underground railway to keep going? Perhaps when they had found someone else special to take over from themselves, they might apply for citizenship.

David had just retrieved his parking ticket from the machine when something caught his eye. Crossing the road from the terminal was a man pushing a wheelchair. The man was familiar. A resemblance to the Camp doctor, An Sang-Ho, but younger. Slumped in the wheelchair was…his daughter…Ruth…yes…it was Ruth.

"Ruth" shouted David. "Ruth, over here. Ruth, Ruth darling, it's Dad. Ruth."

There was no response, not a flicker, nothing. Perhaps she was ill. She was on an I.V. drip. David ran towards his daughter as fast as he could. Nothing stood in his way. Nothing was going to stop him. He could see nothing other than the man pushing the wheelchair towards the private ambulance.

Suddenly David tripped over the luggage trolley pushed by Alex MacLean.

"Ruth" he screamed as he plunged through the air.

David hit the ground so hard he blacked out instantly.

***

Paul was first on the scene and first to recover David's crumpled body. A large bruise was already showing on the side of David's head.

"I am so sorry." Exclaimed Alex MacLean. "He came out of nowhere".

"He thought he saw his daughter, Ruth." Said Paul, cradling his son's head.

"Is he okay? Inquired Sarah, trying to hush Rebecca, who was crying.

"Should I call an ambulance? Asked Alex.

At that moment, David opened his eyes and fixed them on Alex.

"You must help us find my daughter. She's being kidnapped."

"What are you saying, David? What did you see exactly? Asked Paul.

"If you can stand up, David, if I can call you that, let's go inside. I am sure we can find a policeman and get to the bottom of this."

"No, no, no police. You must help us without resorting to the police. These are dangerous people, and my daughter's life is at risk."

"Let's go inside anyway and talk about how I can help. We can go through this systematically, and you can tell me the whole story. How about that?

"But my daughter needs my help". Replied David, shaking his sore head.

"I can help with that if I know the full story."

"Come on, David; this man says he can help. Let's trust him." Said his father.

David looked across at Sarah for assurance, and she said the same.

"We need help David; we can't do anything ourselves."

***

When Leanne MacLean saw her husband enter the international terminal of Auckland Airport supporting a man hobbling badly, she knew instantly that Alex had found himself in another crisis. When there is trouble around, it always finds Alex first. Pushing the luggage trolley closer, with Patrick sleeping in his buggy trailing behind, she followed her husband to the Retro Espresso Coffee stand near the taxi stand exit.

"Problems, Alex?"

"Yes, this man's daughter has been kidnapped just outside in the car park."

"Shouldn't we call the police?"

"It's more complicated than that, Leanne. This is David; he spotted his daughter in a wheelchair being taken away by a man and bundled into a private ambulance. He tried to run after them and tripped over my luggage cart. Which I see I didn't need anyway."

Alex turned to face the other members of the family. "This is er…"

"Hi, I'm Sarah, David's wife; this is Rebecca. This young man here," she said, pointing to Paul, "is David's father."

"Let me look after your luggage trolley Leanne, so you have two hands free should the youngster awaken."

"Thanks for that." Replied Leanne.

"So, coffee?" Asked Alex.

"No thanks," said Sarah, "black teas all around, please."

While they waited for the drinks, David started their story.

"My father and I are refugees from North Korea. Just after my thirtieth birthday, I was accused of criticising the government and the Great Leader, Kim Jong-un. It was a trumped-up charge because we were Christians, an outlawed religion. North Korea has a system of social control that is called collective responsibility, or the *yeon-jwa-je*, the three-generation family incarceration system, arresting whole families. So, within 48 hours, twenty-one family members, including myself, my wife Rachel, my son Joseph, and my daughter Ruth were sent to Camp 22, Hoeryong concentration camp. On the first day, the women and children were separated from the men and taken away. We never saw them again. All the fit men were taken to the Chungbong coal mine. My brother Simon did not survive the beating he received on the first day. The mine was a slave labour camp where we lived on cabbage gruel and hard bread. We quickly lost muscle mass because of the starvation diet. We, my father here, Paul, and my brother Luke decided to escape. My father-in-law, who had already had frostbitten fingers and toes, committed suicide rather than jeopardise our escape. After travelling through China, we eventually reached South Korea and freedom."

The drinks had arrived, and everyone valued timeout from the distressing story.

"So, tell me about the guy you think was pushing your daughter?"

"On the first day, after being separated into groups of men and women, the camp doctor, An Sang-Ho, came over and inspected the women, only the women. He singled out my wife and hissed something at her, which made her cringe, he then stuck a pencil under her chin. I could see it had hurt her, so I stepped forward. One of the guards hit me across the nose with his rifle twice. The doctor, I think the camp inmates called him doctor death, stared at me, his eyes cold and heartless. I'll never forget it. He said if I moved again, he would kill me himself. I learned from another prisoner much later that my wife died in a nerve gas experiment."

David took a mouthful of tea to calm himself before continuing his story.

"I wasn't that far from the guy pushing the wheelchair. I could see my daughter; I know it was her, a little older, but it was definitely her." David looked at Alex for reassurance. "Honestly. As for the guy, it was not the camp doctor. Really it was not. But the resemblance was uncanny. He was younger, slimmer, and maybe a bit taller. It must be either his son or a much younger brother; it had to be.

"So, we have a North Korean concentration camp doctor smuggling a semi-conscious prisoner into New Zealand, who may have been subjected to human experimentation." Said Leanne rather bluntly.

If Alex had access to her shins under the table, he would have kicked her, and she would have been rubbing them as soon as the last syllable left her lips. However, the glaring look on his face conveyed the same message.

"So sorry," said Leanne, her face turning red. "just thinking out loud, please forgive me?"

Paul put his hand on her shoulder for reassurance but said nothing.

Tears had already started to form in the corner of David's eyes after he had finished speaking. Now, they flowed freely down his face. Comforted by Sarah, he turned to Alex.

"Can you help us; please, can you help us?"

"I will certainly try my best. I am sure this guy has entered the country dishonestly by telling lies on his visa application and that of your daughter. Irrespective of the legitimacy of his documentation, he cannot deny the DNA match to you, David being her father. So, first, we must find her; second, we must ascertain why she is here, thirdly we must take her into the state's care. There is certainly great urgency required here, so

307

can I have your cell phone number and details, and I will get back to you."

19. The Hunt

Alex left David and his family with Leanne at the café and walked along the concourse to the escalators that lead to the upper floor. From there, he went through the departure gate and showed the airport security officer his secret intelligence service credentials.

"Where is the security office, please?" inquired Alex.

"Let me get a replacement, and I will take you myself. My name is Bob Dwyer, by the way."

"Alex MacLean, nice to meet you."

While they waited, Alex gave Bob a brief explanation of what he needed and relayed the need for urgency. Once the replacement turned up, Bob led the way through a maze of several turns and locked doors to a room packed with a huge number of CCTV monitors. Almost twenty staff were sitting at desks staring at them. Each staff member was in charge of four screens and could select each camera using a series of buttons and direct the cameras with a joystick through almost 360 degrees. Some cameras were directed at the tarmac where the aeroplanes were parked. These covered the planes, the baggage holds, the baggage handlers, fuelling and the cargo pods. Nearly all of the exterior fence was covered too. Inside the terminal, there were two distinct areas. The most heavily covered area was the departure area and the arrivals area. This included the immigration booths, the customs and the bio-security area. Some of the most densely covered areas were the duty-free shops. Outside the security areas, the public areas were covered by fewer cameras, but what Alex needed, the arrivals hall, the taxi rank and the mini-bus areas, were all well covered.

Bob Dwyer introduced Alex to the shift supervisor Alan Taylor.

Hi Alan, this is Alex MacLean with the New Zealand spooks. He believes there has been an illegal entry by a foreign national who has kidnapped a young girl.

"Okay, Alex, what do you need?

"Firstly, can I have the video and details of a North Korean pushing a wheelchair that landed from Shanghai on an Air New Zealand flight this morning?"

"That would be NZ288 landed 0645 this morning. That's no problem; all the data is collected and stored in our cloud system so that I can access everything from my terminal here. If you sit at this desk here, I can directly relay what is on my screen to your screen. So, give me a second."

"There you go. Chinese National Li Jie and his daughter Li Min. The reason on the Visa is the daughter is here for a kidney transplant at the Ascension Medical Clinic on Gillies Avenue, Newmarket."

"Well, that's bogus; they are both North Korean. Can I have photocopies of the passports and their visas, please?"

"Yes, my pleasure. Bob, do the honour, please. The printer is over in the corner. Thanks.

"Do you have access to SABRE?"

"Yes, do you want me to check for Li Jie?

"Please."

SABRE is an international computer program that records details of airline passengers'; their names, their addresses, phone numbers, date of birth, their flight history, who paid for the ticket, when they paid for it and how they paid for it.

"Okay, Li Jie has been to New Zealand four times in the past year, and each time has spent three weeks here before returning to Shanghai. This is weird. The first time with his wife for a partial liver transplant, the second with his son for a bone marrow transplant, and the third with a nephew for eye surgery. How the hell did immigration miss that buddle of crap?"

"Please check for any surgeons travelling from China around those same dates."

"Yes, on all three occasions. Do you want their names?"

"Not yet. Can you check for all surgeons entering from China?"

"Yes. 26 in the eighteen months, all on holiday visas, all staying for exactly three weeks, all from Shanghai."

"Was there a surgeon on this flight?"

"Yes, Donghai Chen."

"Can you please print me off all the surgeons' details?"

"Yep."

"Can you give me pictures of them passing through customs and bio-security, just in case they have a helper?"

"Yes, they have a helper."

Alan returned to his immigration screen and discovered the helper was Zhang Yǔchén – a Chinese national whose passport details seemed genuine.

"Has he always accompanied Li Jie?"

"Yes"

"Lastly, can you please give me pictures of them leaving the terminal?"

"Certainly, coming up."

"That rego, KEA645, can you run that through the police database, please?"

"Yes, that is legitimate; it is owned by the Ascension Medical Clinic on Gillies Avenue.

***

Having gathered all his material and being escorted out by Bob Dwyer, Alex MacLean paid his parking ticket, sat in his car for a moment, and rang his wife, Leanne.

"Hi, my love. Did you get home okay?

"Yes, no problem. A tearful goodbye to David and his family took a while. Patrick was as good as gold; he really was. I got a taxi. The charge was…wait for it…\$107. And I had to carry the bags myself. How did you get on?

"Great, there is something very illegal going on. I have to see my boss at the office, lay out the facts that I have, and dig up a few more, then we should have enough to make some arrests. So, got to go; see you later." Alex rang off before Leanne could reply.

Because of the traffic, it took Alex nearly an hour to get to his office, just off Wellesley Street in the Auckland CBD. Having parked in his allotted space, he took the lift to the fourth floor and tapped on his boss's door. Tane Oakura, ex-military, had been with the NZSIS for 15 years. Tall, at over 1.8 metres, he was soft-spoken with greying long hair tied in a plait that hung down his back to his belt. Proud of his Māori heritage, a magnificent jade Mere pounamu presented to him by the Prime Minister for his work against terrorism, had pride of place at the front of his desk.

It took only ten minutes to convince Tane that David Ko's story had merit, that his daughter's life was in danger, and they had to move fast.

"I suggest you get on to the Visa card records of these surgeons on your list. See where they have been, see what they have been doing. Same for this other character, Li Jie, or whatever his real name is. Get Stephen Marsh to run down what this Ascension Medical Clinic is trading in; is it legitimate? Get him to check what they purchase regarding medical supplies, the big, specialised stuff necessary for transplant surgery and recovery. I am sure there must be specialised drugs for that.

Tane thought for a moment before continuing.

"I will use my contacts to alert the people we need; the Judiciary, Police, Immigration, and Institute of Environmental Science and Research. We will need a DNA swab from David Ko, so I will send a tech over to his place immediately. So, Alex, what are you waiting for?

Alex soon got access to Visa and gained the records for the 26 Chinese surgeons. It was the weirdest cover story he had ever seen. They had all been to the same places; Sky City Casino, Christchurch, and Queenstown on the same days of their 'holiday' in New Zealand; day 7, day 11, and day 18. They had stayed in the same hotels, been to the same restaurants almost at the exact times, and had the same excursions. Alex could predict where Donghai Chen was going, what he was going to do and almost when he was going to do it. The so-called Li Jie had followed the same pattern, so Alex had nailed down the fact that if Li Jie was bogus, so were the surgeons. The surgeons entered New Zealand on holiday visas, so could he prove the Ascension Medical Clinic paid them? He needed to access their bank records, which would require a court order, and he was pretty sure they would be paid offshore. However, it wouldn't hurt to look. A quick call to Tane Oakura was all it took to obtain a warrant to access the bank records.

It was eight o'clock when Alex found the needle in the haystack. For some obscure reason, the Ascension Medical Clinic had paid one of the surgeons $14,500 on day 8 of his stay. Cross-checking his Visa revealed what had happened; he had lost money at the casino on day 7, leaving his Visa credit low, so the clinic had made an emergency payment to make up the shortfall. The link between Ascension and the surgeons was made.

Stephen Marsh came into Alex's office just after nine.

"I have managed to get some great stuff on Ascension. By in large, they are a legitimate medical clinic. They undertake about 100 hip replacements a year, 200 corrective knee surgeries, 300 eye surgeries, 200 plastic and reconstructive surgeries, 100 gynaecology and 200 urology surgeries, but no transplant surgeries. However, what is really weird they consume large quantities of immunosuppressant medications; for example, Prograf, Cyclosporine, Rapamune and Cellcept, to name but a few. They have had a couple of fatalities that have been subject to a coroner's report, although it was found to be not suspicious. I have found a huge list of surgeons who have worked there. However, two stood out. They are local Chinese surgeons, New Zealanders, both kidney transplant experts, who have worked in this non-transplant clinic twenty months ago."

"Well, I think we had better go and see these gentlemen."

"But it's eleven o'clock."

"No time like the present. I'll square it with the boss first.

The first of the surgeons, Liu Xiang, lived in Beach Road, Howick. The lights were still on, so Alex assumed he was still awake. He answered the door immediately, and he ushered them in on seeing the security passes.

"I wondered how long it would take before this would happen."

"You have been expecting our visit?"

"Yes, both me and my colleague Yao Ming."

"So why do you think we are here?"

"You have come about the illegal kidney transplants at the Ascension Medical Clinic."

"When did this happen?"

We were forced to do this by the Triads twenty months ago, both Yao Ming and I. They had our families and said they would kill them if we didn't do as they said. Thank God we only had to undertake one each.

"Tell me how it was organised."

"They flew a live donor in from China. The donor was North Korean. A technician accompanied the donor. The donor had been given a toxin to make her compliant. This was administered intravenously. When they were in the clinic, an antidote was given in the IV and another drug that they said would recondition the organs and help with immunosuppression. It took nearly five days for the toxin to be flushed out of the body and the reconditioning of the organs to take effect. An MRI was used to confirm that the organs were perfectly normal. After that, the transplant went as normal, except that the donor was alive and unwilling to donate their kidney."

Liu Xiang paused to take stock of what he had just said. With his family asleep upstairs, he knew another nightmarish chapter in his life was about to start.

"After the surgery, the donor was given the toxin again, and then the technician and the donor would fly back to China.

"Were you or your colleague paid for this operation?

"No."

"Why not? Others are?

"We got our families back alive. Hold on a minute, do you mean this shit is still going on?"

"Why did you think it would stop?"

"I just assumed that it had stopped because we were not asked again."

"Why didn't you come forward with this information?"

"Because they said they would rape my wife and daughter in front of me before killing us all, that's why.

"Thank you, Liu Xiang. We will see ourselves out.

"But what happens now?" Pleaded Liu Xiang.

"To be honest, sir, I couldn't say. I have recorded our conversation and will have to report what you said to my boss. What happens next is up to him and his boss, I presume. You certainly have extenuating circumstances, and I am sure these will be taken into consideration. Goodnight, sir."

As Alex and Stephen got in the car, it was twenty past midnight. If they wanted to move on the clinic this morning, they needed to move fast.

While Alex drove towards the second surgeon's house, who lived on Sea Spray Drive, Bucklands Beach, a few minutes away, Stephen rang their boss Tane Oakura and played back the interview recording. As they pulled up outside the second surgeon's house, Tane Oakura had finished listening to the interview.

"That's great work, boys. Forget the other surgeon for the moment. Get back here. I'll get the squad we need, together with the warrants. We'll move on this today, in fact, as early as I can make it happen. See you soon."

20. The Raid

Without complaint, Judge Orell Waio signed the warrants at 0200 hrs, worried for the young girl that they might not be quick enough to save her. By 0330 hrs, the team was assembled at the NZSIS underground garage on Wellesley Street in the Auckland CBD. There were four SIS officers, including Tane Oakura, Alex MacLean and Stephen Marsh. The fourth was a man Alex had never seen before who was not introduced and kept to himself in the shadows. There were eighteen police armed offender squad (AOS), all in civilian dress, with another ten unarmed police officers, including a superintendent and a sergeant, all in uniform. The police had the warrants to enter and search. Also in the team were four immigration officers; two of senior rank and two of junior rank. Immigration officers have the power of entry without warrants if they suspected an offence against the immigration laws was being committed. Last, they had a forensic doctor and nurse who would care for the girl Li Min when they found her. So, with all the bases covered, they had the personnel for the task.

Alex MacLean had an enlarged plan of the Ascension Medical Clinic on an easel at the front of the seated task group. He marked all the entrances with a bold red marker pen and allocated pairs of the armed offender squad to each of the entrances. He marked all the treatment rooms and operating theatres in yellow and assigned a team of police officers, one armed, one not, to each group of these rooms. The same procedure was followed for storerooms. Patient rooms highlighted in green would be checked by one of the armed police officers and one of the SIS officers. Everyone was given photographs of; Li Min, the daughter; Li Jie, the doctor from Camp 22; Zhang Yǔchén, the doctor's bodyguard; and Donghai Chen, the Chinese surgeon.

"A word of caution, I have no idea how our Camp doctor will react, violently or passively. It's anyone's guess; bullies can go either way. However, I want him alive. The bodyguard is a big unit. He was chosen because of his size, and so we must assume he will put up a fight. Be careful; this is a hospital with innocent people incapacitated, unable to move out of the way. Taser him if you must, but no firearms indoors, please. The surgeon will probably not be there when we move in. So once the primary phase is over, remain hidden and quiet until we capture his ass. This may be around 0700 hrs. Now, our primary target is the kidnapped girl Li Min. Study the photograph. We need her alive at all costs. Don't let anyone mess with her when you find her. Now check your radios; SIS, police and immigration will use channel 7, and the AOS to use channel 8."

Alex looked around the room at the assembled team with some trepidation, wondering what rewards or disasters the next few hours would bring.

"Are there any questions?"

Everyone in the group were top professionals; they had done something like this many times. There were no questions.

***

At 0500hrs, the AOS took charge of the exits to the Ascension Medical Clinic. Led by a senior immigration officer, flanked by a member of the AOS, Tane Oakura and the police superintendent, the team entered the front of the building and fronted up to reception. Looking down the barrel of an AR15, the woman at the front desk looked as white as a sheet. Alex thought she was about to faint.

"Madam," the superintendent declared, "we have warrants to search these premises and to seize evidence purporting to an alleged kidnapping yesterday at Auckland Airport. Where in the building are these two people?" He demanded, showing her the photographs of; Li Min, Li Jie, Zhang Yǔchén and Donghai Chen.

"Emm…the…er…girl is…in 217, she is being prepped for…er…surgery later this morning. The two men are in the room next to hers, er…218. That's upstairs. The surgeon, Mr Chen, is coming in at six this morning to see the girl and see that she is ready for surgery."

"What is the surgery?" Asked Tane Oakura.

"She is willingly donating a kidney to her sister, who lives here in New Zealand, Li Juan."

With the search underway, Tane, Alex, the senior immigration officer Ken James and an AOS officer crashed open room 218. Li Jie and Zhang Yǔchén were still asleep and did not wake until shaken vigorously by Alex.

"Li Jie," announced Ken James you are under arrest for offences under the New Zealand Immigration Act 2009, whereby you entered the country illegally under a false name using false documents. You have the right to remain silent. You do not have to make any statement. Anything you say will be recorded and may be given in evidence in court. You have the right to speak with a lawyer without delay and in private before deciding whether to answer any questions. The police have a list of lawyers you may speak to for free."

Li Jie looked panicked, like a rabbit caught in a car's headlights.

"I, I…have diplomatic immunity. I am a citizen of North Korea."

"Let me see your passport, please." Said Ken ignoring the diplomatic immunity nonsense."

After rummaging in his bag for several minutes, Li eventually produced his passport and handed it to Ken.

"This is a Chinese passport, and it declares you to be Li Jie, a Chinese citizen born ten years ago."

Alex couldn't help smiling at the typing mistake on the Chinese passport. When it was scanned at the airport, the electronic record was correct. However, the typo was missed by the inspecting immigration officer would get a bollocking for their mistake.

"This is a fake passport Mr Li, and you are no diplomat from North Korea. You, Mr Li, are under arrest.

Alex went behind Li and pulled his hands behind his back, then slid them through the plastic cuffs and tightened them, just enough for discomfort but not sufficient to inhibit the circulation.

"Now, Mr Zhang, your passport, please."

Zhang was not fazed by the intrusion of armed police or immigration; he had been there, done that, and had the tee shirt. He handed his passport to Ken James.

325

"This all seems to be genuine, Mr Zhang; however, your visa was granted for holidays only. Empty your pockets, Mr Zhang."

Zhang Yŭchén emptied his pockets, and apart from some bric-a-brac, there was a roll of New Zealand currency. Ken James passed it to Alex to count.

"Well, Mr Zhang, $11,400 is a fair buddle of cash; where did you get it?"

Zhang turned to Li Jie and said something in Chinese. He faced Ken James again and said nothing.

"So, you got it from Li Jie, did you." Declared Ken. "Yes, I can speak Chinese too; I can read it as well. You see, my grandmother insisted we were fluent in her birth language. Funny that, when dealing with triad criminals like you."

After Zhang was handcuffed, Alex, Tane and the superintendent of police, the doctor and the nurse moved next door to 217.

***

The room was darkened; the blinds were drawn against the morning light rising over the eastern horizon. The patient was connected to an intravenous drip in the bed, with wires attached to various monitors for her heart, breathing and blood pressure. Sitting on a lounge chair in the corner was a nurse, fully awake, holding the patient's hand. When the group entered the room, the nurse did not move a muscle, nor was she shocked by the AR15 pointing at her heart.

"Who are you?" Enquired Tane.

"I am the duty nurse Anne Calder."

"What are you doing to this patient?"

"I am praying for her and trying to calm her before she dies."

"Why is she dying?"

"She isn't yet. But look at her chart. She will undergo surgery to remove both her kidneys, liver, bone marrow and corneas. The surgeon who is harvesting her organs is going to kill her."

The forensic doctor, Laura Bishop, stepped forward and addressed Nurse Calder.

"What is in the drip?"

"They give these patients a toxin to make them compliant; the toxin is seated in the brain. However, before they can harvest any of the organs, they have to give an antidote and a drug that refurbishes the system

327

and helps the recipient of the organs with immunosuppression. This used to take a week. But they found that increasing the refurbishing drug enhanced the antidote and reduced the time needed to flush out the toxin."

"So, was Li Min due for surgery this morning?

"Her name is not Li Min; she is Ruth Ha Hye-Su, from North Korea. She was captive in a concentration camp called Camp 22 near Hoeryong. The man who brought her here is the camp's medical doctor, in charge of human medical experimentation. His Name is An Sang-Ki. He tried to rape her twelve months or so ago, but she can't remember exactly. But he carries her scar on his penis and tongue from when she fought him off. She told me that this multiple organ donation is how he wants to kill her."

"Why isn't she awake now?"

"They sedated her early this morning, so they wouldn't have to tie her to the bed as the compliance toxin wore off. They were worried that she would try to kill herself or harm herself before they could take her organs."

"Have you witnessed this thing before?"

"Live donations, from one living donor to a recipient. The donor recovers and returns to their native country. Yes, I've seen that before. But when I started asking questions about the number of foreign surgeons coming and going, my shifts were altered, and I was moved to other patients."

"Why are you here now, then?"

"A friend of mine went home sick, and I took her place. This is murder and has turned my stomach. I came on at ten o'clock and only found out what was happening at midnight. I didn't know what to do. Especially with that big goon Zhang guarding her most of the time. I was going to ring the police but didn't know what to say. Boy, am I glad to see you are here now."

"We will need to interview you formally, Ms Calder and make a statement." Announced Tane Oakura.

Laura Bishop turned to Tane and said, "I think we should move Ruth to another hospital; I suggest Southern Cross Hospital, North Harbour. I am there all this week and will be able to look after her. Is that Okay?

"Yes," replied Tane, "I'll call an Ambulance."

***

At six o'clock, the Ascension Medical Clinic's entrance opened and in strode the immaculately dressed and haughty figure of Donghai Chen.

"Is my patient ready?" he barked at the receptionist.

"Yes…Doc…Doctor, room 217."

As Donghai Chen flung open the door of 217, he looked puzzled as there was no patient in the bed – just some guy with long plaited hair.

"Ahh, Doctor Chen, we've been waiting for you."

Chen turned to leave but was suddenly confronted with the barrel of an AR15 aimed at his face. The haughty surgeon fainted and fell in a heap at the feet of Alex MacLean.

21. The Reunion

David Ko, Sarah, his wife and his father Paul were allowed to visit Ruth at the North Harbour, Southern Cross Hospital, as soon as his daughter came round from the sedative and Dr Laura Bishop had examined her.

Speaking to the doctor, David Ko asked about his daughter's health before entering Ruth's private room.

"Considering where she has been incarcerated, she is in remarkable condition. She is a little malnourished and a little dehydrated, but other than that, she is fine. Her past has not been so great. She has suffered broken ribs on a least two separate occasions. She has a few teeth missing from trauma, and she has recently had a broken arm; although this was set crudely, I think it is wise that we operate on her arm to correct this properly."

"How long will Ruth be in the hospital?" Asked David.

"I have a slot to correct the arm tomorrow morning. It's not a big operation, as long as there are no complications and nothing arises from the toxins her captors have given her perhaps four or five days."

"Thank you, doctor."

An Sang-Ki, a.k.a. Li Jie, was stripped naked in front of the SIS, immigration and police investigators, who noted the scar at the base of his penis before they gave him a set of coveralls and sat him in a chair.

"Open your mouth for us, Mr Li, please." Instructed the duty doctor.

Sang-Ki did as he was told. The scar on his tongue was noted. A DNA swab was taken for the paternity test. Then the doctor measured Sang-Ki's temperature, heart rate, blood pressure and lung efficiency.

"You need to give up smoking, Mr Li." Said the doctor, having finished his examination.

With a quick nod to the investigators, the doctor left the room. In the corner of the well-lit room, Alex MacLean searched Li's clothes and luggage. His clothes held nothing except a packet of Camels, a Dunhill Hobnail gold lighter, probably worth $1000, and a gold money clip holding eleven $1000 U.S. dollar notes. There were some New Zealand notes amounting to $247.

In his luggage were two medical packs – the first containing the toxin and the antidote written in

Chinese and North Korean. The third phial in this pack contained the dry reconditioning powder, which had to be reconstituted with sterile saline. The second medical pack, which had been opened, contained a test kit for detecting the toxin material, whatever this was.

Also in the suitcase, beside his clothes, all designer brands, were three bundles of American dollars totalling $175,000. Sealed in the lining were four account books for banks in Singapore, The Maldives, Bangkok and Hong Kong. The four accounts held over four million U.S. dollars in the name of Li Jie.

In the middle of the desk around which they were all seated was the Polycom teleconference unit that connected the interviewers to two interpreters, one Mandarin Chinese and the other North Korean. The questions started in Korean.

"Mr Li, what was the purpose of your visit to New Zealand?" Asked Ken James, the senior immigration officer.

An Sang-Ki did not reply to the Korean interpreter's question. Neither did he respond to the Chinese interpreter's question.

"This is very unfortunate, as we must establish who you are and what you are doing here if you wish to keep any of the money you have brought into the country."

"My name is Li Jie, just as my passport declares." He said in perfect English. "I am a citizen of South Korea. I came here so my daughter Li Min could receive a kidney transplant. That is what the $175,000 is for. The money in the bank account books is from my businesses in Korea."

"Well, whoever helped you with this counterfeit passport probably made the date of birth mistake on purpose so that the banks would not let you access any money with this document. They had you on, Mr Li, hook, line and sinker. As for Li Min being your daughter, we will have to see about that. The swabs the doctor took from you will be tested to see if you are a DNA match to her."

At that moment, a knock on the door and a secretary brought in a message for Tane Oakura, the SIS chief. He opened the note before passing it to the other group members.

"Courier has just delivered a message to the Ascension Medical Clinic from Dr Mavis Baker, an associate professor at the University of Auckland, Bowers Institute for Medical Research. She reports; sorry the results are late. However, the sample received is completely prion free. Kind regards, Mavis." Tane stared at Sang-Ki, waiting for him to answer what this meant.

"Alex, get over to the Bowers Institute and interview Professor Baker. Please find out how she is connected to this lot. Take the two medical packs with you; if she is kosher, perhaps she can understand it all. Hurry up, though. I want this trash charged with something before 72 hours is up."

Alex grabbed the two packs and left.

"So, Mr Li, we have packs of medical gear containing toxins and antidotes in your suitcase and test results returned from the University telling you that the patient, allegedly your daughter, is prion free. How do you explain that, Mr Li?"

"Those things are not mine. I know nothing about poisoning my daughter and toxins."

***

Alex found Professor Baker in her office on the third floor of the new science building of the University of Auckland situated off Symonds Street. After showing the sixty-year-old Professor his SIS identity card, the academic was taken aback but said she would help however she could.

"The test you did for the Ascension Medical Clinic today have you done any of these tests before." Asked Alex.

"Yes, that is the twenty-seventh."

"How did it all start?"

"A guy from the clinic named Doctor Li Jie came to the institute and said that they had a problem with a prion toxin that had spread from farm animals to humans. He explained they had developed an anti-toxin to combat the prion. He said they had also developed a test to detect the prion in blood samples that required a specialised laboratory like ours. He gave the institute a $100,000 U.S. donation and would pay us $5,000 per test. Of course, such funding was gladly received, and we said yes. We don't research prions, they're too dangerous, but the Ascension Medical Clinic supplies the testing materials and the methodology, so it's easy money for us.

"Is this the man who commissioned the work?" Inquired Alex, showing the Professor a photograph of An Sang-Ki from his phone.

"Yes, that is him. He is also the guy who dropped off the blood sample and the test kit early this morning for me to carry out the test."

"You work that late?"

"Not usually. It was all prearranged."

"There is no way of telling you this gently. This man is not who he claims to be, Doctor Li Jie. He is An Sang-Ki, the camp doctor of a concentration camp called Camp 22 near Hoeryong, North Korea. He has been running some illegal organ trafficking trade using prisoners from his camp. We suspect through China with the aid of the Chinese Triads."

"Oh, my goodness." Exclaimed the Professor covering her mouth.

"I am afraid we haven't $10,000 to give you, but we would like you to analyse what there is in these phials. From the labels, we suspect A; contains the toxin; I think you said the prion. B; contains the antidote, and C; contains some reconditioning powder that has something to do with helping immunosuppression following the transplantation of an organ like a kidney."

"Yes, we will gladly do that. As I said, we do not research prions, so we must be cautious with phial A, but we will do our best. Who do we send the report to?"

Alex gave her his card. "You had better send any leftover materials to us with the report. Thanks, Professor Baker."

"Glad to help."

As Alex left the Professor, all her phones, her landlines and her cell phones were monitored for the next 72 hours to see if she contacted anyone suspicious that may be part of the illegal organ trafficking trade.

There were none. As far as the SIS was concerned, she was kosher.

***

When David Ko and his father met Ruth at the North Harbour, Southern Cross Hospital, she wore a lilac tee-shirt and denim jeans. Her left arm was in a sling. But she was on her feet, her brown eyes were bright, her short black hair shone in the overhead lights, and her smile would have won any Miss World contest. When Ruth and her father embraced, all the years of pain and suffering fell away, and their hearts fused and beat as one. Tears flooded down the faces of David and his father. David could not let his daughter go. The daughter he never thought he would ever see again. Paul came next as David sank into a chair sobbing. When Paul had told the escapees in China to keep the faith that they would see their families again, he did not believe it himself, and he scolded himself for even thinking it. But here was the reality of that dream. Ruth was alive.

***

In her house on Frost Road, Waitoki, Sarah Ko sat in her lounge diner, cradling a hot cup of coffee, looking across the green undulating pastures and listening to the endless bird song she had always adored about this property. Then her thoughts turned to Ruth as she lamented that the view from her windows would be so alien to her. She felt a deep sense of insecurity and apprehension about meeting Ruth. Will she like me, she wondered. Her mother was dead; would she resent David marrying again to someone Chinese as well? Her struggle for survival would damage Ruth and need tenderness without being smothered or treated like a child. How would she react to Rebecca? Her new sister?

When she heard the front door open, her heart skipped a beat and thundered in her chest. She stood up and faced the entrance, and there stood David with his beautiful daughter Ruth. Even as skinny as she was, her beauty shone through. The resemblance to her father was uncanny. She smiled at Sarah and stepped forward.

"Sarah, it is so nice to meet you. My father has told me a lot about you on the way here. He said you were beautiful. He was right; you are." Ruth said in Korean.

"Welcome home, Ruth. I am so happy to meet you at long last. Your father has shared much about your childhood in Korea. Today is the start of your new life in New Zealand." Sarah replied in Korean.

When Sarah and Ruth embraced, it was as if they were long-lost sisters with an instantly forged bond.

David reappeared from one of the bedrooms with a wriggling bundle in his arms and introduced his sleepy daughter Rebecca: more hugs, more tears and big love.

Epilogue

Ruth Ko graduated from the University of Auckland with a first-class honours degree in engineering. She has worked on many civil engineering projects, including the light-rail network in Auckland. She is married to a consultant paediatrician and has two children, a boy and a girl. Nurse Anne Calder is the Godmother to both of her children.

Sang-Ki, a.k.a. Li Jie, was deported to South Korea, where he was arrested, on arrival, by the South Korean National Intelligence Service. Following interrogation, he was identified as An Sang-Ki, the son of Doctor Death, An Sang-Ho. Several witnesses, who were themselves, escapees from Camp 22, identified An Sang-Ki as one of the doctors from Camp 22 that had experimented on live human prisoners. He was convicted of crimes against humanity and given a life sentence. He served two years in isolation for his own protection before it was deemed safe for him to be placed in the general prison population. He died of stab wounds within a week of the placement. The Korean National Intelligence Service seized the money in the offshore accounts of Li Jie. Several significant charities benefitted from large anonymous U.S. dollar donations that year.

Doctor Donghai Chen gave up all the details of the illicit organ trafficking organised by the triads based in

Harbin. He gave names, money transactions, bank accounts he knew about, contacts in the prefecture, the whole works. He was sentenced to life imprisonment because he signed the organ donation forms, which would have led to Ruth's death. He spent six months in Paremoremo, maximum security prison, before being deported back to China. Within a month, his body was found floating in the Tumen River near Sinhakpo Station.

With evidence from Donghai Chen, a letter from the New Zealand Prime Minister was sent to the Chinese Premier, condemning the behaviour of Chinese citizens conducting illicit organ trafficking in New Zealand, organised by the triads based in Harbin. Within a month, the triads in Harbin had been eliminated by the Guoanbu, the Chinese Secret Police. This was conveyed to the New Zealand SIS and the Prime Minister. However, such elimination was just a cursory gesture; the triads like cancer, regrow, metastasise, and manifest elsewhere.

Two of the Ascension Medical Clinic directors were found guilty of aiding and abetting illicit organ trafficking and were sentenced to life imprisonment. Their assets gained from this trade, houses, cars, and a boat, were seized and sold under forfeiture law. The Ascension Medical Clinic and the remaining staff and directors were found innocent of any wrongdoing. The two renal doctors blackmailed by the triads to conduct the first renal transplants at the Ascension Medical

Clinic were censured by the Medical Council of New Zealand, but no further action was taken.

Zhang Yǔchén, who had a valid Chinese passport and had not committed any crime in New Zealand that could be proven, was deported immediately to China. He was never heard of again.

**

Although the characters in this story are fictitious, Camp 22 is not. Camp 22 still exists. Chungbong Mine still exists. Criticising the government and the Great Leader, Kim Jong-un, still carries the penalty of re-education and hard labour for life. Christianity is a banned religion that carries the sentence of death or life imprisonment. North Korea still has a system of social control called collective responsibility, or the *yeon-jwa-je*, arresting whole families, the three-generation family-incarceration system. Camp 22 is not the only concentration camp in North Korea. Amnesty International estimates there are between 13-16, although some are purportedly closed, this is difficult to confirm.

Hoeryong concentration camp - Wikipedia

Human rights in North Korea Amnesty International

North Korea's prisons: How harsh are conditions? - BBC News

Prisons in North Korea - Wikipedia

Warren Miner-Williams has a doctorate in clinical biochemistry and has published many scientific papers in prestigious journals and co-authored chapters in nutritional textbooks. He holds a master's degree in education and has published a number of educational textbooks in the U.K., helping teachers conduct and assess scientific research in schools. Allied to this in the 1990's he was a member of the Royal Society of Chemistry's Committee awarding grants for research projects in U.K. schools. He now lives in New Zealand with his wife and two married daughters. Amongst his many hobbies he has drawn expertise from Kendo; Sub-aqua diving*; Caving*; Cave diving; Hang gliding; Motorcycle racing; Parachuting; Skiing* and Photography both underwater and caving, (* as an instructor).